The Descent of Man, and Other Stories

Edith Wharton

Table of Contents

Table of Contents

The Descent of Man, and Other Stories

Edith Wharton

The Descent of Man

I

WHEN Professor Linyard came back from his holiday in the Maine woods the air of rejuvenation he brought with him was due less to the influences of the climate than to the companionship he had enjoyed on his travels. To Mrs. Linyard's observant eye he had appeared to set out alone; but an invisible traveller had in fact accompanied him, and if his heart beat high it was simply at the pitch of his adventure: for the Professor had eloped with an idea.

No one who has not tried the experiment can divine its exhilaration. Professor Linyard would not have changed places with any hero of romance pledged to a flesh−and−blood abduction. The most fascinating female is apt to be encumbered with luggage and scruples: to take up a good deal of room in the present and overlap inconveniently into the future; whereas an idea can accommodate itself to a single molecule of the brain or expand to the circumference of the horizon. The Professor's companion had to the utmost this quality of adaptability. As the express train whirled him away from the somewhat inelastic circle of Mrs. Linyard's affections, his idea seemed to be sitting opposite him, and their eyes met every moment or two in a glance of joyous complicity; yet when a friend of the family presently joined him and began to talk about college matters, the idea slipped out of sight in a flash, and the Professor would have had no difficulty in proving that he was alone.

But if, from the outset, he found his idea the most agreeable of fellow–travellers, it was only in the aromatic solitude of the woods that he tasted the full savour of his adventure. There, during the long cool August days, lying full length on the pine–needles and gazing up into the sky, he would meet the eyes of his companion bending over him like a nearer heaven. And what eyes they were! — clear yet unfathomable, bubbling with inexhaustible laughter, yet drawing their freshness and sparkle from the central depths of thought! To a man who for twenty years had faced an eye reflecting the obvious with perfect accuracy, these escapes into the inscrutable had always been peculiarly inviting; but hitherto the Professor's mental infidelities had been restricted by an unbroken and relentless domesticity. Now, for the first time since his marriage, chance had given him six weeks to himself, and he was coming home with his lungs full of liberty.

It must not be inferred that the Professor's domestic relations were defective: they were in fact so complete that it was almost impossible to get away from them. It is the happy husbands who are really in bondage; the little rift within the lute is often a passage to freedom. Marriage had given the Professor exactly what he had sought in it; a comfortable lining to life. The impossibility of rising to sentimental crises had made him scrupulously careful not to shirk the practical obligations of the bond. He took as it were a sociological view of his case, and modestly regarded himself as a brick in that foundation on which the state is supposed to rest. Perhaps if Mrs. Linyard had cared about entomology, or had taken sides in the war over the transmission of acquired characteristics, he might have had a less impersonal notion of marriage; but he was unconscious of any deficiency in their relation, and if consulted would probably have declared that he didn't want any woman bothering with his beetles. His real life had always lain in the universe of thought, in that enchanted region which, to those who have lingered there, comes to have so much more colour and substance than the painted curtain hanging before it. The Professor's particular veil of Maia was a narrow strip of homespun woven in a monotonous pattern; but he had only to lift it to step into an empire.

This unseen universe was thronged with the most seductive shapes: the Professor moved Sultan–like through a seraglio of ideas. But of all the lovely apparitions that wove their spells about him, none had ever worn quite so persuasive an aspect as this latest favourite. For the others were mostly rather grave companions, serious–minded and elevating enough to have passed muster in a Ladies' Debating Club; but this new fancy of the Professor's was simply one embodied laugh. It was, in other words, the smile of relaxation at the end of a long day's toil: the flash of irony that the laborious mind

2

projects, irresistibly, over labour conscientiously performed. The Professor had always been a hard worker. If he was an indulgent friend to his ideas, he was also a stern task–master to them. For, in addition to their other duties, they had to support his family: to pay the butcher and baker, and provide for Jack's schooling and Millicent's dresses. The Professor's household was a modest one, yet it tasked his ideas to keep it up to his wife's standard. Mrs. Linyard was not an exacting wife, and she took enough pride in her husband's attainments to pay for her honours by turning Millicent's dresses and darning Jack's socks, and going to the College receptions year after year in the same black silk with shiny seams. It consoled her to see an occasional mention of Professor Linyard's remarkable monograph on the Ethical Reactions of the Infusoria, or an allusion to his investigations into the Unconscious Cerebration of the Amoeba.

Still there were moments when the healthy indifference of Jack and Millicent reacted on the maternal sympathies; when Mrs. Linyard would have made her husband a railway–director, if by this transformation she might have increased her boy's allowance and given her daughter a new hat, or a set of furs such as the other girls were wearing. Of such moments of rebellion the Professor himself was not wholly unconscious. He could not indeed understand why any one should want a new hat; and as to an allowance, he had had much less money at college than Jack, and had yet managed to buy a microscope and collect a few "specimens"; while Jack was free from such expensive tastes! But the Professor did not let his want of sympathy interfere with the discharge of his paternal obligations. He worked hard to keep the wants of his family gratified, and it was precisely in the endeavor to attain this end that he at length broke down and had to cease from work altogether.

To cease from work was not to cease from thought of it; and in the unwonted pause from effort the Professor found himself taking a general survey of the field he had travelled. At last it was possible to lift his nose from the loom, to step a moment in front of the tapestry he had been weaving. From this first inspection of the pattern so long wrought over from behind, it was natural to glance a little farther and seek its reflection in the public eye. It was not indeed of his special task that he thought in this connection. He was but one of the great army of weavers at work among the threads of that cosmic woof; and what he sought was the general impression their labour had produced.

When Professor Linyard first plied his microscope, the audience of the man of science had been composed of a few fellow–students, sympathetic or hostile as their habits of mind predetermined, but versed in the jargon of the profession and familiar with the point of departure. In the intervening quarter of a century, however, this little group had been swallowed up in a larger public. Every one now read scientific books and expressed an opinion on them. The ladies and the clergy had taken them up first; now they had passed to the school–room and the kindergarten. Daily life was regulated on scientific principles; the daily papers had their "Scientific Jottings"; nurses passed examinations in hygienic science, and babies were fed and dandled according to the new psychology.

The very fact that scientific investigation still had, to some minds, a flavour of heterodoxy, gave it a perennial interest. The mob had broken down the walls of tradition to batten in the orchard of forbidden knowledge. The inaccessible goddess whom the Professor had served in his youth now offered her charms in the market–place. And yet it was not the same goddess after all, but a pseudo–science masquerading in the garb of the real divinity. This false goddess had her ritual and her literature. She had her sacred books, written by false priests and sold by millions to the faithful. In the most successful of these works, ancient dogma and modern discovery were depicted in a close embrace under the lime–lights of a hazy transcendentalism; and the tableau never failed of its effect. Some of the books designed on this popular model had lately fallen into the Professor's hands, and they filled him with mingled rage and hilarity. The rage soon died: he came to regard this mass of pseudo–literature as protecting the truth from desecration. But the hilarity remained, and flowed into the form of his idea. And the idea — the divine, incomparable idea — was simply that he should avenge his goddess by satirizing her false interpreters. He would write a skit on the "popular" scientific book; he would so heap platitude on platitude, fallacy on fallacy, false analogy on false analogy, so use his superior knowledge to abound in the sense of the ignorant, that even the gross crowd would join in the laugh against its augurs. And the laugh should be something more than the distension of mental muscles; it should be the trumpet–blast bringing down the walls of ignorance, or at least the little stone striking the giant between the eyes.

II

THE Professor, on presenting his card, had imagined that it would command prompt access to the publisher's sanctuary; but the young man who read his name was not moved to immediate action. It was clear that Professor Linyard of Hillbridge University was not a specific figure to the purveyors of popular literature. But the publisher was an old friend; and when the card had finally drifted to his office on the languid tide of routine he came forth at once to greet his visitor.

The warmth of his welcome convinced the Professor that he had been right in bringing his manuscript to Ned Harviss. He and Harviss had been at Hillbridge together, and the future publisher had been one of the wildest spirits in that band of college outlaws which yearly turns out so many inoffensive citizens and kind husbands and fathers. The Professor knew the taming qualities of life. He was aware that many of his most reckless comrades had been transformed into prudent capitalists or cowed wage–earners; but he was almost sure that he could count on Harviss. So rare a sense of irony, so keen a perception of relative values, could hardly have been blunted even by twenty years' intercourse with the obvious.

The publisher's appearance was a little disconcerting. He looked as if he had been fattened on popular fiction; and his fat was full of optimistic creases. The Professor seemed to see him bowing into his office a long train of spotless heroines laden with the maiden tribute of the hundredth thousand volume.

Nevertheless, his welcome was reassuring. He did not disown his early enormities, and capped his visitor's tentative allusions by such flagrant references to the past that the Professor produced his manuscript without a scruple.

"What — you don't mean to say you've been doing something in our line?"

The Professor smiled. "You publish scientific books sometimes, don't you?"

The publisher's optimistic creases relaxed a little. "H'm — it all depends — I'm afraid you're a little too scientific for us. We have a big sale for scientific breakfast foods, but not for the concentrated essences. In your case, of course, I should be delighted to stretch a point; but in your own interest I ought to tell you that perhaps one of the educational houses would do you better."

The Professor leaned back, still smiling luxuriously.

"Well, look it over — I rather think you'll take it."

"Oh, we'll take it, as I say; but the terms might not — "

"No matter about the terms — "

The publisher threw his head back with a laugh. "I had no idea that science was so profitable; we find our popular novelists are the hardest hands at a bargain."

"Science is disinterested," the Professor corrected him. "And I have a fancy to have you publish this thing."

"That's immensely good of you, my dear fellow. Of course your name goes with a certain public — and I rather like the originality of our bringing out a work so out of our line. I daresay it may boom us both." His creases deepened at the thought, and he shone encouragingly on the Professor's leave−taking.

Within a fortnight, a line from Harviss recalled the Professor to town. He had been looking forward with immense zest to this second meeting; Harviss's college roar was in his tympanum, and he pictured himself following up the protracted chuckle which would follow his friend's progress through the manuscript. He was proud of the adroitness with which he had kept his secret from Harviss, had maintained to the last the pretense of a serious work, in order to give the keener edge to his reader's enjoyment. Not since under−graduate days had the Professor tasted such a draught of pure fun as his anticipations now poured for him.

This time his card brought instant admission. He was bowed into the office like a successful novelist, and Harviss grasped him with both hands.

"Well — do you mean to take it?" he asked, with a lingering coquetry.

"Take it? Take it, my dear fellow? It's in press already — you'll excuse my not waiting to consult you? There will be no difficulty about terms, I assure you, and we had barely time to catch the autumn market. My dear Linyard, why didn't you tell me?" His voice sank to a reproachful solemnity, and he pushed forward his own arm−chair.

The Professor dropped into it with a chuckle. "And miss the joy of letting you find out?"

"Well — it was a joy." Harviss held out a box of his best cigars. "I don't know when I've had a bigger sensation. It was so deucedly unexpected — and, my dear fellow, you've brought it so exactly to the right shop."

"I'm glad to hear you say so," said the Professor modestly.

Harviss laughed in rich appreciation. "I don't suppose you had a doubt of it; but of course I was quite unprepared. And it's so extraordinarily out of your line — "

The Professor took off his glasses and rubbed them with a slow smile.

"Would you have thought it so — at college?"

Harviss stared. "At college? — Why, you were the most iconoclastic devil — "

There was a perceptible pause. The Professor restored his glasses and looked at his friend. "Well — ?" he said simply.

"Well — ?" echoed the other, still staring. "Ah — I see; you mean that that's what explains it. The swing of the pendulum, and so forth. Well, I admit it's not an uncommon phenomenon. I've conformed myself, for example; most of our crowd have, I believe; but somehow I hadn't expected it of you."

The close observer might have detected a faint sadness under the official congratulation of his tone; but the Professor was too amazed to have an ear for such fine shades.

"Expected it of me? Expected what of me?" he gasped. "What in heaven do you think this thing is?" And he struck his fist on the manuscript which lay between them.

Harviss had recovered his optimistic creases. He rested a benevolent eye on the document.

"Why, your apologia — your confession of faith, I should call it. You surely must have seen which way you were going? You can't have written it in your sleep?"

"Oh, no, I was wide awake enough," said the Professor faintly.

"Well, then, why are you staring at me as if I were not?" Harviss leaned forward to lay a reassuring hand on his visitor's worn coat-sleeve. "Don't mistake me, my dear Linyard. Don't fancy there was the least unkindness in my allusion to your change of front. What is growth but the shifting of the stand-point? Why should a man be expected to look at life with the same eyes at twenty and at — our age? It never occurred to me that you could feel the least delicacy in admitting that you have come round a little — have fallen into line, so to speak."

But the Professor had sprung up as if to give his lungs more room to expand; and from them there issued a laugh which shook the editorial rafters.

"Oh, Lord, oh Lord — is it really as good as that?" he gasped.

Harviss had glanced instinctively toward the electric bell on his desk; it was evident that he was prepared for an emergency.

"My dear fellow — " he began in a soothing tone.

"Oh, let me have my laugh out, do," implored the Professor. "I'll — I'll quiet down in a minute; you needn't ring for the young man." He dropped into his chair again, and grasped its arms to steady his shaking. "This is the best laugh I've had since college," he brought out between his paroxysms. And then, suddenly, he sat up with a groan. "But if it's as good as that it's a failure!" he exclaimed.

Harviss, stiffening a little, examined the tip of his cigar. "My dear Linyard," he said at length, "I don't understand a word you're saying."

The Professor succumbed to a fresh access, from the vortex of which he managed to fling out — "But that's the very core of the joke!"

Harviss looked at him resignedly. "What is?"

"Why, your not seeing — your not understanding — "

"Not understanding what?"

8

"Why, what the book is meant to be." His laughter subsided again and he sat gazing thoughtfully at the publisher. "Unless it means," he wound up, "that I've over–shot the mark."

"If I am the mark, you certainly have," said Harviss, with a glance at the clock.

The Professor caught the glance and interpreted it. "The book is a skit," he said, rising.

The other stared. "A skit? It's not serious, you mean?"

"Not to me — but it seems you've taken it so."

"You never told me — " began the publisher in a ruffled tone.

"No, I never told you," said the Professor.

Harviss sat staring at the manuscript between them. "I don't pretend to be up in such recondite forms of humour," he said, still stiffly. "Of course you address yourself to a very small class of readers."

"Oh, infinitely small," admitted the Professor, extending his hand toward the manuscript.

Harviss appeared to be pursuing his own train of thought. "That is," he continued, "if you insist on an ironical interpretation."

"If I insist on it — what do you mean?"

The publisher smiled faintly. "Well — isn't the book susceptible of another? If I read it without seeing — "

"Well?" murmured the other, fascinated.

— "why shouldn't the rest of the world?" declared Harviss boldly. "I represent the Average Reader — that's my business, that's what I've been training myself to do for the last twenty years. It's a mission like another — the thing is to do it thoroughly; not to cheat and compromise. I know fellows who are publishers in business hours and

9

dilettantes the rest of the time. Well, they never succeed: convictions are just as necessary in business as in religion. But that's not the point — I was going to say that if you'll let me handle this book as a genuine thing I'll guarantee to make it go."

The Professor stood motionless, his hand still on the manuscript.

"A genuine thing?" he echoed.

"A serious piece of work — the expression of your convictions. I tell you there's nothing the public likes as much as convictions — they'll always follow a man who believes in his own ideas. And this book is just on the line of popular interest. You've got hold of a big thing. It's full of hope and enthusiasm: it's written in the religious key. There are passages in it that would do splendidly in a Birthday Book — things that popular preachers would quote in their sermons. If you'd wanted to catch a big public you couldn't have gone about it in a better way. The thing's perfect for my purpose — I wouldn't let you alter a word of it. It'll sell like a popular novel if you'll let me handle it in the right way."

III

WHEN the Professor left Harviss's office, the manuscript remained behind. He thought he had been taken by the huge irony of the situation — by the enlarged circumference of the joke. In its original form, as Harviss had said, the book would have addressed itself to a very limited circle: now it would include the world. The elect would understand; the crowd would not; and his work would thus serve a double purpose. And, after all, nothing was changed in the situation; not a word of the book was to be altered. The change was merely in the publisher's point of view, and in the "tip" he was to give the reviewers. The Professor had only to hold his tongue and look serious.

These arguments found a strong reinforcement in the large premium which expressed Harviss's sense of his opportunity. As a satire, the book would have brought its author nothing; in fact, its cost would have come out of his own pocket, since, as Harviss assured him, no publisher would have risked taking it. But as a profession of faith, as the recantation of an eminent biologist, whose leanings had hitherto been supposed to be toward a cold determinism, it would bring in a steady income to author and publisher.

The offer found the Professor in a moment of financial perplexity. His illness, his unwonted holiday, the necessity of postponing a course of well–paid lectures, had combined to diminish his resources; and when Harviss offered him an advance of a thousand dollars the esoteric savour of the joke became irresistible. It was still as a joke that he persisted in regarding the transaction; and though he had pledged himself not to betray the real intent of the book, he held in petto the notion of some day being able to take the public into his confidence. As for the initiated, they would know at once: and however long a face he pulled, his colleagues would see the tongue in his cheek. Meanwhile it fortunately happened that, even if the book should achieve the kind of triumph prophesied by Harviss, it would not appreciably injure its author's professional standing. Professor Linyard was known chiefly as a microscopist. On the structure and habits of a certain class of coleoptera he was the most distinguished living authority; but none save his intimate friends knew what generalizations on the destiny of man he had drawn from these special studies. He might have published a treatise on the Filioque without disturbing the confidence of those on whose approval his reputation rested; and moreover he was sustained by the thought that one glance at his book would let them into its secret. In fact, so sure was he of this that he wondered the astute Harviss had cared to risk such speedy exposure. But Harviss had probably reflected that even in this reverberating age the opinions of the laboratory do not easily reach the street; and the Professor, at any rate, was not bound to offer advice on this point.

The determining cause of his consent was the fact that the book was already in press. The Professor knew little about the workings of the press, but the phrase gave him a sense of finality, of having been caught himself in the toils of that mysterious engine. If he had had time to think the matter over, his scruples might have dragged him back; but his conscience was eased by the futility of resistance.

IV

MRS. LINYARD did not often read the papers; and there was therefore a special significance in her approaching her husband one evening after dinner with a copy of the New York Investigator in her hand. Her expression lent solemnity to the act: Mrs. Linyard had a limited but distinctive set of expressions, and she now looked as she did when the President of the University came to dine.

"You didn't tell me of this, Samuel," she said in a slightly tremulous voice.

"Tell you of what?" returned the Professor, reddening to the margin of his baldness.

"That you had published a book — I might never have heard of it if Mrs. Pease hadn't brought me the paper."

Her husband rubbed his eye–glasses with a groan. "Oh, you would have heard of it," he said gloomily.

Mrs. Linyard stared. "Did you wish to keep it from me, Samuel?" And as he made no answer, she added with irresistible pride: "Perhaps you don't know what beautiful things have been said about it."

He took the paper with a reluctant hand. "Has Pease been saying beautiful things about it?"

"The Professor? Mrs. Pease didn't say he had mentioned it."

The author heaved a sigh of relief. His book, as Harviss had prophesied, had caught the autumn market: had caught and captured it. The publisher had conducted the campaign like an experienced strategist. He had completely surrounded the enemy. Every newspaper, every periodical, held in ambush an advertisement of "The Vital Thing." Weeks in advance the great commander had begun to form his lines of attack. Allusions to the remarkable significance of the coming work had appeared first in the scientific and literary reviews, spreading thence to the supplements of the daily journals. Not a moment passed without a quickening touch to the public consciousness: seventy millions of people were forced to remember at least once a day that Professor Linyard's book was on the verge of appearing. Slips emblazoned with the question: Have you read "The Vital Thing"? fell from the pages of popular novels and whitened the floors of crowded street–cars. The query, in large lettering, assaulted the traveller at the railway bookstall, confronted him on the walls of "elevated" stations, and seemed, in its ascending scale, about to supplant the interrogations as to soap and stove–polish which animate our rural scenery.

The Descent of Man, and Other Stories

On the day of publication, the Professor had withdrawn to his laboratory. The shriek of the advertisements was in his ears, and his one desire was to avoid all knowledge of the event they heralded. A reaction of self–consciousness had set in, and if Harviss's cheque had sufficed to buy up the first edition of "The Vital Thing" the Professor would gladly have devoted it to that purpose. But the sense of inevitableness gradually subdued him, and he received his wife's copy of the Investigator with a kind of impersonal curiosity. The review was a long one, full of extracts: he saw, as he glanced over them, how well they would look in a volume of "Selections." The reviewer began by thanking his author "for sounding with no uncertain voice that note of ringing optimism, of faith in man's destiny and the supremacy of good, which has too long been silenced by the whining chorus of a decadent nihilism. . . . It is well," the writer continued, "when such reminders come to us not from the moralist but from the man of science — when from the desiccating atmosphere of the laboratory there rises this glorious cry of faith and reconstruction."

The review was minute and exhaustive. Thanks no doubt to Harviss's diplomacy, it had been given to the Investigator's "best man," and the Professor was startled by the bold eye with which his emancipated fallacies confronted him. Under the reviewer's handling they made up admirably as truths, and their author began to understand Harviss's regret that they should be used for any less profitable purpose.

The Investigator, as Harviss phrased it, "set the pace," and the other journals followed, finding it easier to let their critical man–of–all–work play a variation on the first reviewer's theme than to secure an expert to "do" the book afresh. But it was evident that the Professor had captured his public, for all the resources of the profession could not, as Harviss gleefully pointed out, have carried the book so straight to the heart of the nation. There was something noble in the way in which Harviss belittled his own share in the achievement, and insisted on the inutility of shoving a book which had started with such headway on.

"All I ask you is to admit that I saw what would happen," he said with a touch of professional pride. "I knew you'd struck the right note — I knew they'd be quoting you from Maine to San Francisco. Good as fiction? It's better — it'll keep going longer."

"Will it?" said the Professor with a slight shudder. He was resigned to an ephemeral triumph, but the thought of the book's persistency frightened him.

"I should say so! Why, you fit in everywhere — science, theology, natural history — and then the all−for−the−best element which is so popular just now. Why, you come right in with the How−to−Relax series, and they sell way up in the millions. And then the book's so full of tenderness — there are such lovely things in it about flowers and children. I didn't know an old Dryasdust like you could have such a lot of sentiment in him. Why, I actually caught myself snivelling over that passage about the snowdrops piercing the frozen earth; and my wife was saying the other day that, since she's read "The Vital Thing," she begins to think you must write the "What−Cheer Column in the Inglenook." He threw back his head with a laugh which ended in the inspired cry: "And, by George, sir, when the thing begins to slow off we'll start somebody writing against it, and that will run us straight into another hundred thousand."

And as earnest of this belief he drew the Professor a supplementary cheque.

V

MRS. LINYARD'S knock cut short the importunities of the lady who had been trying to persuade the Professor to be taken by flashlight at his study table for the Christmas number of the Inglenook. On this point the Professor had fancied himself impregnable; but the unwonted smile with which he welcomed his wife's intrusion showed that his defences were weakening.

The lady from the Inglenook took the hint with professional promptness, but said brightly, as she snapped the elastic around her note−book: "I shan't let you forget me, Professor."

The groan with which he followed her retreat was interrupted by his wife's question: "Do they pay you for these interviews, Samuel?"

The Professor looked at her with sudden attention. "Not directly," he said, wondering at her expression.

She sank down with a sigh. "Indirectly, then?"

"What is the matter, my dear? I gave you Harviss's second cheque the other day — "

Her tears arrested him. "Don't be hard on the boy, Samuel! I really believe your success has turned his head."

"The boy — what boy? My success — ? Explain yourself, Susan!"

"It's only that Jack has — has borrowed some money — which he can't repay. But you mustn't think him altogether to blame, Samuel. Since the success of your book he has been asked about so much — it's given the children quite a different position. Millicent says that wherever they go the first question asked is, 'Are you any relation of the author of "The Vital Thing"?' Of course we're all very proud of the book; but it entails obligations which you may not have thought of in writing it."

The Professor sat gazing at the letters and newspaper clippings on the study–table which he had just successfully defended from the camera of the Inglenook. He took up an envelope bearing the name of a popular weekly paper.

"I don't know that the Inglenook would help much," he said, "but I suppose this might."

Mrs. Linyard's eyes glowed with maternal avidity.

"What is it, Samuel?"

"A series of 'Scientific Sermons' for the Round–the–Gas–Log column of The Woman's World. I believe that journal has a larger circulation than any other weekly, and they pay in proportion."

He had not even asked the extent of Jack's indebtedness. It had been so easy to relieve recent domestic difficulties by the timely production of Harviss's two cheques, that it now seemed natural to get Mrs. Linyard out of the room by promising further reinforcements. The Professor had indignantly rejected Harviss's suggestion that he should follow up his success by a second volume on the same lines. He had sworn not to lend more than a passive support to the fraud of "The Vital Thing"; but the temptation to free himself from Mrs. Linyard prevailed over his last scruples, and within an hour he was at work on the Scientific Sermons.

The Professor was not an unkind man. He really enjoyed making his family happy; and it was his own business if his reward for so doing was that it kept them out of his way. But the success of "The Vital Thing" gave him more than this negative satisfaction. It enlarged his own existence and opened new doors into other lives. The Professor, during fifty virtuous years, had been cognizant of only two types of women: the fond and foolish, whom one married, and the earnest and intellectual, whom one did not. Of the two, he infinitely preferred the former, even for conversational purposes. But as a social instrument woman was unknown to him; and it was not till he was drawn into the world on the tide of his literary success that he discovered the deficiencies in his classification of the sex. Then he learned with astonishment of the existence of a third type: the woman who is fond without foolishness and intellectual without earnestness. Not that the Professor inspired, or sought to inspire, sentimental emotions; but he expanded in the warm atmosphere of personal interest which some of his new acquaintances contrived to create about him. It was delightful to talk of serious things in a setting of frivolity, and to be personal without being domestic.

Even in this new world, where all subjects were touched on lightly, and emphasis was the only indelicacy, the Professor found himself constrained to endure an occasional reference to his book. It was unpleasant at first; but gradually he slipped into the habit of hearing it talked of, and grew accustomed to telling pretty women just how "it had first come to him."

Meanwhile the success of the Scientific Sermons was facilitating his family relations. His photograph in the Inglenook, to which the lady of the note-book had succeeded in appending a vivid interview, carried his fame to circles inaccessible even to "The Vital Thing"; and the Professor found himself the man of the hour. He soon grew used to the functions of the office, and gave out hundred-dollar interviews on every subject, from labour-strikes to Babism, with a frequency which reacted agreeably on the domestic exchequer. Presently his head began to figure in the advertising pages of the magazines. Admiring readers learned the name of the only breakfast-food in use at his table, of the ink with which "The Vital Thing" had been written, the soap with which the author's hands were washed, and the tissue-builder which fortified him for further effort. These confidences endeared the Professor to millions of readers, and his head passed in due course from the magazine and the newspaper to the biscuit-tin and the chocolate-box.

VI

THE Professor, all the while, was leading a double life. While the author of "The Vital Thing" reaped the fruits of popular approval, the distinguished microscopist continued his laboratory work unheeded save by the few who were engaged in the same line of investigations. His divided allegiance had not hitherto affected the quality of his work: it seemed to him that he returned to the laboratory with greater zest after an afternoon in a drawing–room where readings from "The Vital Thing" had alternated with plantation melodies and tea. He had long ceased to concern himself with what his colleagues thought of his literary career. Of the few whom he frequented, none had referred to "The Vital Thing"; and he knew enough of their lives to guess that their silence might as fairly be attributed to indifference as to disapproval. They were intensely interested in the Professor's views on beetles, but they really cared very little what he thought of the Almighty.

The Professor entirely shared their feelings, and one of his chief reasons for cultivating the success which accident had bestowed on him, was that it enabled him to command a greater range of appliances for his real work. He had known what it was to lack books and instruments; and "The Vital Thing" was the magic wand which summoned them to his aid. For some time he had been feeling his way along the edge of a discovery: balancing himself with professional skill on a plank of hypothesis flung across an abyss of uncertainty. The conjecture was the result of years of patient gathering of facts: its corroboration would take months more of comparison and classification. But at the end of the vista victory loomed. The Professor felt within himself that assurance of ultimate justification which, to the man of science, makes a life–time seem the mere comma between premiss and deduction. But he had reached the point where his conjectures required formulation. It was only by giving them expression, by exposing them to the comment and criticism of his associates, that he could test their final value; and this inner assurance was confirmed by the only friend whose confidence he invited.

Professor Pease, the husband of the lady who had opened Mrs. Linyard's eyes to the triumph of "The Vital Thing," was the repository of her husband's scientific experiences. What he thought of "The Vital Thing" had never been divulged; and he was capable of such vast exclusions that it was quite possible that pervasive work had not yet reached him. In any case, it was not likely to affect his judgment of the author's professional capacity.

"You want to put that all in a book, Linyard," was Professor Pease's summing–up. "I'm sure you've got hold of something big; but to see it clearly yourself you ought to outline it for others. Take my advice — chuck everything else and get to work tomorrow. It's time you wrote a book, anyhow."

It's time you wrote a book, anyhow! The words smote the Professor with mingled pain and ecstasy: he could have wept over their significance. But his friend's other phrase reminded him with a start of Harviss. "You have got hold of a big thing — " it had been the publisher's first comment on "The Vital Thing." But what a world of meaning lay between the two phrases! It was the world in which the powers who fought for the Professor were destined to wage their final battle; and for the moment he had no doubt of the outcome.

"By George, I'll do it, Pease!" he said, stretching his hand to his friend.

The next day he went to town to see Harviss. He wanted to ask for an advance on the new popular edition of "The Vital Thing." He had determined to drop a course of supplementary lectures at the University, and to give himself up for a year to his book. To do this, additional funds were necessary; but thanks to "The Vital Thing" they would be forthcoming.

The publisher received him as cordially as usual; but the response to his demand was not as prompt as his previous experience had entitled him to expect.

"Of course we'll be glad to do what we can for you, Linyard; but the fact is, we've decided to give up the idea of the new edition for the present."

"You've given up the new edition?"

"Why, yes — we've done pretty well by 'The Vital Thing,' and we're inclined to think it's your turn to do something for it now."

The Professor looked at him blankly. "What can I do for it?" he asked — "what more" his accent added.

"Why, put a little new life in it by writing something else. The secret of perpetual motion hasn't yet been discovered, you know, and it's one of the laws of literature that books which start with a rush are apt to slow down sooner than the crawlers. We've kept 'The Vital Thing' going for eighteen months — but, hang it, it ain't so vital any more. We simply couldn't see our way to a new edition. Oh, I don't say it's dead yet — but it's moribund, and you're the only man who can resuscitate it."

The Professor continued to stare. "I — what can I do about it?" he stammered.

"Do? Why write another like it — go it one better: you know the trick. The public isn't tired of you by any means; but you want to make yourself heard again before anybody else cuts in. Write another book — write two, and we'll sell them in sets in a box: The Vital Thing Series. That will take tremendously in the holidays. Try and let us have a new volume by October — I'll be glad to give you a big advance if you'll sign a contract on that."

The Professor sat silent: there was too cruel an irony in the coincidence.

Harviss looked up at him in surprise.

"Well, what's the matter with taking my advice — you're not going out of literature, are you?"

The Professor rose from his chair. "No — I'm going into it," he said simply.

"Going into it?"

"I'm going to write a real book — a serious one."

"Good Lord! Most people think 'The Vital Thing' 's serious."

"Yes — but I mean something different."

"In your old line — beetles and so forth?"

"Yes," said the Professor solemnly.

Harviss looked at him with equal gravity. "Well, I'm sorry for that," he said, "because it takes you out of our bailiwick. But I suppose you've made enough money out of 'The Vital Thing' to permit yourself a little harmless amusement. When you want more cash come back to us — only don't put it off too long, or some other fellow will have stepped into your shoes. Popularity don't keep, you know; and the hotter the success the quicker the commodity perishes."

He leaned back, cheerful and sententious, delivering his axioms with conscious kindliness.

The Professor, who had risen and moved to the door, turned back with a wavering step.

"When did you say another volume would have to be ready?" he faltered.

"I said October — but call it a month later. You don't need any pushing nowadays."

"And — you'd have no objection to letting me have a little advance now? I need some new instruments for my real work."

Harviss extended a cordial hand. "My dear fellow, that's talking — I'll write the cheque while you wait; and I daresay we can start up the cheap edition of 'The Vital Thing' at the same time, if you'll pledge yourself to give us the book by November. — How much?" he asked, poised above his cheque–book.

In the street, the Professor stood staring about him, uncertain and a little dazed.

"After all, it's only putting it off for six months," he said to himself; "and I can do better work when I get my new instruments."

He smiled and raised his hat to the passing victoria of a lady in whose copy of "The Vital Thing" he had recently written:

Labor est etiam ipsa voluptas.

The Other Two

I

WAYTHORN, on the drawing-room hearth, waited for his wife to come down to dinner.

It was their first night under his own roof, and he was surprised at his thrill of boyish agitation. He was not so old, to be sure — his glass gave him little more than the five-and-thirty years to which his wife confessed — but he had fancied himself already in the temperate zone; yet here he was listening for her step with a tender sense of all it symbolized, with some old trail of verse about the garlanded nuptial door-posts floating through his enjoyment of the pleasant room and the good dinner just beyond it.

They had been hastily recalled from their honeymoon by the illness of Lily Haskett, the child of Mrs. Waythorn's first marriage. The little girl, at Waythorn's desire, had been transferred to his house on the day of her mother's wedding, and the doctor, on their arrival, broke the news that she was ill with typhoid, but declared that all the symptoms were favorable. Lily could show twelve years of unblemished health, and the case promised to be a light one. The nurse spoke as reassuringly, and after a moment of alarm Mrs. Waythorn had adjusted herself to the situation. She was very fond of Lily — her affection for the child had perhaps been her decisive charm in Waythorn's eyes — but she had the perfectly balanced nerves which her little girl had inherited, and no woman ever wasted less tissue in unproductive worry. Waythorn was therefore quite prepared to see her come in presently, a little late because of a last look at Lily, but as serene and well-appointed as if her good-night kiss had been laid on the brow of health. Her composure was restful to him; it acted as ballast to his somewhat unstable sensibilities. As he pictured her bending over the child's bed he thought how soothing her presence must be in illness: her very step would prognosticate recovery.

His own life had been a gray one, from temperament rather than circumstance, and he had been drawn to her by the unperturbed gayety which kept her fresh and elastic at an age when most women's activities are growing either slack or febrile. He knew what was said about her; for, popular as she was, there had always been a faint undercurrent of detraction. When she had appeared in New York, nine or ten years earlier, as the pretty Mrs. Haskett whom Gus Varick had unearthed somewhere — was it in Pittsburgh or

Utica? — society, while promptly accepting her, had reserved the right to cast a doubt on its own discrimination. Inquiry, however, established her undoubted connection with a socially reigning family, and explained her recent divorce as the natural result of a runaway match at seventeen; and as nothing was known of Mr. Haskett it was easy to believe the worst of him.

Alice Haskett's remarriage with Gus Varick was a passport to the set whose recognition she coveted, and for a few years the Varicks were the most popular couple in town. Unfortunately the alliance was brief and stormy, and this time the husband had his champions. Still, even Varick's stanchest supporters admitted that he was not meant for matrimony, and Mrs. Varick's grievances were of a nature to bear the inspection of the New York courts. A New York divorce is in itself a diploma of virtue, and in the semi–widowhood of this second separation Mrs. Varick took on an air of sanctity, and was allowed to confide her wrongs to some of the most scrupulous ears in town. But when it was known that she was to marry Waythorn there was a momentary reaction. Her best friends would have preferred to see her remain in the role of the injured wife, which was as becoming to her as crape to a rosy complexion. True, a decent time had elapsed, and it was not even suggested that Waythorn had supplanted his predecessor. Still, people shook their heads over him, and one grudging friend, to whom he affirmed that he took the step with his eyes open, replied oracularly: "Yes — and with your ears shut."

Waythorn could afford to smile at these innuendoes. In the Wall Street phrase, he had "discounted" them. He knew that society has not yet adapted itself to the consequences of divorce, and that till the adaptation takes place every woman who uses the freedom the law accords her must be her own social justification. Waythorn had an amused confidence in his wife's ability to justify herself. His expectations were fulfilled, and before the wedding took place Alice Varick's group had rallied openly to her support. She took it all imperturbably: she had a way of surmounting obstacles without seeming to be aware of them, and Waythorn looked back with wonder at the trivialities over which he had worn his nerves thin. He had the sense of having found refuge in a richer, warmer nature than his own, and his satisfaction, at the moment, was humorously summed up in the thought that his wife, when she had done all she could for Lily, would not be ashamed to come down and enjoy a good dinner.

The anticipation of such enjoyment was not, however, the sentiment expressed by Mrs. Waythorn's charming face when she presently joined him. Though she had put on her most engaging teagown she had neglected to assume the smile that went with it, and Waythorn thought he had never seen her look so nearly worried.

"What is it?" he asked. "Is anything wrong with Lily?"

"No; I've just been in and she's still sleeping." Mrs. Waythorn hesitated. "But something tiresome has happened."

He had taken her two hands, and now perceived that he was crushing a paper between them.

"This letter?"

"Yes — Mr. Haskett has written — I mean his lawyer has written."

Waythorn felt himself flush uncomfortably. He dropped his wife's hands.

"What about?"

"About seeing Lily. You know the courts — "

"Yes, yes," he interrupted nervously.

Nothing was known about Haskett in New York. He was vaguely supposed to have remained in the outer darkness from which his wife had been rescued, and Waythorn was one of the few who were aware that he had given up his business in Utica and followed her to New York in order to be near his little girl. In the days of his wooing, Waythorn had often met Lily on the doorstep, rosy and smiling, on her way "to see papa."

"I am so sorry," Mrs. Waythorn murmured.

He roused himself. "What does he want?"

"He wants to see her. You know she goes to him once a week."

"Well — he doesn't expect her to go to him now, does he?"

"No — he has heard of her illness; but he expects to come here."

"Here?"

Mrs. Waythorn reddened under his gaze. They looked away from each other.

"I'm afraid he has the right. . . . You'll see. . . ." She made a proffer of the letter.

Waythorn moved away with a gesture of refusal. He stood staring about the softly lighted room, which a moment before had seemed so full of bridal intimacy.

"I'm so sorry," she repeated. "If Lily could have been moved — "

"That's out of the question," he returned impatiently.

"I suppose so."

Her lip was beginning to tremble, and he felt himself a brute.

"He must come, of course," he said. "When is — his day?"

"I'm afraid — to-morrow."

"Very well. Send a note in the morning."

The butler entered to announce dinner.

Waythorn turned to his wife. "Come — you must be tired. It's beastly, but try to forget about it," he said, drawing her hand through his arm.

"You're so good, dear. I'll try," she whispered back.

Her face cleared at once, and as she looked at him across the flowers, between the rosy candle-shades, he saw her lips waver back into a smile.

"How pretty everything is!" she sighed luxuriously.

He turned to the butler. "The champagne at once, please. Mrs. Waythorn is tired."

In a moment or two their eyes met above the sparkling glasses. Her own were quite clear and untroubled: he saw that she had obeyed his injunction and forgotten.

II

WAYTHORN, the next morning, went down town earlier than usual. Haskett was not likely to come till the afternoon, but the instinct of flight drove him forth. He meant to stay away all day — he had thoughts of dining at his club. As his door closed behind him he reflected that before he opened it again it would have admitted another man who had as much right to enter it as himself, and the thought filled him with a physical repugnance.

He caught the "elevated" at the employees' hour, and found himself crushed between two layers of pendulous humanity. At Eighth Street the man facing him wriggled out and another took his place. Waythorn glanced up and saw that it was Gus Varick. The men were so close together that it was impossible to ignore the smile of recognition on Varick's handsome overblown face. And after all — why not? They had always been on good terms, and Varick had been divorced before Waythorn's attentions to his wife began. The two exchanged a word on the perennial grievance of the congested trains, and when a seat at their side was miraculously left empty the instinct of self-preservation made Waythorn slip into it after Varick.

The latter drew the stout man's breath of relief.

"Lord — I was beginning to feel like a pressed flower." He leaned back, looking unconcernedly at Waythorn. "Sorry to hear that Sellers is knocked out again."

"Sellers?" echoed Waythorn, starting at his partner's name.

Varick looked surprised. "You didn't know he was laid up with the gout?"

"No. I've been away — I only got back last night." Waythorn felt himself reddening in anticipation of the other's smile.

"Ah — yes; to be sure. And Sellers's attack came on two days ago. I'm afraid he's pretty bad. Very awkward for me, as it happens, because he was just putting through a rather important thing for me."

"Ah?" Waythorn wondered vaguely since when Varick had been dealing in "important things." Hitherto he had dabbled only in the shallow pools of speculation, with which Waythorn's office did not usually concern itself.

It occurred to him that Varick might be talking at random, to relieve the strain of their propinquity. That strain was becoming momentarily more apparent to Waythorn, and when, at Cortlandt Street, he caught sight of an acquaintance, and had a sudden vision of the picture he and Varick must present to an initiated eye, he jumped up with a muttered excuse.

"I hope you'll find Sellers better," said Varick civilly, and he stammered back: "If I can be of any use to you — " and let the departing crowd sweep him to the platform.

At his office he heard that Sellers was in fact ill with the gout, and would probably not be able to leave the house for some weeks.

"I'm sorry it should have happened so, Mr. Waythorn," the senior clerk said with affable significance. "Mr. Sellers was very much upset at the idea of giving you such a lot of extra work just now."

"Oh, that's no matter," said Waythorn hastily. He secretly welcomed the pressure of additional business, and was glad to think that, when the day's work was over, he would have to call at his partner's on the way home.

He was late for luncheon, and turned in at the nearest restaurant instead of going to his club. The place was full, and the waiter hurried him to the back of the room to capture the only vacant table. In the cloud of cigar–smoke Waythorn did not at once distinguish his neighbors; but presently, looking about him, he saw Varick seated a few feet off. This time, luckily, they were too far apart for conversation, and Varick, who faced another way, had probably not even seen him; but there was an irony in their renewed nearness.

Varick was said to be fond of good living, and as Waythorn sat despatching his hurried luncheon he looked across half enviously at the other's leisurely degustation of his meal. When Waythorn first saw him he had been helping himself with critical deliberation to a bit of Camembert at the ideal point of liquefaction, and now, the cheese removed, he was just pouring his cafe double from its little two–storied earthen pot. He poured slowly, his ruddy profile bent above the task, and one beringed white hand steadying the lid of the coffee–pot; then he stretched his other hand to the decanter of cognac at his elbow, filled a liqueur–glass, took a tentative sip, and poured the brandy into his coffee–cup.

Waythorn watched him in a kind of fascination. What was he thinking of — only of the flavor of the coffee and the liqueur? Had the morning's meeting left no more trace in his thoughts than on his face? Had his wife so completely passed out of his life that even this odd encounter with her present husband, within a week after her remarriage, was no more than an incident in his day? And as Waythorn mused, another idea struck him: had Haskett ever met Varick as Varick and he had just met? The recollection of Haskett perturbed him, and he rose and left the restaurant, taking a circuitous way out to escape the placid irony of Varick's nod.

It was after seven when Waythorn reached home. He thought the footman who opened the door looked at him oddly.

"How is Miss Lily?" he asked in haste.

"Doing very well, sir. A gentleman — "

"Tell Barlow to put off dinner for half an hour," Waythorn cut him off, hurrying upstairs.

He went straight to his room and dressed without seeing his wife. When he reached the drawing–room she was there, fresh and radiant. Lily's day had been good; the doctor was not coming back that evening.

At dinner Waythorn told her of Sellers's illness and of the resulting complications. She listened sympathetically, adjuring him not to let himself be overworked, and asking vague feminine questions about the routine of the office. Then she gave him the chronicle of Lily's day; quoted the nurse and doctor, and told him who had called to inquire. He had never seen her more serene and unruffled. It struck him, with a curious pang, that she was very happy in being with him, so happy that she found a childish pleasure in rehearsing the trivial incidents of her day.

After dinner they went to the library, and the servant put the coffee and liqueurs on a low table before her and left the room. She looked singularly soft and girlish in her rosy pale dress, against the dark leather of one of his bachelor armchairs. A day earlier the contrast would have charmed him.

He turned away now, choosing a cigar with affected deliberation.

"Did Haskett come?" he asked, with his back to her.

"Oh, yes — he came."

"You didn't see him, of course?"

She hesitated a moment. "I let the nurse see him."

That was all. There was nothing more to ask. He swung round toward her, applying a match to his cigar. Well, the thing was over for a week, at any rate. He would try not to think of it. She looked up at him, a trifle rosier than usual, with a smile in her eyes.

"Ready for your coffee, dear?"

He leaned against the mantelpiece, watching her as she lifted the coffee–pot. The lamplight struck a gleam from her bracelets and tipped her soft hair with brightness. How light and slender she was, and how each gesture flowed into the next! She seemed a creature all compact of harmonies. As the thought of Haskett receded, Waythorn felt himself yielding again to the joy of possessorship. They were his, those white hands with their flitting motions, his the light haze of hair, the lips and eyes. . . .

She set down the coffee–pot, and reaching for the decanter of cognac, measured off a liqueur–glass and poured it into his cup.

Waythorn uttered a sudden exclamation.

"What is the matter?" she said, startled.

"Nothing; only — I don't take cognac in my coffee."

"Oh, how stupid of me," she cried.

Their eyes met, and she blushed a sudden agonized red.

III

TEN DAYS later, Mr. Sellers, still house–bound, asked Waythorn to call on his way downtown.

The senior partner, with his swaddled foot propped up by the fire, greeted his associate with an air of embarrassment.

"I'm sorry, my dear fellow; I've got to ask you to do an awkward thing for me."

Waythorn waited, and the other went on, after a pause apparently given to the arrangement of his phrases: "The fact is, when I was knocked out I had just gone into a rather complicated piece of business for — Gus Varick."

"Well?" said Waythorn, with an attempt to put him at his ease.

"Well — it's this way: Varick came to me the day before my attack. He had evidently had an inside tip from somebody, and had made about a hundred thousand. He came to me for advice, and I suggested his going in with Vanderlyn."

"Oh, the deuce!" Waythorn exclaimed. He saw in a flash what had happened. The investment was an alluring one, but required negotiation. He listened intently while Sellers put the case before him, and, the statement ended, he said: "You think I ought to see Varick?"

"I'm afraid I can't as yet. The doctor is obdurate. And this thing can't wait. I hate to ask you, but no one else in the office knows the ins and outs of it."

Waythorn stood silent. He did not care a farthing for the success of Varick's venture, but the honor of the office was to be considered, and he could hardly refuse to oblige his partner.

"Very well," he said, "I'll do it."

That afternoon, apprised by telephone, Varick called at the office. Waythorn, waiting in his private room, wondered what the others thought of it. The newspapers, at the time of Mrs. Waythorn's marriage, had acquainted their readers with every detail of her previous matrimonial ventures, and Waythorn could fancy the clerks smiling behind Varick's back as he was ushered in.

Varick bore himself admirably. He was easy without being undignified, and Waythorn was conscious of cutting a much less impressive figure. Varick had no head for business, and the talk prolonged itself for nearly an hour while Waythorn set forth with scrupulous precision the details of the proposed transaction.

"I'm awfully obliged to you," Varick said as he rose. "The fact is I'm not used to having much money to look after, and I don't want to make an ass of myself — " He smiled, and Waythorn could not help noticing that there was something pleasant about his smile. "It feels uncommonly queer to have enough cash to pay one's bills. I'd have sold my soul for it a few years ago!"

Waythorn winced at the allusion. He had heard it rumored that a lack of funds had been one of the determining causes of the Varick separation, but it did not occur to him that Varick's words were intentional. It seemed more likely that the desire to keep clear of embarrassing topics had fatally drawn him into one. Waythorn did not wish to be outdone in civility.

"We'll do the best we can for you," he said. "I think this is a good thing you're in."

"Oh, I'm sure it's immense. It's awfully good of you — " Varick broke off, embarrassed. "I suppose the thing's settled now — but if — "

"If anything happens before Sellers is about, I'll see you again," said Waythorn quietly. He was glad, in the end, to appear the more self–possessed of the two.

The course of Lily's illness ran smooth, and as the days passed Waythorn grew used to the idea of Haskett's weekly visit. The first time the day came round, he stayed out late, and questioned his wife as to the visit on his return. She replied at once that Haskett had merely seen the nurse downstairs, as the doctor did not wish any one in the child's sick-room till after the crisis.

The following week Waythorn was again conscious of the recurrence of the day, but had forgotten it by the time he came home to dinner. The crisis of the disease came a few days later, with a rapid decline of fever, and the little girl was pronounced out of danger. In the rejoicing which ensued the thought of Haskett passed out of Waythorn's mind and one afternoon, letting himself into the house with a latchkey, he went straight to his library without noticing a shabby hat and umbrella in the hall.

In the library he found a small effaced-looking man with a thinnish gray beard sitting on the edge of a chair. The stranger might have been a piano-tuner, or one of those mysteriously efficient persons who are summoned in emergencies to adjust some detail of the domestic machinery. He blinked at Waythorn through a pair of gold-rimmed spectacles and said mildly: "Mr. Waythorn, I presume? I am Lily's father."

Waythorn flushed. "Oh — " he stammered uncomfortably. He broke off, disliking to appear rude. Inwardly he was trying to adjust the actual Haskett to the image of him projected by his wife's reminiscences. Waythorn had been allowed to infer that Alice's first husband was a brute.

"I am sorry to intrude," said Haskett, with his over-the- counter politeness.

"Don't mention it," returned Waythorn, collecting himself. "I suppose the nurse has been told?"

"I presume so. I can wait," said Haskett. He had a resigned way of speaking, as though life had worn down his natural powers of resistance.

Waythorn stood on the threshold, nervously pulling off his gloves.

"I'm sorry you've been detained. I will send for the nurse," he said; and as he opened the door he added with an effort: "I'm glad we can give you a good report of Lily." He winced as the we slipped out, but Haskett seemed not to notice it.

"Thank you, Mr. Waythorn. It's been an anxious time for me."

"Ah, well, that's past. Soon she'll be able to go to you." Waythorn nodded and passed out.

In his own room, he flung himself down with a groan. He hated the womanish sensibility which made him suffer so acutely from the grotesque chances of life. He had known when he married that his wife's former husbands were both living, and that amid the multiplied contacts of modern existence there were a thousand chances to one that he would run against one or the other, yet he found himself as much disturbed by his brief encounter with Haskett as though the law had not obligingly removed all difficulties in the way of their meeting.

Waythorn sprang up and began to pace the room nervously. He had not suffered half so much from his two meetings with Varick. It was Haskett's presence in his own house that made the situation so intolerable. He stood still, hearing steps in the passage.

"This way, please," he heard the nurse say. Haskett was being taken upstairs, then: not a corner of the house but was open to him. Waythorn dropped into another chair, staring vaguely ahead of him. On his dressing–table stood a photograph of Alice, taken when he had first known her. She was Alice Varick then — how fine and exquisite he had thought her! Those were Varick's pearls about her neck. At Waythorn's instance they had been returned before her marriage. Had Haskett ever given her any trinkets — and what had become of them, Waythorn wondered? He realized suddenly that he knew very little of Haskett's past or present situation; but from the man's appearance and manner of speech he could reconstruct with curious precision the surroundings of Alice's first marriage. And it startled him to think that she had, in the background of her life, a phase of existence so different from anything with which he had connected her. Varick, whatever his faults, was a gentleman, in the conventional, traditional sense of the term: the sense which at that moment seemed, oddly enough, to have most meaning to Waythorn. He and Varick had the same social habits, spoke the same language, understood the same allusions. But this other man . . . it was grotesquely uppermost in Waythorn's mind that Haskett had worn a made–up tie attached with an elastic. Why should that ridiculous detail symbolize the whole man? Waythorn was exasperated by his own paltriness, but the fact of the tie expanded, forced itself on him, became as it were the key to Alice's past. He could see her, as Mrs. Haskett, sitting in a "front parlor" furnished in plush, with a pianola, and a copy of "Ben Hur" on the centre−table. He could see her going to the theatre with Haskett — or perhaps even to a "Church Sociable" — she in a "picture hat" and Haskett in a black frock−coat, a little creased, with the made−up tie on an elastic. On the way home they would stop and look at the illuminated shop−windows, lingering over the photographs of New York actresses. On Sunday afternoons Haskett would take her for a walk, pushing Lily ahead of them in a white enameled perambulator, and Waythorn had a vision of the people they would stop and talk to. He could fancy how pretty Alice must have looked, in a dress adroitly constructed from the hints of a New York fashion−paper; how she must have looked down on the other women, chafing at her life, and secretly feeling that she belonged in a bigger place.

For the moment his foremost thought was one of wonder at the way in which she had shed the phase of existence which her marriage with Haskett implied. It was as if her whole aspect, every gesture, every inflection, every allusion, were a studied negation of that period of her life. If she had denied being married to Haskett she could hardly have stood more convicted of duplicity than in this obliteration of the self which had been his wife.

Waythorn started up, checking himself in the analysis of her motives. What right had he to create a fantastic effigy of her and then pass judgment on it? She had spoken vaguely of her first marriage as unhappy, had hinted, with becoming reticence, that Haskett had wrought havoc among her young illusions. . . . It was a pity for Waythorn's peace of mind that Haskett's very inoffensiveness shed a new light on the nature of those illusions. A man would rather think that his wife has been brutalized by her first husband than that the process has been reversed.

IV

"MR. WAYTHORN, I don't like that French governess of Lily's."

Haskett, subdued and apologetic, stood before Waythorn in the library, revolving his shabby hat in his hand.

Waythorn, surprised in his armchair over the evening paper, stared back perplexedly at his visitor.

"You'll excuse my asking to see you," Haskett continued. "But this is my last visit, and I thought if I could have a word with you it would be a better way than writing to Mrs. Waythorn's lawyer."

Waythorn rose uneasily. He did not like the French governess either; but that was irrelevant.

"I am not so sure of that," he returned stiffly; "but since you wish it I will give your message to — my wife." He always hesitated over the possessive pronoun in addressing Haskett.

The latter sighed. "I don't know as that will help much. She didn't like it when I spoke to her."

Waythorn turned red. "When did you see her?" he asked.

"Not since the first day I came to see Lily — right after she was taken sick. I remarked to her then that I didn't like the governess."

Waythorn made no answer. He remembered distinctly that, after that first visit, he had asked his wife if she had seen Haskett. She had lied to him then, but she had respected his wishes since; and the incident cast a curious light on her character. He was sure she would not have seen Haskett that first day if she had divined that Waythorn would object, and the fact that she did not divine it was almost as disagreeable to the latter as the discovery that she had lied to him.

"I don't like the woman," Haskett was repeating with mild persistency. "She ain't straight, Mr. Waythorn — she'll teach the child to be underhand. I've noticed a change in Lily — she's too anxious to please — and she don't always tell the truth. She used to be the straightest child, Mr. Waythorn — " He broke off, his voice a little thick. "Not but what I want her to have a stylish education," he ended.

Waythorn was touched. "I'm sorry, Mr. Haskett; but frankly, I don't quite see what I can do."

Haskett hesitated. Then he laid his hat on the table, and advanced to the hearth–rug, on which Waythorn was standing. There was nothing aggressive in his manner; but he had the solemnity of a timid man resolved on a decisive measure.

"There's just one thing you can do, Mr. Waythorn," he said. "You can remind Mrs. Waythorn that, by the decree of the courts, I am entitled to have a voice in Lily's bringing up." He paused, and went on more deprecatingly: "I'm not the kind to talk about enforcing my rights, Mr. Waythorn. I don't know as I think a man is entitled to rights he hasn't known how to hold on to; but this business of the child is different. I've never let go there — and I never mean to."

The scene left Waythorn deeply shaken. Shamefacedly, in indirect ways, he had been finding out about Haskett; and all that he had learned was favorable. The little man, in order to be near his daughter, had sold out his share in a profitable business in Utica, and accepted a modest clerkship in a New York manufacturing house. He boarded in a shabby street and had few acquaintances. His passion for Lily filled his life. Waythorn felt that this exploration of Haskett was like groping about with a dark–lantern in his wife's past; but he saw now that there were recesses his lantern had not explored. He had never inquired into the exact circumstances of his wife's first matrimonial rupture. On the surface all had been fair. It was she who had obtained the divorce, and the court had given her the child. But Waythorn knew how many ambiguities such a verdict might cover. The mere fact that Haskett retained a right over his daughter implied an unsuspected compromise. Waythorn was an idealist. He always refused to recognize unpleasant contingencies till he found himself confronted with them, and then he saw them followed by a special train of consequences. His next days were thus haunted, and he determined to try to lay the ghosts by conjuring them up in his wife's presence.

When he repeated Haskett's request a flame of anger passed over her face; but she subdued it instantly and spoke with a slight quiver of outraged motherhood.

"It is very ungentlemanly of him," she said.

The word grated on Waythorn. "That is neither here nor there. It's a bare question of rights."

She murmured: "It's not as if he could ever be a help to Lily — "

35

Waythorn flushed. This was even less to his taste. "The question is," he repeated, "what authority has he over her?"

She looked downward, twisting herself a little in her seat. "I am willing to see him — I thought you objected," she faltered.

In a flash he understood that she knew the extent of Haskett's claims. Perhaps it was not the first time she had resisted them.

"My objecting has nothing to do with it," he said coldly; "if Haskett has a right to be consulted you must consult him."

She burst into tears, and he saw that she expected him to regard her as a victim.

Haskett did not abuse his rights. Waythorn had felt miserably sure that he would not. But the governess was dismissed, and from time to time the little man demanded an interview with Alice. After the first outburst she accepted the situation with her usual adaptability. Haskett had once reminded Waythorn of the piano–tuner, and Mrs. Waythorn, after a month or two, appeared to class him with that domestic familiar. Waythorn could not but respect the father's tenacity. At first he had tried to cultivate the suspicion that Haskett might be "up to" something, that he had an object in securing a foothold in the house. But in his heart Waythorn was sure of Haskett's single–mindedness; he even guessed in the latter a mild contempt for such advantages as his relation with the Waythorns might offer. Haskett's sincerity of purpose made him invulnerable, and his successor had to accept him as a lien on the property.

Mr. Sellers was sent to Europe to recover from his gout, and Varick's affairs hung on Waythorn's hands. The negotiations were prolonged and complicated; they necessitated frequent conferences between the two men, and the interests of the firm forbade Waythorn's suggesting that his client should transfer his business to another office.

Varick appeared well in the transaction. In moments of relaxation his coarse streak appeared, and Waythorn dreaded his geniality; but in the office he was concise and clear–headed, with a flattering deference to Waythorn's judgment. Their business relations being so affably established, it would have been absurd for the two men to ignore each other in society. The first time they met in a drawing–room, Varick took up their intercourse in the same easy key, and his hostess's grateful glance obliged Waythorn to respond to it. After that they ran across each other frequently, and one evening at a ball Waythorn, wandering through the remoter rooms, came upon Varick seated beside his wife. She colored a little, and faltered in what she was saying; but Varick nodded to Waythorn without rising, and the latter strolled on.

In the carriage, on the way home, he broke out nervously: "I didn't know you spoke to Varick."

Her voice trembled a little. "It's the first time — he happened to be standing near me; I didn't know what to do. It's so awkward, meeting everywhere — and he said you had been very kind about some business."

"That's different," said Waythorn.

She paused a moment. "I'll do just as you wish," she returned pliantly. "I thought it would be less awkward to speak to him when we meet."

Her pliancy was beginning to sicken him. Had she really no will of her own — no theory about her relation to these men? She had accepted Haskett — did she mean to accept Varick? It was "less awkward," as she had said, and her instinct was to evade difficulties or to circumvent them. With sudden vividness Waythorn saw how the instinct had developed. She was "as easy as an old shoe" — a shoe that too many feet had worn. Her elasticity was the result of tension in too many different directions. Alice Haskett — Alice Varick — Alice Waythorn — she had been each in turn, and had left hanging to each name a little of her privacy, a little of her personality, a little of the inmost self where the unknown god abides.

"Yes — it's better to speak to Varick," said Waythorn wearily.

V

THE WINTER wore on, and society took advantage of the Waythorns' acceptance of Varick. Harassed hostesses were grateful to them for bridging over a social difficulty, and Mrs. Waythorn was held up as a miracle of good taste. Some experimental spirits could not resist the diversion of throwing Varick and his former wife together, and there were those who thought he found a zest in the propinquity. But Mrs. Waythorn's conduct remained irreproachable. She neither avoided Varick nor sought him out. Even Waythorn could not but admit that she had discovered the solution of the newest social problem.

He had married her without giving much thought to that problem. He had fancied that a woman can shed her past like a man. But now he saw that Alice was bound to hers both by the circumstances which forced her into continued relation with it, and by the traces it had left on her nature. With grim irony Waythorn compared himself to a member of a syndicate. He held so many shares in his wife's personality and his predecessors were his partners in the business. If there had been any element of passion in the transaction he would have felt less deteriorated by it. The fact that Alice took her change of husbands like a change of weather reduced the situation to mediocrity. He could have forgiven her for blunders, for excesses; for resisting Hackett, for yielding to Varick; for anything but her acquiescence and her tact. She reminded him of a juggler tossing knives; but the knives were blunt and she knew they would never cut her.

And then, gradually, habit formed a protecting surface for his sensibilities. If he paid for each day's comfort with the small change of his illusions, he grew daily to value the comfort more and set less store upon the coin. He had drifted into a dulling propinquity with Haskett and Varick and he took refuge in the cheap revenge of satirizing the situation. He even began to reckon up the advantages which accrued from it, to ask himself if it were not better to own a third of a wife who knew how to make a man happy than a whole one who had lacked opportunity to acquire the art. For it was an art, and made up, like all others, of concessions, eliminations and embellishments; of lights judiciously thrown and shadows skillfully softened. His wife knew exactly how to manage the lights, and he knew exactly to what training she owed her skill. He even tried to trace the source of his obligations, to discriminate between the influences which had combined to produce his domestic happiness: he perceived that Haskett's commonness had made Alice worship good breeding, while Varick's liberal construction of the marriage bond had taught her to value the conjugal virtues; so that he was directly indebted to his predecessors for the devotion which made his life easy if not inspiring.

From this phase he passed into that of complete acceptance. He ceased to satirize himself because time dulled the irony of the situation and the joke lost its humor with its sting. Even the sight of Haskett's hat on the hall table had ceased to touch the springs of epigram. The hat was often seen there now, for it had been decided that it was better for Lily's father to visit her than for the little girl to go to his boarding–house. Waythorn, having acquiesced in this arrangement, had been surprised to find how little difference it made. Haskett was never obtrusive, and the few visitors who met him on the stairs were unaware of his identity. Waythorn did not know how often he saw Alice, but with himself Haskett was seldom in contact.

One afternoon, however, he learned on entering that Lily's father was waiting to see him. In the library he found Haskett occupying a chair in his usual provisional way. Waythorn always felt grateful to him for not leaning back.

"I hope you'll excuse me, Mr. Waythorn," he said rising. "I wanted to see Mrs. Waythorn about Lily, and your man asked me to wait here till she came in."

"Of course," said Waythorn, remembering that a sudden leak had that morning given over the drawing–room to the plumbers.

He opened his cigar–case and held it out to his visitor, and Haskett's acceptance seemed to mark a fresh stage in their intercourse. The spring evening was chilly, and Waythorn invited his guest to draw up his chair to the fire. He meant to find an excuse to leave Haskett in a moment; but he was tired and cold, and after all the little man no longer jarred on him.

The two were inclosed in the intimacy of their blended cigar– smoke when the door opened and Varick walked into the room. Waythorn rose abruptly. It was the first time that Varick had come to the house, and the surprise of seeing him, combined with the singular inopportuneness of his arrival, gave a new edge to Waythorn's blunted sensibilities. He stared at his visitor without speaking.

Varick seemed too preoccupied to notice his host's embarrassment.

"My dear fellow," he exclaimed in his most expansive tone, "I must apologize for tumbling in on you in this way, but I was too late to catch you down town, and so I thought — " He stopped short, catching sight of Haskett, and his sanguine color deepened to a flush which spread vividly under his scant blond hair. But in a moment he recovered himself and nodded slightly. Haskett returned the bow in silence, and Waythorn was still groping for speech when the footman came in carrying a tea–table.

The intrusion offered a welcome vent to Waythorn's nerves. "What the deuce are you bringing this here for?" he said sharply.

"I beg your pardon, sir, but the plumbers are still in the drawing–room, and Mrs. Waythorn said she would have tea in the library." The footman's perfectly respectful tone implied a reflection on Waythorn's reasonableness.

"Oh, very well," said the latter resignedly, and the footman proceeded to open the folding tea–table and set out its complicated appointments. While this interminable process continued the three men stood motionless, watching it with a fascinated stare, till Waythorn, to break the silence, said to Varick: "Won't you have a cigar?"

He held out the case he had just tendered to Haskett, and Varick helped himself with a smile. Waythorn looked about for a match, and finding none, proffered a light from his own cigar. Haskett, in the background, held his ground mildly, examining his cigar–tip now and then, and stepping forward at the right moment to knock its ashes into the fire.

The footman at last withdrew, and Varick immediately began: "If I could just say half a word to you about this business — "

"Certainly," stammered Waythorn; "in the dining–room — "

But as he placed his hand on the door it opened from without, and his wife appeared on the threshold.

She came in fresh and smiling, in her street dress and hat, shedding a fragrance from the boa which she loosened in advancing.

"Shall we have tea in here, dear?" she began; and then she caught sight of Varick. Her smile deepened, veiling a slight tremor of surprise. "Why, how do you do?" she said with a distinct note of pleasure.

As she shook hands with Varick she saw Haskett standing behind him. Her smile faded for a moment, but she recalled it quickly, with a scarcely perceptible side–glance at

Waythorn.

"How do you do, Mr. Haskett?" she said, and shook hands with him a shade less cordially.

The three men stood awkwardly before her, till Varick, always the most self-possessed, dashed into an explanatory phrase.

"We — I had to see Waythorn a moment on business," he stammered, brick-red from chin to nape.

Haskett stepped forward with his air of mild obstinacy. "I am sorry to intrude; but you appointed five o'clock — " he directed his resigned glance to the time-piece on the mantel.

She swept aside their embarrassment with a charming gesture of hospitality.

"I'm so sorry — I'm always late; but the afternoon was so lovely." She stood drawing her gloves off, propitiatory and graceful, diffusing about her a sense of ease and familiarity in which the situation lost its grotesqueness. "But before talking business," she added brightly, "I'm sure every one wants a cup of tea."

She dropped into her low chair by the tea-table, and the two visitors, as if drawn by her smile, advanced to receive the cups she held out.

She glanced about for Waythorn, and he took the third cup with a laugh.

Expiation

I.

"I CAN never," said Mrs. Fetherel, "hear the bell ring without a shudder."

Her unruffled aspect — she was the kind of woman whose emotions never communicate themselves to her clothes — and the conventional background of the New York drawing-room, with its pervading implication of an imminent tea-tray and of an atmosphere in which the social functions have become purely reflex, lent to her declaration a relief not lost on her cousin Mrs. Clinch, who, from the other side of the fireplace, agreed with a glance at the clock,that it was the hour for bores.

"Bores!" cried Mrs. Fetherel impatiently. "If I shuddered at them>, I should have a chronic ague!"

She leaned forward and laid a sparkling finger on her cousin's shabby black knee. "I mean the newspaper clippings," she whispered.

Mrs. Clinch returned a glance of intelligence. "They've begun already?"

"Not yet; but they're sure to now, at any minute, my publisher tells me."

Mrs. Fetherel's look of apprehension sat oddly on her small features, which had an air of neat symmetry somehow suggestive of being set in order every morning by the housemaid. Some one (there were rumors that it was her cousin) had once said that Paula Fetherel would have been very pretty if she hadn't looked so like a moral axiom in a copy-book hand.

Mrs. Clinch received her confidence with a smile. "Well," she said, "I suppose you were prepared for the consequences of authorship?"

Mrs. Fetherel blushed brightly. "It isn't their coming," she owned — "it's their coming now."

"Now?"

"The Bishop's in town."

Mrs. Clinch leaned back and shaped her lips to a whistle which deflected in a laugh. "Well!" she said.

"You see!" Mrs. Fetherel triumphed.

"Well — weren't you prepared for the Bishop?"

"Not now — at least, I hadn't thought of his seeing the clippings."

"And why should he see them?"

"Bella — won't you understand? It's John."

"John?"

"Who has taken the most unexpected tone — one might almost say out of perversity."

"Oh, perversity — " Mrs. Clinch murmured, observing her cousin between lids wrinkled by amusement. "What tone has John taken?"

Mrs. Fetherel threw out her answer with the desperate gesture of a woman who lays bare the traces of a marital fist. "The tone of being proud of my book."

The measure of Mrs. Clinch's enjoyment overflowed in laughter.

"Oh, you may laugh," Mrs. Fetherel insisted, "but it's no joke to me. In the first place, John's liking the book is so — so — such a false note — it puts me in such a ridiculous position; and then it has set him watching for the reviews — who would ever have suspected John of knowing that books were reviewed? Why, he's actually found out about the Clipping Bureau, and whenever the postman rings I hear John rush out of the library to see if there are any yellow envelopes. Of course, when they do come he'll bring them into the drawing–room and read them aloud to everybody who happens to be here — and the Bishop is sure to happen to be here!"

Mrs. Clinch repressed her amusement. "The picture you draw is a lurid one," she conceded, "but your modesty strikes me as abnormal, especially in an author. The chances are that some of the clippings will be rather pleasant reading. The critics are not all union men."

Mrs. Fetherel stared. "Union men?"

"Well, I mean they don't all belong to the well-known Society-for-the-Persecution-of-Rising-Authors. Some of them have even been known to defy its regulations and say a good word for a new writer."

"Oh, I dare say," said Mrs. Fetherel, with the laugh her cousin's epigram exacted. "But you don't quite see my point. I'm not at all nervous about the success of my book — my publisher tells me I have no need to be — but I am afraid of its being a succés de scandale."

"Mercy!" said Mrs. Clinch, sitting up.

The butler and footman at this moment appeared with the tea-tray, and when they had withdrawn, Mrs. Fetherel, bending her brightly rippled head above the kettle, continued in a murmur of avowal, "The title, even, is a kind of challenge."

"'Fast and Loose,'" Mrs. Clinch mused. "Yes, it ought to take."

"I didn't choose it for that reason!" the author protested. "I should have preferred something quieter — less pronounced; but I was determined not to shirk the responsibility of what I had written. I want people to know beforehand exactly what kind of book they are buying."

"Well," said Mrs. Clinch, "that's a degree of conscientiousness that I've never met with before. So few books fulfil the promise of their titles that experienced readers never expect the fare to come up to the menu."

"'Fast and Loose' will be no disappointment on that score,"her cousin significantly returned. "I've handled the subject without gloves. I've called a spade a spade."

"You simply make my mouth water! And to think I haven't been able to read it yet because every spare minute of my time has been given to correcting the proofs of 'How the Birds Keep Christmas'! There's an instance of the hardships of an author's life!"

Mrs. Fetherel's eye clouded. "Don't joke, Bella, please. I suppose to experienced authors there's always something absurd in the nervousness of a new writer, but in my case so much is at stake; I've put so much of myself into this book and I'm so afraid of being misunderstood . . . of being, as it were, in advance of my time . . . like poor Flaubert. . . . I know you'll think me ridiculous . . . and if only my own reputation were at stake, I should never give it a thought . . . but the idea of dragging John's name through the mire . . ."

Mrs. Clinch, who had risen and gathered her cloak about her, stood surveying from her genial height her cousin's agitated countenance.

"Why did you use John's name, then?"

"That's another of my difficulties! I had to. There would have been no merit in publishing such a book under an assumed name; it would have been an act of moral cowardice. 'Fast and Loose' is not an ordinary novel. A writer who dares to show up the hollowness of social conventions must have the courage of her convictions and be willing to accept the consequences of defying society. Can you imagine Ibsen or Tolstoy writing under a false name?" Mrs. Fetherel lifted a tragic eye to her cousin. "You don't know, Bella, how often I've envied you since I began to write. I used to wonder sometimes — you won't mind my saying so? — why, with all your cleverness, you hadn't taken up some more exciting subject than natural history; but I see now how wise you were. Whatever happens, you will never be denounced by the press!"

"Is that what you're afraid of?" asked Mrs. Clinch, as she grasped the bulging umbrella which rested against her chair. "My dear, if I had ever had the good luck to be denounced by the press, my brougham would be waiting at the door for me at this very moment, and I shouldn't have to ruin this umbrella by using it in the rain. Why, you innocent, if I'd ever felt the slightest aptitude for showing up social conventions, do you suppose I should waste my time writing 'Nests Ajar' and 'How to Smell the Flowers'? There's a fairly steady demand for pseudo-science and colloquial ornithology, but it's nothing, simply nothing, to the ravenous call for attacks on social institutions — especially by those inside the institutions!"

There was often, to her cousin, a lack of taste in Mrs. Clinch's pleasantries, and on this occasion they seemed more than usually irrelevant.

"'Fast and Loose' was not written with the idea of a large sale."

Mrs. Clinch was unperturbed. "Perhaps that's just as well,"she returned, with a philosophic shrug. "The surprise will be all the pleasanter, I mean. For of course it's going to sell tremendously; especially if you can get the press to denounce it."

"Bella, how can you? I sometimes think you say such things expressly to tease me; and yet I should think you of all women would understand my purpose in writing such a book. It has always seemed to me that the message I had to deliver was not for myself alone, but for all the other women in the world who have felt the hollowness of our social shams, the ignominy of bowing down to the idols of the market, but have lacked either the courage or the power to proclaim their independence; and I have fancied,Bella dear, that, however severely society might punish me for revealing its weaknesses, I could count on the sympathy of those who, like you" — Mrs. Fetherel's voice sank — "have passed through the deep waters."

Mrs. Clinch gave herself a kind of canine shake, as though to free her ample shoulders from any drop of the element she was supposed to have traversed.

"Oh, call them muddy rather than deep," she returned; "and you'll find, my dear, that women who've had any wading to do are rather shy of stirring up mud. It sticks — especially on white clothes."

Mrs. Fetherel lifted an undaunted brow. "I'm not afraid," she proclaimed; and at the same instant she dropped her tea–spoon with a clatter and shrank back into her seat. "There's the bell," she exclaimed, "and I know it's the Bishop!"

It was in fact the Bishop of Ossining, who, impressively announced by Mrs. Fetherel's butler, now made an entry that may best be described as not inadequate to the expectations the announcement raised. The Bishop always entered a room well; but,when unannounced, or preceded by a Low Church butler who gave him his surname, his appearance lacked the impressiveness conferred on it by the due specification of his diocesan dignity. The Bishop was very fond of his niece Mrs. Fetherel, and one of the traits he most valued in her was the possession of a butler who knew how to announce a bishop.

Mrs. Clinch was also his niece; but, aside from the fact that she possessed no butler at all, she had laid herself open to her uncle's criticism by writing insignificant little books which had a way of going into five or ten editions, while the fruits of his own episcopal leisure — "The Wail of Jonah" (twenty cantos in blank verse), and "Through a Glass Brightly; or, How to Raise Funds fora Memorial Window" — inexplicably languished on the back shelves of a publisher noted for his dexterity in pushing "devotional goods." Even this indiscretion the Bishop might, however, have condoned,had his niece thought fit to turn to him for support and advice at the painful juncture of her history when, in her own words, it became necessary for her to invite Mr. Clinch to look out for another situation. Mr. Clinch's misconduct was of the kind especially designed by Providence to test the fortitude of a Christian wife and mother, and the Bishop was absolutely distended with seasonable advice and edification; so that when Bella met his tentative exhortations with the curt remark that she preferred to do her own housecleaning unassisted, her uncle's grief at her ingratitude was not untempered with sympathy for Mr. Clinch.

It is not surprising, therefore, that the Bishop's warmest greetings were always reserved for Mrs. Fetherel; and on this occasion Mrs. Clinch thought she detected, in the salutation which fell to her share, a pronounced suggestion that her own presence was superfluous — a hint which she took with her usual imperturbable good humor.

II.

Left alone with the Bishop, Mrs. Fetherel sought the nearest refuge from conversation by offering him a cup of tea. The Bishop accepted with the preoccupied air of a man to whom, for the moment,tea is but a subordinate incident. Mrs. Fetherel's nervousness increased; and knowing that the surest way of distracting attention from one's own affairs is to affect an interest in those of one's companion, she hastily asked if her uncle had come to town on business.

"On business — yes — " said the Bishop in an impressive tone. "I had to see my publisher, who has been behaving rather unsatisfactorily in regard to my last book."

"Ah — your last book?" faltered Mrs. Fetherel, with a sickening sense of her inability to recall the name or nature of the work in question, and a mental vow never again to be caught in such ignorance of a colleague's productions.

"'Through a Glass Brightly,'" the Bishop explained, with an emphasis which revealed his detection of her predicament. "You may remember that I sent you a copy last Christmas?"

"Of course I do!" Mrs. Fetherel brightened. "It was that delightful story of the poor consumptive girl who had no money, and two little brothers to support — "

"Sisters — idiot sisters — " the Bishop gloomily corrected.

"I mean sisters; and who managed to collect money enough to put up a beautiful memorial window to her — her grandfather, whom she had never seen — "

"But whose sermons had been her chief consolation and support during her long struggle with poverty and disease." The Bishop gave the satisfied sigh of the workman who reviews his completed task. "A touching subject, surely; and I believe I did it justice;at least, so my friends assured me."

"Why, yes — I remember there was a splendid review of it in the 'Reredos'!" cried Mrs. Fetherel, moved by the incipient instinct of reciprocity.

"Yes — by my dear friend Mrs. Gollinger, whose husband, the late Dean Gollinger, was under very particular obligations to me. Mrs. Gollinger is a woman of rare literary acumen, and her praise of my book was unqualified; but the public wants more highly seasoned fare, and the approval of a thoughtful churchwoman carries less weight than the sensational comments of an illiterate journalist." The Bishop lent a meditative eye on his spotless gaiters. "At the risk of horrifying you, my dear," he added, with a slight laugh, "I will confide to you that my best chance of a popular success would be to have my book denounced by the press."

"Denounced?" gasped Mrs. Fetherel. "On what ground?"

"On the ground of immorality." The Bishop evaded her startled gaze. "Such a thing is inconceivable to you, of course; but I am only repeating what my publisher tells me. If, for instance, a critic could be induced — I mean, if a critic were to be found, who called in question the morality of my heroine in sacrificing her own health and that of her idiot sisters in order to put up a memorial window to her grandfather, it would probably raise a general controversy in the newspapers, and I might count on a sale of ten or fifteen thousand within the next year. If he described her as morbid or decadent, it might even run to twenty thousand;but that is more than I permit myself to hope. In fact, I should be satisfied with any general charge of immorality." The Bishop sighed again. "I need hardly tell you that I am actuated by no mere literary ambition. Those whose opinion I most value have assured me that the book is not without merit; but, though it does not become me to dispute their verdict, I can truly say that my vanity as an author is not at stake. I have, however, a special reason for wishing to increase the circulation of 'Through a Glass Brightly'; it was written for a purpose — a purpose I have greatly at heart — "

"I know," cried his niece sympathetically. "The chantry window — ?"

"Is still empty, alas! and I had great hopes that, under Providence, my little book might be the means of filling it. All our wealthy parishioners have given lavishly to the cathedral, and it was for this "`reason that, in writing 'Through a Glass,' I addressed my appeal more especially to the less well–endowed, hoping by the example of my heroine to stimulate the collection of small sums throughout the entire diocese, and perhaps beyond it. I am sure," the Bishop feelingly concluded, "the book would have a wide–spread influence if people could only be induced to read it!"

His conclusion touched a fresh thread of association in Mrs.Fetherel's vibrating nerve–centers. "I never thought of that!" she cried.

The Bishop looked at her inquiringly.

"That one's books may not be read at all! How dreadful!" she exclaimed.

He smiled faintly. "I had not forgotten that I was addressing an authoress," he said. "Indeed, I should not have dared to inflict my troubles on any one not of the craft."

Mrs. Fetherel was quivering with the consciousness of her involuntary self–betrayal. "Oh, uncle!" she murmured.

"In fact," the Bishop continued, with a gesture which seemed to brush away her scruples, "I came here partly to speak to you about your novel. 'Fast and Loose,' I think you call it?"

Mrs. Fetherel blushed assentingly.

"And is it out yet?" the Bishop continued.

"It came out about a week ago. But you haven't touched your tea, and it must be quite cold. Let me give you another cup . . ."

"My reason for asking," the Bishop went on, with the bland inexorableness with which, in his younger days, he had been known to continue a sermon after the senior warden had looked four times at his watch — "my reason for asking is, that I hoped I might not be too late to induce you to change the title."

Mrs. Fetherel set down the cup she had filled. "The title?"she faltered.

The Bishop raised a reassuring hand. "Don't misunderstand me,dear child; don't for a moment imagine that I take it to be in anyway indicative of the contents of the book. I know you too well for that. My first idea was that it had probably been forced on you by an unscrupulous publisher — I know too well to what ignoble compromises one may be driven in such cases! . . ." He paused, as though to give her the opportunity of confirming this conjecture,but she preserved an apprehensive silence, and he went on, as though taking up the second point in his sermon — "Or, again, the name may have taken your fancy without your realizing all that it implies to minds more alive than yours to offensive innuendoes. It is — ahem — excessively suggestive, and I hope I am not too late to warn you of the false impression it is likely to produce on the very readers whose approbation you would most value. My friend Mrs. Gollinger, for instance — "

Mrs. Fetherel, as the publication of her novel testified, was in theory a woman of independent views; and if in practise she sometimes failed to live up to her standard, it was rather from an irresistible tendency to adapt herself to her environment than from any conscious lack of moral courage. The Bishop's exordium had excited in her that sense of opposition which such admonitions are apt to provoke; but as he went on she felt herself gradually enclosed in an atmosphere in which her theories vainly gasped for breath. The Bishop had the immense dialectical advantage of invalidating any conclusions at variance with his own by always assuming that his premises were among the necessary laws of thought. This method, combined with the habit of ignoring any classifications but his own, created an element in which the first condition of existence was the immediate adoption of his standpoint; so that his niece, as she listened, seemed to feel Mrs.Gollinger's Mechlin cap spreading its conventual shadow over her rebellious brow and the "Revue de Paris" at her elbow turning into a copy of the "Reredos." She had meant to assure her uncle that she was quite aware of the significance of the title she had chosen, that it had been deliberately selected as indicating the subject of her novel, and that the book itself had been written indirect defiance of the class of readers for whose susceptibilities she was alarmed. The words were almost on her lips when the irresistible suggestion conveyed by the Bishop's tone and language deflected them into the apologetic murmur, "Oh, uncle, you mustn't think — I never meant — " How much farther this current of reaction might have carried her, the historian is unable to computer, for at this point the door opened and her husband entered the room.

"The first review of your book!" he cried, flourishing a yellow envelope. "My dear Bishop, how lucky you're here!"

Though the trials of married life have been classified and catalogued with exhaustive accuracy, there is one form of conjugal misery which has perhaps received inadequate attention; and that is the suffering of the versatile woman whose husband is not equally adapted to all her moods. Every woman feels for the sister who is compelled to wear a bonnet which does not "go" with her gown; but how much sympathy is given to her whose husband refuses to harmonize with the pose of the moment? Scant justice has, for instance, been done to the misunderstood wife whose husband persists in understanding her; to the submissive helpmate whose taskmaster shuns every opportunity of browbeating her; and to the generous and impulsive being whose bills are paid with philosophic calm. Mrs. Fetherel, as wives go, had been fairly exempt from trials of this nature, for her husband, if undistinguished by pronounced brutality or indifference, had at least the negative merit of being her intellectual inferior. Landscape gardeners, who are aware of the usefulness of a valley in emphasizing the height of a hill, can form an idea of the account to which an accomplished woman may turn such deficiencies; and it need scarcely be said that Mrs. Fetherel had made the most of her opportunities. It was agreeably obvious to every one, Fetherel included, that he was not the man to appreciate such a woman; but there are no limits to man's perversity, and he did his best to invalidate this advantage by admiring her without pretending to understand her. What she most suffered from was this fatuous approval: the maddening sense that, however she conducted herself, he would always admire her. Had he belonged to the class whose conversational supplies are drawn from the domestic circle, his wife's name would never have been off his lips; and to Mrs. Fetherel's sensitive perceptions his frequent silences were indicative of the fact that she was his one topic.

It was, in part, the attempt to escape this persistent approbation that had driven Mrs. Fetherel to authorship. She had fancied that even the most infatuated husband might be counted onto resent, at least negatively, an attack on the sanctity of the hearth; and her anticipations were heightened by a sense of the unpardonableness of her act. Mrs. Fetherel's relations with her husband were in fact complicated by an irrepressible tendency to be fond of him; and there was a certain pleasure in the prospect of a situation that justified the most explicit expiation.

These hopes Fetherel's attitude had already defeated. He read the book with enthusiasm, he pressed it on his friends, he sent a copy to his mother; and his very soul now hung on the verdict of the reviewers. It was perhaps this proof of his general ineptitude that made his wife doubly alive to his special defects; so that his inopportune entrance was aggravated by the very sound of his voice and the hopeless aberration of his smile. Nothing, to the observant, is more indicative of a man's character and circumstances than his way of entering a room. The Bishop of Ossining, for instance, brought with him not only an atmosphere of episcopal authority, but an implied opinion on the verbal inspiration of the Scriptures, and on the attitude of the church toward divorce; while the appearance of Mrs. Fetherel's husband produced an immediate impression of domestic felicity. His mere aspect implied that there was a well–filled nursery upstairs; that this wife, if she did not sew on his buttons, at least superintended the performance of that task; that they both went to church regularly, and that they dined with his mother every Sunday evening punctually at seven o'clock.

All this and more was expressed in the affectionate gesture with which he now raised the yellow envelope above Mrs. Fetherel's clutch; and knowing the uselessness of begging him not to be silly,she said, with a dry despair, "You're boring the Bishop horribly."

Fetherel turned a radiant eye on that dignitary. "She bores us all horribly, doesn't she, sir?" he exulted.

"Have you read it?" said his wife, uncontrollably.

"Read it? Of course not — it's just this minute come. I say,Bishop, you're not going — ?"

"Not till I've heard this," said the Bishop, settling himself in his chair with an indulgent smile.

His niece glanced at him despairingly. "Don't let John's nonsense detain you," she entreated.

"Detain him? That's good," guffawed Fetherel. "It isn't as long as one of his sermons — won't take me five minutes to read. Here, listen to this, ladies and gentlemen: 'In this age of festering pessimism and decadent depravity, it is no surprise to the nauseated reviewer to open one more volume saturated with the fetid emanations of the sewer — '"

Fetherel, who was not in the habit of reading aloud, paused with a gasp, and the Bishop glanced sharply at his niece, who kept her gaze fixed on the tea-cup she had not yet succeeded in transferring to his hand.

— "'Of the sewer,'" her husband resumed; "'but his wonder is proportionately great when he lights on a novel as sweetly inoffensive as Paula Fetherel's "Fast and Loose." Mrs. Fetherel is, we believe, a new hand at fiction, and her work reveals frequent traces of inexperience; but these are more than atoned for by her pure, fresh view of life and her altogether unfashionable regard for the reader's moral susceptibilities. Let no one be induced by its distinctly misleading title to forego the enjoyment of this pleasant picture of domestic life, which, in spite of a total lack of force in character-drawing and of consecutiveness in incident, may be described as a distinctly pretty story.'"

III.

It was several weeks later that Mrs. Clinch once more brought the plebeian aroma of heated tram-cars and muddy street-crossings into the violet-scented atmosphere of her cousin's drawing-room.

"Well," she said, tossing a damp bundle of proof into the corner of a silk-cushioned bergère, "I've read it at last and I'm not so awfully shocked!"

Mrs. Fetherel, who sat near the fire with her head propped on a languid hand, looked up without speaking.

"Mercy, Paula," said her visitor, "you're ill."

Mrs. Fetherel shook her head. "I was never better," she said,mournfully.

"Then may I help myself to tea? Thanks."

Mrs. Clinch carefully removed her mended glove before taking a buttered tea–cake; then she glanced again at her cousin.

"It's not what I said just now — ?" she ventured.

"Just now?"

"About 'Fast and Loose'? I came to talk it over."

Mrs. Fetherel sprang to her feet. "I never," she cried dramatically, "want to hear it mentioned again!"

"Paula!" exclaimed Mrs. Clinch, setting down her cup.

Mrs. Fetherel slowly turned on her an eye brimming with the incommunicable; then, dropping into her seat again, she added, with a tragic laugh, "There's nothing left to say."

"Nothing — ?" faltered Mrs. Clinch, longing for another tea–cake, but feeling the inappropriateness of the impulse in an atmosphere so charged with the portentous. "Do you mean that everything has been said?" She looked tentatively at her cousin. "Haven't they been nice?"

"They've been odious — odious — " Mrs. Fetherel burst out, with an ineffectual clutch at her handkerchief. "It's been perfectly intolerable!"

Mrs. Clinch, philosophically resigning herself to the propriety of taking no more tea, crossed over to her cousin and laid a sympathizing hand on that lady's agitated shoulder.

"It is a bore at first," she conceded; "but you'll be surprised to see how soon one gets used to it."

"I shall — never — get — used to it — " Mrs. Fetherel brokenly declared.

"Have they been so very nasty — all of them?"

"Every one of them!" the novelist sobbed.

"I'm so sorry, dear; it does hurt, I know — but hadn't you rather expected it?"

"Expected it?" cried Mrs. Fetherel, sitting up.

Mrs. Clinch felt her way warily. "I only mean, dear, that I fancied from what you said before the book came out — that you rather expected — that you'd rather discounted — "

"Their recommending it to everybody as a perfectly harmless story?"

"Good gracious! Is that what they've done?"

Mrs. Fetherel speechlessly nodded.

"Every one of them?"

"Every one — "

"Whew!" said Mrs. Clinch, with an incipient whistle.

"Why, you've just said it yourself!" her cousin suddenly reproached her.

"Said what?"

"That you weren't so awfully shocked — "

"I? Oh, well — you see, you'd keyed me up to such a pitch that it wasn't quite as bad as I expected — "

Mrs. Fetherel lifted a smile steeled for the worst. "Why not say at once," she suggested, "that it's a distinctly pretty story?"

"They haven't said that?"

"They've all said it."

"My poor Paula!"

"Even the Bishop — "

"The Bishop called it a pretty story?"

"He wrote me — I've his letter somewhere. The title rather scared him — he wanted me to change it; but when he'd read the book he wrote that it was all right and that he'd sent several copies to his friends."

"The old hypocrite!" cried Mrs. Clinch. "That was nothing but professional jealousy."

"Do you think so?" cried her cousin, brightening.

"Sure of it, my dear. His own books don't sell, and he knew the quickest way to kill yours was to distribute it through the diocese with his blessing."

"Then you don't really think it's a pretty story?"

"Dear me, no! Not nearly as bad as that — "

"You're so good, Bella — but the reviewers?"

"Oh, the reviewers," Mrs. Clinch jeered. She gazed meditatively at the cold remains of her tea−cake. "Let me see,"she said, suddenly; "do you happen to remember if the first review came out in an important paper?"

"Yes — the 'Radiator.'"

"That's it! I thought so. Then the others simply followed suit: they often do if a big paper sets the pace. Saves a lot of trouble. Now if you could only have got the 'Radiator' to denounce you — "

"That's what the Bishop said!" cried Mrs. Fetherel.

"He did?"

"He said his only chance of selling 'Through a Glass Brightly' was to have it denounced on the ground of immorality."

"H'm," said Mrs. Clinch. "I thought he knew a trick or two." She turned an illuminated eye on her cousin. "You ought to get him to denounce 'Fast and Loose'!" she cried.

Mrs. Fetherel looked at her suspiciously. "I suppose every book must stand or fall on its own merits," she said in an unconvinced tone.

"Bosh! That view is as extinct as the post–chaise and the packet–ship — it belongs to the time when people read books. Nobody does that now; the reviewer was the first to set the example, and the public were only too thankful to follow it. At first they read the reviews; now they read only the publishers' extracts from them. Even these are rapidly being replaced by paragraphs borrowed from the vocabulary of commerce. I often have to look twice before I am sure if I am reading a department–store advertisement or the announcement of a new batch of literature. The publishers will soon be having their 'fall and spring openings' and their 'special importations for Horse–Show Week.' But the Bishop is right, of course — nothing helps a book like a rousing attack on its morals;and as the publishers can't exactly proclaim the impropriety of their own wares, the task has to be left to the press or the pulpit."

"The pulpit — ?" Mrs. Fetherel mused.

"Why, yes — look at those two novels in England last year — "

Mrs. Fetherel shook her head hopelessly. "There is so much more interest in literature in England than here."

"Well, we've got to make the supply create the demand. The Bishop could run your novel up into the hundred thousands in no time."

"But if he can't make his own sell — ?"

"My dear, a man can't very well preach against his own writings!"

Mrs. Clinch rose and picked up her proofs.

"I'm awfully sorry for you, Paula dear," she concluded, "but I can't help being thankful that there's no demand for pessimism in the field of natural history. Fancy having to write 'The Fall of a Sparrow,' or 'How the Plants Misbehave!'"

IV.

Mrs. Fetherel, driving up to the Grand Central Station one morning about five months later, caught sight of the distinguished novelist, Archer Hynes, hurrying into the waiting–room ahead of her. Hynes, on his side, recognizing her brougham, turned back to greet her as the footman opened the carriage–door.

"My dear colleague! Is it possible that we are traveling together?"

Mrs. Fetherel blushed with pleasure. Hynes had given her two columns of praise in the Sunday "Meteor," and she had not yet learned to disguise her gratitude.

"I am going to Ossining," she said, smilingly.

"So am I. Why, this is almost as good as an elopement."

"And it will end where elopements ought to — in church."

"In church? You're not going to Ossining to go to church?"

"Why not? There's a special ceremony in the cathedral — the chantry window is to be unveiled."

"The chantry window? How picturesque! What is a chantry? And why do you want to see it unveiled? Are you after copy — doing something in the Huysmans manner? 'La Cathédrale,' eh?"

"Oh, no." Mrs. Fetherel hesitated. "I'm going simply to please my uncle," she said, at last.

"Your uncle?"

"The Bishop, you know." She smiled.

"The Bishop — the Bishop of Ossining? Why, wasn't he the chap who made that ridiculous attack on your book? Is that prehistoric ass your uncle? Upon my soul, I think you're mighty forgiving to travel all the way to Ossining for one of his stained–glass sociables!"

Mrs. Fetherel's smile flowed into a gentle laugh. "Oh, I've never allowed that to interfere with our friendship. My uncle felt dreadfully about having to speak publicly against my book — it was a great deal harder for him than for me — but he thought it his duty to do so. He has the very highest sense of duty."

"Well," said Hynes, with a shrug, "I don't know that he didn't do you a good turn. Look at that!"

They were standing near the book–stall, and he pointed to a placard surmounting the counter and emblazoned with the conspicuous announcement: "Fast and Loose. New Edition with Author's Portrait. Hundred and Fiftieth Thousand."

Mrs. Fetherel frowned impatiently. "How absurd! They've no right to use my picture as a poster!"

"There's our train," said Hynes; and they began to push their way through the crowd surging toward one of the inner doors.

As they stood wedged between circumferent shoulders, Mrs.Fetherel became conscious of the fixed stare of a pretty girl who whispered eagerly to her companion: "Look Myrtle! That's Paula Fetherel right behind us — I knew her in a minute!"

"Gracious — where?" cried the other girl, giving her head a twist which swept her Gainsborough plumes across Mrs. Fetherel's face.

The first speaker's words had carried beyond her companion's ear, and a lemon–colored woman in spectacles, who clutched a copy of the "Journal of Psychology" on one drab–cotton–gloved hand, stretched her disengaged hand across the intervening barrier of humanity.

"Have I the privilege of addressing the distinguished author of 'Fast and Loose'? If so, let me thank you in the name of the Woman's Psychological League of Peoria for your magnificent courage in raising the standard of revolt against — "

"You can tell us the rest in the car," said a fat man, pressing his good–humored bulk against the speaker's arm.

Mrs. Fetherel, blushing, embarrassed and happy, slipped into the space produced by this displacement, and a few moments later had taken her seat in the train.

She was a little late, and the other chairs were already filled by a company of elderly ladies and clergymen who seemed to belong to the same party, and were still busy exchanging greetings and settling themselves in their places.

One of the ladies, at Mrs. Fetherel's approach, uttered an exclamation of pleasure and advanced with outstretched hand. "My dear Mrs. Fetherel! I am so delighted to see you here. May I hope you are going to the unveiling of the chantry window? The dear Bishop so hoped that you would do so! But perhaps I ought to introduce myself. I am Mrs. Gollinger" — she lowered her voice expressively — "one of your uncle's oldest friends, one who has stood close to him through all this sad business, and who knows what he suffered when he felt obliged to sacrifice family affection to the call of duty."

Mrs. Fetherel, who had smiled and colored slightly at the beginning of this speech, received its close with a deprecating gesture.

"Oh, pray don't mention it," she murmured. "I quite understood how my uncle was placed — I bore him no ill will for feeling obliged to preach against my book."

"He understood that, and was so touched by it! He has often told me that it was the hardest task he was ever called upon to perform — and, do you know, he quite feels that this unexpected gift of the chantry window is in some way a return for his courage in

60

preaching that sermon."

Mrs. Fetherel smiled faintly. "Does he feel that?"

"Yes; he really does. When the funds for the window were so mysteriously placed at his disposal, just as he had begun to despair of raising them, he assured me that he could not help connecting the fact with his denunciation of your book."

"Dear uncle!" sighed Mrs. Fetherel. "Did he say that?"

"And now," continued Mrs. Gollinger, with cumulative rapture — "now that you are about to show, by appearing at the ceremony to–day, that there has been no break in your friendly relations, the dear Bishop's happiness will be complete. He was so longing to have you come to the unveiling!"

"He might have counted on me," said Mrs. Fetherel, still smiling.

"Ah, that is so beautifully forgiving of you!" cried Mrs.Gollinger, enthusiastically. "But then, the Bishop has always assured me that your real nature was very different from that which — if you will pardon my saying so — seems to be revealed by your brilliant but — er — rather subversive book. 'If you only knew my niece, dear Mrs. Gollinger,' he always said, 'you would see that her novel was written in all innocence of heart;' and to tell you the truth, when I first read the book I didn't think it so very, very shocking. It wasn't till the dear Bishop had explained tome — but, dear me, I mustn't take up your time in this way when so many others are anxious to have a word with you."

Mrs. Fetherel glanced at her in surprise, and Mrs. Gollinger continued, with a playful smile: "You forget that your face is familiar to thousands whom you have never seen. We all recognized you the moment you entered the train, and my friends here are so eager to make your acquaintance — even those" — her smile deepened — "who thought the dear Bishop not quite unjustified in his attack on your remarkable novel."

V.

A religious light filled the chantry of Ossining Cathedral,filtering through the linen curtain which veiled the central window, and mingling with the blaze of tapers on the richly adorned altar.

In this devout atmosphere, agreeably laden with the incense–like aroma of Easter lilies and forced lilacs, Mrs. Fetherel knelt with a sense of luxurious satisfaction. Beside her sat Archer Hynes, who had remembered that there was to be a church scene in his next novel, and that his impressions of the devotional environment needed refreshing. Mrs. Fetherel was very happy. She was conscious that her entrance had sent a thrill through the female devotees who packed the chantry, and she had humor enough to enjoy the thought that, but for the good Bishop's denunciation of her book, the heads of his flock would not have been turned so eagerly in her direction. Moreover, as she had entered she had caught sight of a society reporter, and she knew that her presence, and the fact that she was accompanied by Hynes, would be conspicuously proclaimed in the morning papers. All these evidences of the success of her handiwork might have turned a calmer head than Mrs. Fetherel's; and though she had now learned to dissemble her gratification, it still filled her inwardly with a delightful glow.

The Bishop was somewhat late in appearing, and she employed the interval in meditating on the plot of her next novel, which was already partly sketched out, but for which she had been unable to find a satisfactory denouement. By a not uncommon process of ratiocination, Mrs. Fetherel's success had convinced her of her vocation. She was sure now that it was her duty to lay bare the secret plague–spots of society, and she was resolved that there should be no doubt as to the purpose of her new book. Experience had shown her that where she had fancied she was calling a spade a spade she had in fact been alluding in guarded terms to the drawing–room shovel. She was determined not to repeat the same mistake, and she flattered herself that her coming novel would not need an episcopal denunciation to insure its sale, however likely it was to receive this crowning evidence of success.

She had reached this point in her meditations when the choir burst into song and the ceremony of the unveiling began. The Bishop, almost always felicitous in his addresses to the fair sex,was never more so than when he was celebrating the triumph of one of his cherished purposes. There was a peculiar mixture of Christian humility and episcopal exultation in the manner with which he called attention to the Creator's promptness in responding to his demand for funds, and he had never been more happily inspired than in eulogizing the mysterious gift of the chantry window.

Though no hint of the donor's identity had been allowed to escape him, it was generally understood that the Bishop knew who had given the window, and the congregation awaited in a flutter of suspense the possible announcement of a name. None came, however,though the Bishop deliciously titillated the curiosity of his flock by circling ever closer about the interesting secret. He would not disguise from them, he said, that the heart which had divined his inmost wish had been a woman's — is it not to woman's intuitions that more than half the happiness of earth is owing? What man is obliged to learn by the laborious process of experience, woman's wondrous instinct tells her at a glance; and so it had been with this cherished scheme, this unhoped-for completion of their beautiful chantry. So much, at least, he was allowed to reveal;and indeed, had he not done so, the window itself would have spoken for him, since the first glance at its touching subject and exquisite design would show it to have originated in a woman's heart. This tribute to the sex was received with an audible sigh of contentment, and the Bishop, always stimulated by such evidence of his sway over his hearers, took up his theme with gathering eloquence.

Yes — a woman's heart had planned the gift, a woman's hand had executed it, and, might he add, without too far withdrawing the veil in which Christian beneficence ever loved to drape its acts — might he add that, under Providence, a book, a simple book, a mere tale, in fact, had had its share in the good work for which they were assembled to give thanks?

At this unexpected announcement, a ripple of excitement ran through the assemblage, and more than one head was abruptly turned in the direction of Mrs. Fetherel, who sat listening in an agony of wonder and confusion. It did not escape the observant novelist at her side that she drew down her veil to conceal an uncontrollable blush, and this evidence of dismay caused him to fix an attentive gaze on her, while from her seat across the aisle, Mrs. Gollinger sent a smile of unctuous approval.

"A book — a simple book — " the Bishop's voice went on above this flutter of mingled emotions. "What is a book? Only a few pages and a little ink — and yet one of the mightiest instruments which Providence has devised for shaping the destinies of man . ... one of the most powerful influences for good or evil which the Creator has placed in the hands of his creatures . . ."

The air seemed intolerably close to Mrs. Fetherel, and she drew out her scent-bottle, and then thrust it hurriedly away, conscious that she was still the center of an unenviable

63

attention. And all the while the Bishop's voice droned on . . .

"And of all forms of literature, fiction is doubtless that which has exercised the greatest sway, for good or ill, over the passions and imagination of the masses. Yes, my friends, I am the first to acknowledge it — no sermon, however eloquent, no theological treatise, however learned and convincing, has ever inflamed the heart and imagination like a novel — a simple novel. Incalculable is the power exercised over humanity by the great magicians of the pen — a power ever enlarging its boundaries and increasing its responsibilities as popular education multiplies the number of readers. . . . Yes, it is the novelist's hand which can pour balm on countless human sufferings, or inoculate mankind with the festering poison of a corrupt imagination. . . ."

Mrs. Fetherel had turned white, and her eyes were fixed with a blind stare of anger on the large—sleeved figure in the center of the chancel.

"And too often, alas, it is the poison and not the balm which the unscrupulous hand of genius proffers to its unsuspecting readers. But, my friends, why should I continue? None know better than an assemblage of Christian women, such as I am now addressing,the beneficent or baleful influences of modern fiction; and so,when I say that this beautiful chantry window of ours owes its existence in part to the romancer's pen" — the Bishop paused, and bending forward, seemed to seek a certain face among the countenances eagerly addressed to his — "when I say that this pen,which for personal reasons it does not become me to celebrate unduly — "

Mrs. Fetherel at this point half rose, pushing back her chair,which scraped loudly over the marble floor; but Hynes involuntarily laid a warning hand on her arm, and she sank down with a confused murmur about the heat.

" — When I confess that this pen, which for once at least has proved itself so much mightier than the sword, is that which was inspired to trace the simple narrative of 'Through a Glass Brightly'" — Mrs. Fetherel looked up with a gasp of mingled relief and anger — "when I tell you, my dear friends, that it was your Bishop's own work which first roused the mind of one of his flock to the crying need of a chantry window, I think you will admit that I am justified in celebrating the triumphs of the pen, even though it be the modest instrument which your own Bishop wields."

64

The Bishop paused impressively, and a faint gasp of surprise and disappointment was audible throughout the chantry. Something very different from this conclusion had been expected, and even Mrs. Gollinger's lips curled with a slightly ironic smile. But Archer Hynes's attention was chiefly reserved for Mrs. Fetherel,whose face had changed with astonishing rapidity from surprise to annoyance, from annoyance to relief, and then back again to something very like indignation.

The address concluded, the actual ceremony of the unveiling was about to take place, and the attention of the congregation soon reverted to the chancel, where the choir had grouped themselves beneath the veiled window, prepared to burst into a chant of praise as the Bishop drew back the hanging. The moment was an impressive one, and every eye was fixed on the curtain. Even Hynes's gaze strayed to it for a moment, but soon returned to his neighbor's face; and then he perceived that Mrs. Fetherel, alone of all the persons present, was not looking at the window. Her eyes were fixed in an indignant stare on the Bishop; a flush of anger burned becomingly under her veil, and her hands nervously crumpled the beautifully printed program of the ceremony.

Hynes broke into a smile of comprehension. He glanced at the Bishop, and back at the Bishop's niece; then, as the episcopal hand was solemnly raised to draw back the curtain, he bent and whispered in Mrs. Fetherel's ear:

"Why, you gave it yourself! You wonderful woman, of course you gave it yourself!"

Mrs. Fetherel raised her eyes to his with a start. Her blush deepened and her lips shaped a hasty "No"; but the denial was deflected into the indignant murmur — "It wasn't his silly book that did it anyhow!"

The Lady's Maid's Bell

I

IT was the autumn after I had the typhoid. I'd been three months in hospital, and when I came out I looked so weak and tottery that the two or three ladies I applied to were afraid to engage me. Most of my money was gone, and after I'd boarded for two months, hanging about the employment–agencies, and answering any advertisement that looked any way respectable, I pretty nearly lost heart, for fretting hadn't made me fatter, and I didn't see why my luck should ever turn. It did though — or I thought so at the time. A Mrs. Railton, a friend of the lady that first brought me out to the States, met me one day and stopped to speak to me: she was one that had always a friendly way with her. She asked me what ailed me to look so white, and when I told her, "Why, Hartley," says she, "I believe I've got the very place for you. Come in to–morrow and we'll talk about it."

The next day, when I called, she told me the lady she'd in mind was a niece of hers, a Mrs. Brympton, a youngish lady, but something of an invalid, who lived all the year round at her country–place on the Hudson, owing to not being able to stand the fatigue of town life.

"Now, Hartley," Mrs. Railton said, in that cheery way that always made me feel things must be going to take a turn for the better — "now understand me; it's not a cheerful place i'm sending you to. The house is big and gloomy; my niece is nervous, vaporish; her husband — well, he's generally away; and the two children are dead. A year ago, I would as soon have thought of shutting a rosy active girl like you into a vault; but you're not particularly brisk yourself just now, are you? and a quiet place, with country air and wholesome food and early hours, ought to be the very thing for you. Don't mistake me," she added, for I suppose I looked a trifle downcast; "you may find it dull, but you won't be unhappy. My niece is an angel. Her former maid, who died last spring, had been with her twenty years and worshipped the ground she walked on. She's a kind mistress to all, and where the mistress is kind, as you know, the servants are generally good–humored, so you'll probably get on well enough with the rest of the household. And you're the very woman I want for my niece: quiet, well–mannered, and educated above your station. You read aloud well, I think? That's a good thing; my niece likes to be read to. She wants a maid that can be something of a companion: her last was, and I can't say how she misses her. It's a lonely life . . . Well, have you decided?"

"Why, ma'am," I said, "I'm not afraid of solitude."

"Well, then, go; my niece will take you on my recommendation. I'll telegraph her at once and you can take the afternoon train. She has no one to wait on her at present, and I don't want you to lose any time."

I was ready enough to start, yet something in me hung back; and to gain time I asked, "And the gentleman, ma'am?"

"The gentleman's almost always away, I tell you," said Mrs. Ralston, quick−like — "and when he's there," says she suddenly, "you've only to keep out of his way."

I took the afternoon train and got out at D — — −station at about four o'clock. A groom in a dog−cart was waiting, and we drove off at a smart pace. It was a dull October day, with rain hanging close overhead, and by the time we turned into the Brympton Place woods the daylight was almost gone. The drive wound through the woods for a mile or two, and came out on a gravel court shut in with thickets of tall black−looking shrubs. There were no lights in the windows, and the house did look a bit gloomy.

I had asked no questions of the groom, for I never was one to get my notion of new masters from their other servants: I prefer to wait and see for myself. But I could tell by the look of everything that I had got into the right kind of house, and that things were done handsomely. A pleasant−faced cook met me at the back door and called the house−maid to show me up to my room. "You'll see madam later," she said. "Mrs. Brympton has a visitor."

I hadn't fancied Mrs. Brympton was a lady to have many visitors, and somehow the words cheered me. I followed the house−maid upstairs, and saw, through a door on the upper landing, that the main part of the house seemed well−furnished, with dark panelling and a number of old portraits. Another flight of stairs led us up to the servants' wing. It was almost dark now, and the house−maid excused herself for not having brought a light. "But there's matches in your room," she said, "and if you go careful you'll be all right. Mind the step at the end of the passage. Your room is just beyond."

I looked ahead as she spoke, and half−way down the passage, I saw a woman standing. She drew back into a doorway as we passed, and the house−maid didn't appear to notice her. She was a thin woman with a white face, and a darkish stuff gown and apron. I took her for the housekeeper and thought it odd that she didn't speak, but just gave me a long look as she went by. My room opened into a square hall at the end of the passage. Facing my door was another which stood open: the house−maid exclaimed when she saw it.

"There — Mrs. Blinder's left that door open again!" said she, closing it.

"Is Mrs. Blinder the housekeeper?"

"There's no housekeeper: Mrs. Blinder's the cook."

"And is that her room?"

"Laws, no," said the house−maid, cross−like. "That's nobody's room. It's empty, I mean, and the door hadn't ought to be open. Mrs. Brympton wants it kept locked."

She opened my door and led me into a neat room, nicely furnished, with a picture or two on the walls; and having lit a candle she took leave, telling me that the servants'−hall tea was at six, and that Mrs. Brympton would see me afterward.

I found them a pleasant−spoken set in the servants' hall, and by what they let fall I gathered that, as Mrs. Railton had said, Mrs. Brympton was the kindest of ladies; but I didn't take much notice of their talk, for I was watching to see the pale woman in the dark gown come in. She didn't show herself, however, and I wondered if she ate apart; but if she wasn't the housekeeper, why should she? Suddenly it struck me that she might be a trained nurse, and in that case her meals would of course be served in her room. If Mrs. Brympton was an invalid it was likely enough she had a nurse. The idea annoyed me, I own, for they're not always the easiest to get on with, and if I'd known, I shouldn't have taken the place. But there I was, and there was no use pulling a long face over it; and not being one to ask questions, I waited to see what would turn up.

When tea was over, the house−maid said to the footman: "Has Mr. Ranford gone?" and when he said yes, she told me to come up with her to Mrs. Brympton.

Mrs. Brympton was lying down in her bedroom. Her lounge stood near the fire and beside it was a shaded lamp. She was a delicate−looking lady, but when she smiled I felt there was nothing I wouldn't do for her. She spoke very pleasantly, in a low voice, asking me my name and age and so on, and if I had everything I wanted, and if I wasn't afraid of feeling lonely in the country.

"Not with you I wouldn't be, madam," I said, and the words surprised me when I'd spoken them, for I'm not an impulsive person; but it was just as if I'd thought aloud.

She seemed pleased at that, and said she hoped I'd continue in the same mind; then she gave me a few directions about her toilet, and said Agnes the house-maid would show me next morning where things were kept.

"I am tired to-night, and shall dine upstairs," she said. "Agnes will bring me my tray, that you may have time to unpack and settle yourself; and later you may come and undress me."

"Very well, ma'am," I said. "You'll ring, I suppose?"

I thought she looked odd.

"No — Agnes will fetch you," says she quickly, and took up her book again.

Well — that was certainly strange: a lady's maid having to be fetched by the house-maid whenever her lady wanted her! I wondered if there were no bells in the house; but the next day I satisfied myself that there was one in every room, and a special one ringing from my mistress's room to mine; and after that it did strike me as queer that, whenever Mrs. Brympton wanted anything, she rang for Agnes, who had to walk the whole length of the servants' wing to call me.

But that wasn't the only queer thing in the house. The very next day I found out that Mrs. Brympton had no nurse; and then I asked Agnes about the woman I had seen in the passage the afternoon before. Agnes said she had seen no one, and I saw that she thought I was dreaming. To be sure, it was dusk when we went down the passage, and she had excused herself for not bringing a light; but I had seen the woman plain enough to know her again if we should meet. I decided that she must have been a friend of the cook's, or of one of the othe* women-servants: perhaps she had come down from town for a night's visit, and the servants wanted it kept secret. Some ladies are very stiff about having their servants' friends in the house overnight. At any rate, I made up my mind to ask no more questions.

In a day or two, another odd thing happened. I was chatting one afternoon with Mrs. Blinder, who was a friendly disposed woman, and had been longer in the house than the other servants, and she asked me if I was quite comfortable and had everything I needed. I said I had no fault to find with my place or with my mistress, but I thought it odd that in so large a house there was no sewing-room for the lady's maid.

"Why," says she, "there is one; the room you're in is the old sewing-room."

"Oh," said I; "and where did the other lady's maid sleep?"

At that she grew confused, and said hurriedly that the servants' rooms had all been changed about last year, and she didn't rightly remember.

That struck me as peculiar, but I went on as if I hadn't noticed: "Well, there's a vacant room opposite mine, and I mean to ask Mrs. Brympton if I mayn't use that as a sewing-room."

To my astonishment, Mrs. Blinder went white, and gave my hand a kind of squeeze. "Don't do that, my dear," said she, trembling-like. "To tell you the truth, that was Emma Saxon's room, and my mistress has kept it closed ever since her death."

"And who was Emma Saxon?"

"Mrs. Brympton's former maid."

"The one that was with her so many years?" said I, remembering what Mrs. Railton had told me.

Mrs. Blinder nodded.

"What sort of woman was she?"

"No better walked the earth," said Mrs. Blinder. "My mistress loved her like a sister."

"But I mean — what did she look like?"

Mrs. Blinder got up and gave me a kind of angry stare. "I'm no great hand at describing," she said; "and I believe my pastry's rising." And she walked off into the kitchen and shut the door after her.

II

I HAD been near a week at Brympton before I saw my master. Word came that he was arriving one afternoon, and a change passed over the whole household. It was plain that nobody loved him below stairs. Mrs. Blinder took uncommon care with the dinner that night, but she snapped at the kitchen—maid in a way quite unusual with her; and Mr. Wace, the butler, a serious, slow—spoken man, went about his duties as if he'd been getting ready for a funeral. He was a great Bible—reader, Mr. Wace was, and had a beautiful assortment of texts at his command; but that day he used such dreadful language that I was about to leave the table, when he assured me it was all out of Isaiah; and I noticed that whenever the master came Mr. Wace took to the prophets.

About seven, Agnes called me to my mistress's room; and there I found Mr. Brympton. He was standing on the hearth; a big fair bull—necked man, with a red face and little bad—tempered blue eyes: the kind of man a young simpleton might have thought handsome, and would have been like to pay dear for thinking it.

He swung about when I came in, and looked me over in a trice. I knew what the look meant, from having experienced it once or twice in my former places. Then he turned his back on me, and went on talking to his wife; and I knew what that meant, too. I was not the kind of morsel he was after. The typhoid had served me well enough in one way: it kept that kind of gentleman at arm's—length.

"This is my new maid, Hartley," says Mrs. Brympton in her kind voice; and he nodded and went on with what he was saying.

In a minute or two he went off, and left my mistress to dress for dinner, and I noticed as I waited on her that she was white, and chill to the touch.

Mr. Brympton took himself off the next morning, and the whole house drew a long breath when he drove away. As for my mistress, she put on her hat and furs (for it was a fine winter morning) and went out for a walk in the gardens, coming back quite fresh and rosy, so that for a minute, before her color faded, I could guess what a pretty young lady she must have been, and not so long ago, either.

She had met Mr. Ranford in the grounds, and the two came back together, I remember, smiling and talking as they walked along the terrace under my window. That was the first time I saw Mr. Ranford, though I had often heard his name mentioned in the hall. He was a neighbor, it appeared, living a mile or two beyond Brympton, at the end of the village; and as he was in the habit of spending his winters in the country he was almost the only company my mistress had at that season. He was a slight tall gentleman of about thirty, and I thought him rather melancholy−looking till I saw his smile, which had a kind of surprise in it, like the first warm day in spring. He was a great reader, I heard, like my mistress, and the two were forever borrowing books of one another, and sometimes (Mr. Wace told me) he would read aloud to Mrs. Brympton by the hour, in the big dark library where she sat in the winter afternoons. The servants all liked him, and perhaps that's more of a compliment than the masters suspect. He had a friendly word for every one of us, and we were all glad to think that Mrs. Brympton had a pleasant companionable gentleman like that to keep her company when the master was away. Mr. Ranford seemed on excellent terms with Mr. Brympton too; though I couldn't but wonder that two gentlemen so unlike each other should be so friendly. But then I knew how the real quality can keep their feelings to themselves.

As for Mr. Brympton, he came and went, never staying more than a day or two, cursing the dulness and the solitude, grumbling at everything, and (as I soon found out) drinking a deal more than was good for him. After Mrs. Brympton left the table he would sit half the night over the old Brympton port and madeira, and once, as I was leaving my mistress's room rather later than usual, I met him coming up the stairs in such a state that I turned sick to think of what some ladies have to endure and hold their tongues about.

The servants said very little about their master; but from what they let drop I could see it had been an unhappy match from the beginning. Mr. Brympton was coarse, loud and pleasure−loving; my mistress quiet, retiring, and perhaps a trifle cold. Not that she was not always pleasant−spoken to him: I thought her wonderfully forbearing; but to a gentleman as free as Mr. Brympton I daresay she seemed a little offish.

Well, things went on quietly for several weeks. My mistress was kind, my duties were light, and I got on well with the other servants. In short, I had nothing to complain of; yet there was always a weight on me. I can't say why it was so, but I know it was not the loneliness that I felt. I soon got used to that; and being still languid from the fever, I was thankful for the quiet and the good country air. Nevertheless, I was never quite easy in my mind. My mistress, knowing I had been ill, insisted that I should take my walk regular, and often invented errands for me: — a yard of ribbon to be fetched from the village, a letter posted, or a book returned to Mr. Ranford. As soon as I was out of doors my spirits rose, and I looked forward to my walks through the bare moist–smelling woods; but the moment I caught sight of the house again my heart dropped down like a stone in a well. It was not a gloomy house exactly, yet I never entered it but a feeling of gloom came over me.

Mrs. Brympton seldom went out in winter; only on the finest days did she walk an hour at noon on the south terrace. Excepting Mr. Ranford, we had no visitors but the doctor, who drove over from D — — –about once a week. He sent for me once or twice to give me some trifling direction about my mistress, and though he never told me what her illness was, I thought, from a waxy look she had now and then of a morning, that it might be the heart that ailed her. The season was soft and unwholesome, and in January we had a long spell of rain. That was a sore trial to me, I own, for I couldn't go out, and sitting over my sewing all day, listening to the drip, drip of the eaves, I grew so nervous that the least sound made me jump. Somehow, the thought of that locked room across the passage began to weigh on me. Once or twice, in the long rainy nights, I fancied I heard noises there; but that was nonsense, of course, and the daylight drove such notions out of my head. Well, one morning Mrs. Brympton gave me quite a start of pleasure by telling me she wished me to go to town for some shopping. I hadn't known till then how low my spirits had fallen. I set off in high glee, and my first sight of the crowded streets and the cheerful–looking shops quite took me out of myself. Toward afternoon, however, the noise and confusion began to tire me, and I was actually looking forward to the quiet of Brympton, and thinking how I should enjoy the drive home through the dark woods, when I ran across an old acquaintance, a maid I had once been in service with. We had lost sight of each other for a number of years, and I had to stop and tell her what had happened to me in the interval. When I mentioned where I was living she rolled up her eyes and pulled a long face.

"What! The Mrs. Brympton that lives all the year at her place on the Hudson? My dear, you won't stay there three months."

"Oh, but I don't mind the country," says I, offended somehow at her tone. "Since the fever I'm glad to be quiet."

She shook her head. "It's not the country I'm thinking of. All I know is she's had four maids in the last six months, and the last one, who was a friend of mine, told me nobody could stay in the house."

"Did she say why?" I asked.

"No — she wouldn't give me her reason. But she says to me, Mrs. Ansey, she says, if ever a young woman as you know of thinks of going there, you tell her it's not worth while to unpack her boxes."

"Is she young and handsome?" said I, thinking of Mr. Brympton.

"Not her! She's the kind that mothers engage when they've gay young gentlemen at college."

Well, though I knew the woman was an idle gossip, the words stuck in my head, and my heart sank lower than ever as I drove up to Brympton in the dusk. There was something about the house — I was sure of it now . . .

When I went in to tea I heard that Mr. Brympton had arrived, and I saw at a glance that there had been a disturbance of some kind. Mrs. Blinder's hand shook so that she could hardly pour the tea, and Mr. Wace quoted the most dreadful texts full of brimstone. Nobody said a word to me then, but when I went up to my room Mrs. Blinder followed me.

"Oh, my dear," says she, taking my hand, "I'm so glad and thankful you've come back to us!"

That struck me, as you may imagine. "Why," said I, "did you think I was leaving for good?"

"No, no, to be sure," said she, a little confused, "but I can't a−bear to have madam left alone for a day even." She pressed my hand hard, and, "Oh, Miss Hartley," says she, "be good to your mistress, as you're a Christian woman." And with that she hurried away, and left me staring.

A moment later Agnes called me to Mrs. Brympton. Hearing Mr. Brympton's voice in her room, I went round by the dressing–room, thinking I would lay out her dinner–gown before going in. The dressing–room is a large room with a window over the portico that looks toward the gardens. Mr. Brympton's apartments are beyond. When I went in, the door into the bedroom was ajar, and I heard Mr. Brympton saying angrily: — "One would suppose he was the only person fit for you to talk to."

"I don't have many visitors in winter," Mrs. Brympton answered quietly.

"You have me!" he flung at her, sneering.

"You are here so seldom," said she.

"Well — whose fault is that? You make the place about as lively as a family vault — "

With that I rattled the toilet–things, to give my mistress warning and she rose and called me in.

The two dined alone, as usual, and I knew by Mr. Wace's manner at supper that things must be going badly. He quoted the prophets something terrible, and worked on the kitchen–maid so that she declared she wouldn't go down alone to put the cold meat in the ice–box. I felt nervous myself, and after I had put my mistress to bed I was half–tempted to go down again and persuade Mrs. Blinder to sit up awhile over a game of cards. But I heard her door closing for the night, and so I went on to my own room. The rain had begun again, and the drip, drip, drip seemed to be dropping into my brain. I lay awake listening to it, and turning over what my friend in town had said. What puzzled me was that it was always the maids who left . . .

After a while I slept; but suddenly a loud noise wakened me. My bell had rung. I sat up, terrified by the unusual sound, which seemed to go on jangling through the darkness. My hands shook so that I couldn't find the matches. At length I struck a light and jumped out of bed. I began to think I must have been dreaming; but I looked at the bell against the wall, and there was the little hammer still quivering.

I was just beginning to huddle on my clothes when I heard another sound. This time it was the door of the locked room opposite mine softly opening and closing. I heard the sound distinctly, and it frightened me so that I stood stock still. Then I heard a footstep hurrying down the passage toward the main house. The floor being carpeted, the sound was very faint, but I was quite sure it was a woman's step. I turned cold with the thought of it, and for a minute or two I dursn't breathe or move. Then I came to my senses.

"Alice Hartley," says I to myself, "someone left that room just now and ran down the passage ahead of you. The idea isn't pleasant, but you may as well face it. Your mistress has rung for you, and to answer her bell you've got to go the way that other woman has gone."

Well — I did it. I never walked faster in my life, yet I thought I should never get to the end of the passage or reach Mrs. Brympton's room. On the way I heard nothing and saw nothing: all was dark and quiet as the grave. When I reached my mistress's door the silence was so deep that I began to think I must be dreaming, and was half-minded to turn back. Then a panic seized me, and I knocked.

There was no answer, and I knocked again, loudly. To my astonishment the door was opened by Mr. Brympton. He started back when he saw me, and in the light of my candle his face looked red and savage.

"You!" he said, in a queer voice. "How many of you are there, in God's name?"

At that I felt the ground give under me; but I said to myself that he had been drinking, and answered as steadily as I could: "May I go in, sir? Mrs. Brympton has rung for me."

"You may all go in, for what I care," says he, and, pushing by me, walked down the hall to his own bedroom. I looked after him as he went, and to my surprise I saw that he walked as straight as a sober man.

I found my mistress lying very weak and still, but she forced a smile when she saw me, and signed to me to pour out some drops for her. After that she lay without speaking, her breath coming quick, and her eyes closed. Suddenly she groped out with her hand, and " Emma," says she, faintly.

"It's Hartley, madam," I said. "Do you want anything?"

She opened her eyes wide and gave me a startled look.

"I was dreaming," she said. "You may go, now, Hartley, and thank you kindly. I'm quite well again, you see." And she turned her face away from me.

III

THERE was no more sleep for me that night, and I was thankful when daylight came.

Soon afterward, Agnes called me to Mrs. Brympton. I was afraid she was ill again, for she seldom sent for me before nine, but I found her sitting up in bed, pale and drawn-looking, but quite herself.

"Hartley," says she quickly, "will you put on your things at once and go down to the village for me? I want this prescription made up — " here she hesitated a minute and blushed — "and I should like you to be back again before Mr. Brympton is up."

"Certainly, madam," I said.

"And — stay a moment — " she called me back as if an idea had just struck her — "while you're waiting for the mixture, you'll have time to go on to Mr. Ranford's with this note."

It was a two-mile walk to the village, and on my way I had time to turn things over in my mind. It struck me as peculiar that my mistress should wish the prescription made up without Mr. Brympton's knowledge; and, putting this together with the scene of the night before, and with much else that I had noticed and suspected, I began to wonder if the poor lady was weary of her life, and had come to the mad resolve of ending it. The idea took such hold on me that I reached the village on a run, and dropped breathless into a chair before the chemist's counter. The good man, who was just taking down his shutters, stared at me so hard that it brought me to myself.

"Mr. Limmel," I says, trying to speak indifferent, "will you run your eye over this, and tell me if it's quite right?"

He put on his spectacles and studied the prescription.

"Why, it's one of Dr. Walton's," says he. "What should be wrong with it?"

"Well — is it dangerous to take?"

"Dangerous — how do you mean?"

I could have shaken the man for his stupidity.

"I mean — if a person was to take too much of it — by mistake of course — " says I, my heart in my throat.

"Lord bless you, no. It's only lime–water. You might feed it to a baby by the bottleful."

I gave a great sigh of relief, and hurried on to Mr. Ranford's. But on the way another thought struck me. If there was nothing to conceal about my visit to the chemist's, was it my other errand that Mrs. Brympton wished me to keep private? Somehow, that thought frightened me worse than the other. Yet the two gentlemen seemed fast friends, and I would have staked my head on my mistress's goodness. I felt ashamed of my suspicions, and concluded that I was still disturbed by the strange events of the night. I left the note at Mr. Ranford's — and, hurrying back to Brympton, slipped in by a side door without being seen, as I thought.

An hour later, however, as I was carrying in my mistress's breakfast, I was stopped in the hall by Mr. Brympton.

"What were you doing out so early?" he says, looking hard at me.

"Early — me, sir?" I said, in a tremble.

"Come, come," he says, an angry red spot coming out on his forehead, "didn't I see you scuttling home through the shrubbery an hour or more ago?"

I'm a truthful woman by nature, but at that a lie popped out ready–made. "No, sir, you didn't," said I, and looked straight back at him.

He shrugged his shoulders and gave a sullen laugh. "I suppose you think I was drunk last night?" he asked suddenly.

"No, sir, I don't," I answered, this time truthfully enough.

He turned away with another shrug. "A pretty notion my servants have of me!" I heard him mutter as he walked off.

Not till I had settled down to my afternoon's sewing did I realize how the events of the night had shaken me. I couldn't pass that locked door without a shiver. I knew I had heard someone come out of it, and walk down the passage ahead of me. I thought of speaking to Mrs. Blinder or to Mr. Wace, the only two in the house who appeared to have an inkling of what was going on, but I had a feeling that if I questioned them they would deny everything, and that I might learn more by holding my tongue and keeping my eyes open. The idea of spending another night opposite the locked room sickened me, and once I was seized with the notion of packing my trunk and taking the first train to town; but it wasn't in me to throw over a kind mistress in that manner, and I tried to go on with my sewing as if nothing had happened.

I hadn't worked ten minutes before the sewing–machine broke down. It was one I had found in the house, a good machine, but a trifle out of order: Mrs. Blinder said it had never been used since Emma Saxon's death. I stopped to see what was wrong, and as I was working at the machine a drawer which I had never been able to open slid forward and a photograph fell out. I picked it up and sat looking at it in a maze. It was a woman's likeness, and I knew I had seen the face somewhere — the eyes had an asking look that I had felt on me before. And suddenly I remembered the pale woman in the passage.

I stood up, cold all over, and ran out of the room. My heart seemed to be thumping in the top of my head, and I felt as if I should never get away from the look in those eyes. I went straight to Mrs. Blinder. She was taking her afternoon nap, and sat up with a jump when I came in.

"Mrs. Blinder," said I, "who is that?" And I held out the photograph.

She rubbed her eyes and stared.

"Why, Emma Saxon," says she. "Where did you find it?"

I looked hard at her for a minute. "Mrs. Blinder," I said, "I've seen that face before."

Mrs. Blinder got up and walked over to the looking–glass. "Dear me! I must have been asleep," she says. "My front is all over one ear. And now do run along, Miss Hartley, dear, for I hear the clock striking four, and I must go down this very minute and put on the Virginia ham for Mr. Brympton's dinner."

IV

TO all appearances, things went on as usual for a week or two. The only difference was that Mr. Brympton stayed on, instead of going off as he usually did, and that Mr. Ranford never showed himself. I heard Mr. Brympton remark on this one afternoon when he was sitting in my mistress's room before dinner.

"Where's Ranford?" says he. "He hasn't been near the house for a week. Does he keep away because I'm here?"

Mrs. Brympton spoke so low that I couldn't catch her answer.

"Well," he went on, "two's company and three's trumpery; I'm sorry to be in Ranford's way, and I suppose I shall have to take myself off again in a day or two and give him a show." And he laughed at his own joke.

The very next day, as it happened, Mr. Ranford called. The footman said the three were very merry over their tea in the library, and Mr. Brympton strolled down to the gate with Mr. Ranford when he left.

I have said that things went on as usual; and so they did with the rest of the household; but as for myself, I had never been the same since the night my bell had rung. Night after night I used to lie awake, listening for it to ring again, and for the door of the locked room to open stealthily. But the bell never rang, and I heard no sound across the passage. At last the silence began to be more dreadful to me than the most mysterious sounds. I felt that someone were cowering there, behind the locked door, watching and listening as

I watched and listened, and I could almost have cried out, "Whoever you are, come out and let me see you face to face, but don't lurk there and spy on me in the darkness!"

Feeling as I did, you may wonder I didn't give warning. Once I very nearly did so; but at the last moment something held me back. Whether it was compassion for my mistress, who had grown more and more dependent on me, or unwillingness to try a new place, or some other feeling that I couldn't put a name to, I lingered on as if spell–bound, though every night was dreadful to me, and the days but little better.

For one thing, I didn't like Mrs. Brympton's looks. She had never been the same since that night, no more than I had. I thought she would brighten up after Mr. Brympton left, but though she seemed easier in her mind, her spirits didn't revive, nor her strength either. She had grown attached to me, and seemed to like to have me about; and Agnes told me one day that, since Emma Saxon's death, I was the only maid her mistress had taken to. This gave me a warm feeling for the poor lady, though after all there was little I could do to help her.

After Mr. Brympton's departure, Mr. Ranford took to coming again, though less often than formerly. I met him once or twice in the grounds, or in the village, and I couldn't but think there was a change in him too; but I set it down to my disordered fancy.

The weeks passed, and Mr. Brympton had now been a month absent. We heard he was cruising with a friend in the West Indies, and Mr. Wace said that was a long way off, but though you had the wings of a dove and went to the uttermost parts of the earth, you couldn't get away from the Almighty. Agnes said that as long as he stayed away from Brympton, the Almighty might have him and welcome; and this raised a laugh, though Mrs. Blinder tried to look shocked, and Mr. Wace said the bears would eat us.

We were all glad to hear that the West Indies were a long way off, and I remember that, in spite of Mr. Wace's solemn looks, we had a very merry dinner that day in the hall. I don't know if it was because of my being in better spirits, but I fancied Mrs. Brympton looked better too, and seemed more cheerful in her manner. She had been for a walk in the morning, and after luncheon she lay down in her room, and I read aloud to her. When she dismissed me I went to my own room feeling quite bright and happy, and for the first time in weeks walked past the locked door without thinking of it. As I sat down to my work I looked out and saw a few snow–flakes falling. The sight was pleasanter than the

81

eternal rain, and I pictured to myself how pretty the bare gardens would look in their white mantle. It seemed to me as if the snow would cover up all the dreariness, indoors as well as out.

The fancy had hardly crossed my mind when I heard a step at my side. I looked up, thinking it was Agnes.

"Well, Agnes — " said I, and the words froze on my tongue; for there, in the door, stood Emma Saxon.

I don't know how long she stood there. I only know I couldn't stir or take my eyes from her. Afterward I was terribly frightened, but at the time it wasn't fear I felt, but something deeper and quieter. She looked at me long and long, and her face was just one dumb prayer to me — but how in the world was I to help her? Suddenly she turned, and I heard her walk down the passage. This time I wasn't afraid to follow — I felt that I must know what she wanted. I sprang up and ran out. She was at the other end of the passage, and I expected her to take the turn toward my mistress's room; but instead of that she pushed open the door that led to the backstairs. I followed her down the stairs, and across the passageway to the back door. The kitchen and hall were empty at that hour, the servants being off duty, except for the footman, who was in the pantry. At the door she stood still a moment, with another look at me; then she turned the handle, and stepped out. For a minute I hesitated. Where was she leading me to? The door had closed softly after her, and I opened it and looked out, half−expecting to find that she had disappeared. But I saw her a few yards off, hurrying across the court−yard to the path through the woods. Her figure looked black and lonely in the snow, and for a second my heart failed me and I thought of turning back. But all the while she was drawing me after her; and catching up an old shawl of Mrs. Blinder's I ran out into the open.

Emma Saxon was in the wood−path now. She walked on steadily, and I followed at the same pace, till we passed out of the gates and reached the high−road. Then she struck across the open fields to the village. By this time the ground was white, and as she climbed the slope of a bare hill ahead of me I noticed that she left no foot−prints behind her. At sight of that, my heart shrivelled up within me, and my knees were water. Somehow, it was worse here than indoors. She made the whole countryside seem lonely as the grave, with none but us two in it, and no help in the wide world.

Once I tried to go back; but she turned and looked at me, and it was as if she had dragged me with ropes. After that I followed her like a dog. We came to the village, and she led me through it, past the church and the blacksmith's shop, and down the lane to Mr. Ranford's. Mr. Ranford's house stands close to the road: a plain old–fashioned building, with a flagged path leading to the door between box–borders. The lane was deserted, and as I turned into it, I saw Emma Saxon pause under the old elm by the gate. And now another fear came over me. I saw that we had reached the end of our journey, and that it was my turn to act. All the way from Brympton I had been asking myself what she wanted of me, but I had followed in a trance, as it were, and not till I saw her stop at Mr. Ranford's gate did my brain begin to clear itself. It stood a little way off in the snow, my heart beating fit to strangle me, and my feet frozen to the ground; and she stood under the elm and watched me.

I knew well enough that she hadn't led me there for nothing. I felt there was something I ought to say or do — but how was I to guess what it was? I had never thought harm of my mistress and Mr. Ranford, but I was sure now that, from one cause or another, some dreadful thing hung over them. She knew what it was; she would tell me if she could; perhaps she would answer if I questioned her.

It turned me faint to think of speaking to her; but I plucked up heart and dragged myself across the few yards between us. As I did so, I heard the house–door open, and saw Mr. Ranford approaching. He looked handsome and cheerful, as my mistress had looked that morning, and at sight of him the blood began to flow again in my veins.

"Why, Hartley," said he, "what's the matter? I saw you coming down the lane just now, and came out to see if you had taken root in the snow." He stopped and stared at me. "What are you looking at?" he says.

I turned toward the elm as he spoke, and his eyes followed me; but there was no one there. The lane was empty as far as the eye could reach.

A sense of helplessness came over me. She was gone, and I had not been able to guess what she wanted. Her last look had pierced me to the marrow; and yet it had not told me! All at once, I felt more desolate than when she had stood there watching me. It seemed as if she had left me all alone to carry the weight of the secret I couldn't guess. The snow went round me in great circles, and the ground fell away from me. . . .

A drop of brandy and the warmth of Mr. Ranford's fire soon brought me to, and I insisted on being driven back at once to Brympton. It was nearly dark, and I was afraid my mistress might be wanting me. I explained to Mr. Ranford that I had been out for a walk and had been taken with a fit of giddiness as I passed his gate. This was true enough; yet I never felt more like a liar than when I said it.

When I dressed Mrs. Brympton for dinner she remarked on my pale looks and asked what ailed me. I told her I had a headache, and she said she would not require me again that evening, and advised me to go to bed.

It was a fact that I could scarcely keep on my feet; yet I had no fancy to spend a solitary evening in my room. I sat downstairs in the hall as long as I could hold my head up; but by nine I crept upstairs, too weary to care what happened if I could but get my head on a pillow. The rest of the household went to bed soon afterward; they kept early hours when the master was away, and before ten I heard Mrs. Blinder's door close, and Mr. Wace's soon after.

It was a very still night, earth and air all muffled in snow. Once in bed I felt easier, and lay quiet, listening to the strange noises that come out in a house after dark. Once I thought I heard a door open and close again below: it might have been the glass door that led to the gardens. I got up and peered out of the window; but it was in the dark of the moon, and nothing visible outside but the streaking of snow against the panes.

I went back to bed and must have dozed, for I jumped awake to the furious ringing of my bell. Before my head was clear I had sprung out of bed, and was dragging on my clothes. It is going to happen now, I heard myself saying; but what I meant I had no notion. My hands seemed to be covered with glue — I thought I should never get into my clothes. At last I opened my door and peered down the passage. As far as my candle–flame carried, I could see nothing unusual ahead of me. I hurried on, breathless; but as I pushed open the baize door leading to the main hall my heart stood still, for there at the head of the stairs was Emma Saxon, peering dreadfully down into the darkness.

For a second I couldn't stir; but my hand slipped from the door, and as it swung shut the figure vanished. At the same instant there came another sound from below stairs — a stealthy mysterious sound, as of a latch–key turning in the house–door. I ran to Mrs. Brympton's room and knocked.

There was no answer, and I knocked again. This time I heard some one moving in the room; the bolt slipped back and my mistress stood before me. To my surprise I saw that she had not undressed for the night. She gave me a startled look.

"What is this, Hartley?" she says in a whisper. "Are you ill? What are you doing here at this hour?"

"I am not ill, madam; but my bell rang."

At that she turned pale, and seemed about to fall.

"You are mistaken," she said harshly; "I didn't ring. You must have been dreaming." I had never heard her speak in such a tone. "Go back to bed," she said, closing the door on me.

But as she spoke I heard sounds again in the hall below: a man's step this time; and the truth leaped out on me.

"Madam," I said, pushing past her, "there is someone in the house — "

"Someone — ?"

"Mr. Brympton, I think — I hear his step below — "

A dreadful look came over her, and without a word, she dropped flat at my feet. I fell on my knees and tried to lift her: by the way she breathed I saw it was no common faint. But as I raised her head there came quick steps on the stairs and across the hall: the door was flung open, and there stood Mr. Brympton, in his travelling-clothes, the snow dripping from him. He drew back with a start as he saw me kneeling by my mistress.

"What the devil is this?" he shouted. He was less high-colored than usual, and the red spot came out on his forehead.

"Mrs. Brympton has fainted, sir," said I.

He laughed unsteadily and pushed by me. "It's a pity she didn't choose a more convenient moment. I'm sorry to disturb her, but — "

I raised myself up, aghast at the man's action.

"Sir," said I, "are you mad? What are you doing?"

"Going to meet a friend," said he, and seemed to make for the dressing-room.

At that my heart turned over. I don't know what I thought or feared; but I sprang up and caught him by the sleeve.

"Sir, sir," said I, "for pity's sake look at your wife!"

He shook me off furiously.

"It seems that's done for me," says he, and caught hold of the dressing-room door.

At that moment I heard a slight noise inside. Slight as it was, he heard it too, and tore the door open; but as he did so he dropped back. On the threshold stood Emma Saxon. All was dark behind her, but I saw her plainly, and so did he. He threw up his hands as if to hide his face from her; and when I looked again she was gone.

He stood motionless, as if the strength had run out of him; and in the stillness my mistress suddenly raised herself, and opening her eyes fixed a look on him. Then she fell back, and I saw the death-flutter pass over her. . . .

We buried her on the third day, in a driving snow-storm. There were few people in the church, for it was bad weather to come from town, and I've a notion my mistress was one that hadn't many near friends. Mr. Ranford was among the last to come, just before they carried her up the aisle. He was in black, of course, being such a friend of the family, and I never saw a gentleman so pale. As he passed me, I noticed that he leaned a trifle on a stick he carried; and I fancy Mr. Brympton noticed it too, for the red spot came out sharp on his forehead, and all through the service he kept staring across the church at Mr. Ranford, instead of following the prayers as a mourner should.

When it was over and we went out to the graveyard, Mr. Ranford had disappeared, and as soon as my poor mistress's body was underground, Mr. Brympton jumped into the carriage nearest the gate and drove off without a word to any of us. I heard him call out, "To the station," and we servants went back alone to the house.

The Mission of Jane

I

LETHBURY, surveying his wife across the dinner table, found his transient conjugal glance arrested by an indefinable change in her appearance.

"How smart you look! Is that a new gown?" he asked.

Her answering look seemed to deprecate his charging her with the extravagance of wasting a new gown on him, and he now perceived that the change lay deeper than any accident of dress. At the same time, he noticed that she betrayed her consciousness of it by a delicate, almost frightened blush. It was one of the compensations of Mrs. Lethbury's protracted childishness that she still blushed as prettily as at eighteen. Her body had been privileged not to outstrip her mind, and the two, as it seemed to Lethbury, were destined to travel together through an eternity of girlishness.

"I don't know what you mean," she said.

Since she never did, he always wondered at her bringing this out as a fresh grievance against him; but his wonder was unresentful, and he said good–humoredly: "You sparkle so that I thought you had on your diamonds."

She sighed and blushed again.

"It must be," he continued, "that you've been to a dressmaker's opening. You're absolutely brimming with illicit enjoyment."

She stared again, this time at the adjective. His adjectives always embarrassed her: their unintelligibleness savored of impropriety.

"In short," he summed up, "you've been doing something that you're thoroughly ashamed of."

To his surprise she retorted: "I don't see why I should be ashamed of it!"

Lethbury leaned back with a smile of enjoyment. When there was nothing better going he always liked to listen to her explanations.

"Well — ?" he said.

She was becoming breathless and ejaculatory. "Of course you'll laugh — you laugh at everything!"

"That rather blunts the point of my derision, doesn't it?" he interjected; but she rushed on without noticing:

"It's so easy to laugh at things."

"Ah," murmured Lethbury with relish, "that's Aunt Sophronia's, isn't it?"

Most of his wife's opinions were heirlooms, and he took a quaint pleasure in tracing their descent. She was proud of their age, and saw no reason for discarding them while they were still serviceable. Some, of course, were so fine that she kept them for state occasions, like her great–grandmother's Crown Derby; but from the lady known as Aunt Sophronia she had inherited a stout set of every–day prejudices that were practically as good as new; whereas her husband's, as she noticed, were always having to be replaced. In the early days she had fancied there might be a certain satisfaction in taxing him with the fact; but she had long since been silenced by the reply: "My dear, I'm not a rich man, but I never use an opinion twice if I can help it."

She was reduced, therefore, to dwelling on his moral deficiencies; and one of the most obvious of these was his refusal to take things seriously. On this occasion, however, some ulterior purpose kept her from taking up his taunt.

"I'm not in the least ashamed!" she repeated, with the air of shaking a banner to the wind; but the domestic atmosphere being calm, the banner drooped unheroically.

"That," said Lethbury judicially, "encourages me to infer that you ought to be, and that, consequently, you've been giving yourself the unusual pleasure of doing something I shouldn't approve of."

She met this with an almost solemn directness. "No," she said. "You won't approve of it. I've allowed for that."

"Ah," he exclaimed, setting down his liqueur-glass. "You've worked out the whole problem, eh?"

"I believe so."

"That's uncommonly interesting. And what is it?"

She looked at him quietly. "A baby."

If it was seldom given her to surprise him, she had attained the distinction for once.

"A baby?"

"Yes."

"A — human baby?"

"Of course!" she cried, with the virtuous resentment of the woman who has never allowed dogs in the house.

Lethbury's puzzled stare broke into a fresh smile. "A baby I sha'n't approve of? Well, in the abstract I don't think much of them, I admit. Is this an abstract baby?"

Again she frowned at the adjective; but she had reached a pitch of exaltation at which such obstacles could not deter her.

"It's the loveliest baby — " she murmured.

"Ah, then it's concrete. It exists. In this harsh world it draws its breath in pain — "

"It's the healthiest child I ever saw!" she indignantly corrected.

"You've seen it, then?"

Again the accusing blush suffused her. "Yes — I've seen it."

"And to whom does the paragon belong?"

And here indeed she confounded him. "To me — I hope," she declared.

He pushed his chair back with an inarticulate murmur. "To you — ?"

"To us," she corrected.

"Good Lord!" he said. If there had been the least hint of hallucination in her transparent gaze — but no: it was as clear, as shallow, as easily fathomable as when he had first suffered the sharp surprise of striking bottom in it.

It occurred to him that perhaps she was trying to be funny: he knew that there is nothing more cryptic than the humor of the unhumorous.

"Is it a joke?" he faltered.

"Oh, I hope not. I want it so much to be a reality — "

He paused to smile at the limitations of a world in which jokes were not realities, and continued gently: "But since it is one already — "

"To us, I mean: to you and me. I want — " her voice wavered, and her eyes with it. "I have always wanted so dreadfully . . . it has been such a disappointment . . . not to . . ."

"I see," said Lethbury slowly.

But he had not seen before. It seemed curious, now, that he had never thought of her taking it in that way, had never surmised any hidden depths beneath her outspread obviousness. He felt as though he had touched a secret spring in her mind.

There was a moment's silence, moist and tremulous on her part, awkward and slightly irritated on his.

"You've been lonely, I suppose?" he began. It was odd, having suddenly to reckon with the stranger who gazed at him out of her trivial eyes.

"At times," she said.

"I'm sorry."

"It was not your fault. A man has so many occupations; and women who are clever — or very handsome — I suppose that's an occupation too. Sometimes I've felt that when dinner was ordered I had nothing to do till the next day."

"Oh," he groaned.

"It wasn't your fault," she insisted. "I never told you — but when I chose that rose–bud paper for the front room upstairs, I always thought — "

"Well — ?"

"It would be such a pretty paper — for a baby — to wake up in. That was years ago, of course; but it was rather an expensive paper . . . and it hasn't faded in the least . . ." she broke off incoherently.

"It hasn't faded?"

"No — and so I thought . . . as we don't use the room for anything . . . now that Aunt Sophronia is dead . . . I thought I might . . . you might . . . oh, Julian, if you could only have seen it just waking up in its crib!"

"Seen what — where? You haven't got a baby upstairs?"

"Oh, no — not yet," she said, with her rare laugh — the girlish bubbling of merriment that had seemed one of her chief graces in the early days. It occurred to him that he had not given her enough things to laugh about lately. But then she needed such very elementary things: it was as difficult to amuse her as a savage. He concluded that he was not sufficiently simple.

"Alice," he said, almost solemnly, "what do you mean?"

She hesitated a moment: he saw her gather her courage for a supreme effort. Then she said slowly, gravely, as though she were pronouncing a sacramental phrase:

"I'm so lonely without a little child — and I thought perhaps you'd let me adopt one. . . . It's at the hospital . . . its mother is dead . . . and I could . . . pet it, and dress it, and do things for it . . . and it's such a good baby . . . you can ask any of the nurses . . . it would never, never bother you by crying . . ."

II

Lethbury accompanied his wife to the hospital in a mood of chastened wonder. It did not occur to him to oppose her wish. He knew, of course, that he would have to bear the brunt of the situation: the jokes at the club, the inquiries, the explanations. He saw himself in the comic role of the adopted father, and welcomed it as an expiation. For in his rapid reconstruction of the past he found himself cutting a shabbier figure than he cared to admit. He had always been intolerant of stupid people, and it was his punishment to be convicted of stupidity. As his mind traversed the years between his marriage and this unexpected assumption of paternity, he saw, in the light of an overheated imagination, many signs of unwonted crassness. It was not that he had ceased to think his wife stupid: she was stupid, limited, inflexible; but there was a pathos in the struggles of her swaddled mind, in its blind reachings toward the primal emotions. He had always thought she would have been happier with a child; but he had thought it mechanically, because it had so often been thought before, because it was in the nature of things to think it of every woman, because his wife was so eminently one of a species that she fitted into all the generalizations on the sex. But he had regarded this generalization as merely typical of the triumph of tradition over experience. Maternity was no doubt the supreme function of primitive woman, the one end to which her whole organism tended; but the law of increasing complexity had operated in both sexes, and he had not seriously supposed that, outside the world of Christmas fiction and anecdotic art, such truisms had any special hold on the feminine imagination. Now he saw that the arts in question were kept alive by the vitality of the sentiments they appealed to.

Lethbury was in fact going through a rapid process of readjustment. His marriage had been a failure, but he had preserved toward his wife the exact fidelity of act that is sometimes supposed to excuse any divagation of feeling; so that, for years, the tie between them had consisted mainly in his abstaining from making love to other women. The abstention had not always been easy, for the world is surprisingly well–stocked with the kind of woman one ought to have married but did not; and Lethbury had not escaped the solicitation of such alternatives. His immunity had been purchased at the cost of taking refuge in the somewhat rarified atmosphere of his perceptions; and his world being thus limited, he had given unusual care to its details, compensating himself for the narrowness of his horizon by the minute finish of his foreground. It was a world of fine shadings and the nicest proportions, where impulse seldom set a blundering foot, and the feast of reason was undisturbed by an intemperate flow of soul. To such a banquet his wife naturally remained uninvited. The diet would have disagreed with her, and she would probably have objected to the other guests. But Lethbury, miscalculating her needs, had hitherto supposed that he had made ample provision for them, and was consequently at liberty to enjoy his own fare without any reproach of mendicancy at his gates. Now he beheld her pressing a starved face against the windows of his life, and in his imaginative reaction he invested her with a pathos borrowed from the sense of his own shortcomings.

In the hospital, the imaginative process continued with increasing force. He looked at his wife with new eyes. Formerly she had been to him a mere bundle of negations, a labyrinth of dead walls and bolted doors. There was nothing behind the walls, and the doors led no–whither: he had sounded and listened often enough to be sure of that. Now he felt like a traveller who, exploring some ancient ruin, comes on an inner cell, intact amid the general dilapidation, and painted with images which reveal the forgotten uses of the building.

His wife stood by a white crib in one of the wards. In the crib lay a child, a year old, the nurse affirmed, but to Lethbury's eye a mere dateless fragment of humanity projected against a background of conjecture. Over this anonymous particle of life Mrs. Lethbury leaned, such ecstasy reflected in her face as strikes up, in Correggio's Night–piece, from the child's body to the mother's countenance. it was a light that irradiated and dazzled her. She looked up at an inquiry of Lethbury's, but as their glances met he perceived that she no longer saw him, that he had become as invisible to her as she had long been to him. He had to transfer his question to the nurse.

"What is the child's name?" he asked.

"We call her Jane," said the nurse.

III

Lethbury, at first, had resisted the idea of a legal adoption; but when he found that his wife's curiously limited imagination prevented her regarding the child as hers till it had been made so by process of law, he promptly withdrew his objection. On one point only he remained inflexible; and that was the changing of the waif's name. Mrs. Lethbury, almost at once, had expressed a wish to rechristen it: she fluctuated between Muriel and Gladys, deferring the moment of decision like a lady wavering between two bonnets. But Lethbury was unyielding. In the general surrender of his prejudices this one alone held out.

"But Jane is so dreadful," Mrs. Lethbury protested.

"Well, we don't know that she won't be dreadful. She may grow up a Jane."

His wife exclaimed reproachfully. "The nurse says she's the loveliest — "

"Don't they always say that?" asked Lethbury patiently. He was prepared to be inexhaustibly patient now that he had reached a firm foothold of opposition.

"It's cruel to call her Jane," Mrs. Lethbury pleaded.

"It's ridiculous to call her Muriel."

"The nurse is sure she must be a lady's child."

Lethbury winced: he had tried, all along, to keep his mind off the question of antecedents.

"Well, let her prove it," he said, with a rising sense of exasperation. He wondered how he could ever have allowed himself to be drawn into such a ridiculous business; for the first time he felt the full irony of it. He had visions of coming home in the afternoon to a house smelling of linseed and paregoric, and of being greeted by a chronic howl as he went up stairs to dress for dinner. He had never been a club–man, but he saw himself becoming one now.

The worst of his anticipations were unfulfilled. The baby was surprisingly well and surprisingly quiet. Such infantile remedies as she absorbed were not potent enough to be perceived beyond the nursery; and when Lethbury could be induced to enter that sanctuary, there was nothing to jar his nerves in the mild pink presence of his adopted daughter. Jars there were, indeed: they were probably inevitable in the disturbed routine of the household; but they occurred between Mrs. Lethbury and the nurses, and Jane contributed to them only a placid stare which might have served as a rebuke to the combatants.

In the reaction from his first impulse of atonement, Lethbury noted with sharpened perceptions the effect of the change on his wife's character. He saw already the error of supposing that it could work any transformation in her. It simply magnified her existing qualities. She was like a dried sponge put in water: she expanded, but she did not change her shape. From the stand–point of scientific observation it was curious to see how her stored instincts responded to the pseudo–maternal call. She overflowed with the petty maxims of the occasion. One felt in her the epitome, the consummation, of centuries of animal maternity, so that this little woman, who screamed at a mouse and was nervous about burglars, came to typify the cave–mother rending her prey for her young.

It was less easy to regard philosophically the practical effects of her borrowed motherhood. Lethbury found with surprise that she was becoming assertive and definite. She no longer represented the negative side of his life; she showed, indeed, a tendency to inconvenient affirmations. She had gradually expanded her assumption of motherhood till it included his own share in the relation, and he suddenly found himself regarded as the father of Jane. This was a contingency he had not foreseen, and it took all his philosophy to accept it; but there were moments of compensation. For Mrs. Lethbury was undoubtedly happy for the first time in years; and the thought that he had tardily contributed to this end reconciled him to the irony of the means.

At first he was inclined to reproach himself for still viewing the situation from the outside, for remaining a spectator instead of a participant. He had been allured, for a moment, by the vision of severed hands meeting over a cradle, as the whole body of domestic fiction bears witness to their doing; and the fact that no such conjunction took place he could explain only on the ground that it was a borrowed cradle. He did not dislike the little girl. She still remained to him a hypothetical presence, a query rather than a fact; but her nearness was not unpleasant, and there were moments when her tentative utterances, her groping steps, seemed to loosen the dry accretions enveloping his inner self. But even at such moments — moments which he invited and caressed — she did not bring him nearer to his wife. He now perceived that he had made a certain place in his life for Mrs. Lethbury, and that she no longer fitted into it. It was too late to enlarge the space, and so she overflowed and encroached. Lethbury struggled against the sense of submergence. He let down barrier after barrier, yielded privacy after privacy; but his wife's personality continued to dilate. She was no longer herself alone: she was herself and Jane. Gradually, in a monstrous fusion of identity, she became herself, himself and Jane; and instead of trying to adapt her to a spare crevice of his character, he found himself carelessly squeezed into the smallest compartment of the domestic economy.

IV

He continued to tell himself that he was satisfied if his wife was happy; and it was not till the child's tenth year that he felt a doubt of her happiness.

Jane had been a preternaturally good child. During the eight years of her adoption she had caused her foster-parents no anxiety beyond those connected with the usual succession of youthful diseases. But her unknown progenitors had given her a robust constitution, and she passed unperturbed through measles, chicken-pox and whooping-cough. If there was any suffering it was endured vicariously by Mrs. Lethbury, whose temperature rose and fell with the patient's, and who could not hear Jane sneeze without visions of a marble angel weeping over a broken column. But though Jane's prompt recoveries continued to belie such premonitions, though her existence continued to move forward on an even keel of good health and good conduct, Mrs. Lethbury's satisfaction showed no corresponding advance. Lethbury, at first, was disposed to add her disappointment to the long list of feminine inconsistencies with which the sententious observer of life builds up his favorite induction; but circumstances presently led him to take a kindlier view of the case.

Hitherto his wife had regarded him as a negligible factor in Jane's evolution. Beyond providing for his adopted daughter, and effacing himself before her, he was not expected to contribute to her well–being. But as time passed he appeared to his wife in a new light. It was he who was to educate Jane. In matters of the intellect, Mrs. Lethbury was the first to declare her deficiencies — to proclaim them, even, with a certain virtuous superiority. She said she did not pretend to be clever, and there was no denying the truth of the assertion. Now, however, she seemed less ready, not to own her limitations, but to glory in them. Confronted with the problem of Jane's instruction, she stood in awe of the child.

"I have always been stupid, you know," she said to Lethbury with a new humility, "and I'm afraid I sha'n't know what is best for Jane. I'm sure she has a wonderfully good mind, and I should reproach myself if I didn't give her every opportunity." She looked at him helplessly. "You must tell me what ought to be done."

Lethbury was not unwilling to oblige her. Somewhere in his mental lumber–room there rusted a theory of education such as usually lingers among the impedimenta of the childless. He brought this out, refurbished it, and applied it to Jane. At first he thought his wife had not overrated the quality of the child's mind. Jane seemed extraordinarily intelligent. Her precocious definiteness of mind was encouraging to her inexperienced preceptor. She had no difficulty in fixing her attention, and he felt that every fact he imparted was being etched in metal. He helped his wife to engage the best teachers, and for a while continued to take an ex–official interest in his adopted daughter's studies. But gradually his interest waned. Jane's ideas did not increase with her acquisitions. Her young mind remained a mere receptacle for facts: a kind of cold–storage from which anything that had been put there could be taken out at a moment's notice, intact but congealed. She developed, moreover, an inordinate pride in the capacity of her mental storehouse, and a tendency to pelt her public with its contents. She was overheard to jeer at her nurse for not knowing when the Saxon Heptarchy had fallen, and she alternately dazzled and depressed Mrs. Lethbury by the wealth of her chronological allusions. She showed no interest in the significance of the facts she amassed: she simply collected dates as another child might have collected stamps or marbles. To her foster–mother she seemed a prodigy of wisdom; but Lethbury saw, with a secret movement of sympathy, how the aptitudes in which Mrs. Lethbury gloried were slowly estranging her from their possessor.

"She is getting too clever for me," his wife said to him, after one of Jane's historical flights, "but I am so glad that she will be a companion to you."

Lethbury groaned in spirit. He did not look forward to Jane's companionship. She was still a good little girl: but there was something automatic and formal in her goodness, as though it were a kind of moral calisthenics that she went through for the sake of showing her agility. An early consciousness of virtue had moreover constituted her the natural guardian and adviser of her elders. Before she was fifteen she had set about reforming the household. She took Mrs. Lethbury in hand first; then she extended her efforts to the servants, with consequences more disastrous to the domestic harmony; and lastly she applied herself to Lethbury. She proved to him by statistics that he smoked too much, and that it was injurious to the optic nerve to read in bed. She took him to task for not going to church more regularly, and pointed out to him the evils of desultory reading. She suggested that a regular course of study encourages mental concentration, and hinted that inconsecutiveness of thought is a sign of approaching age.

To her adopted mother her suggestions were equally pertinent. She instructed Mrs. Lethbury in an improved way of making beef stock, and called her attention to the unhygienic qualities of carpets. She poured out distracting facts about bacilli and vegetable mould, and demonstrated that curtains and picture–frames are a hot–bed of animal organisms. She learned by heart the nutritive ingredients of the principal articles of diet, and revolutionized the cuisine by an attempt to establish a scientific average between starch and phosphates. Four cooks left during this experiment, and Lethbury fell into the habit of dining at his club.

Once or twice, at the outset, he had tried to check Jane's ardor; but his efforts resulted only in hurting his wife's feelings. Jane remained impervious, and Mrs. Lethbury resented any attempt to protect her from her daughter. Lethbury saw that she was consoled for the sense of her own inferiority by the thought of what Jane's intellectual companionship must be to him; and he tried to keep up the illusion by enduring with what grace he might the blighting edification of Jane's discourse.

V

As Jane grew up, he sometimes avenged himself by wondering if his wife was still sorry that they had not called her Muriel. Jane was not ugly; she developed, indeed, a kind of categorical prettiness that might have been a pro–jection of her mind. She had a creditable collection of features, but one had to take an inventory of them to find out that she was good–looking. The fusing grace had been omitted.

Mrs. Lethbury took a touching pride in her daughter's first steps in the world. She expected Jane to take by her complexion those whom she did not capture by her learning. But Jane's rosy freshness did not work any perceptible ravages. Whether the young men guessed the axioms on her lips and detected the encyclopaedia in her eye, or whether they simply found no intrinsic interest in these features, certain it is, that, in spite of her mother's heroic efforts, and of incessant calls on Lethbury's purse, Jane, at the end of her first season, had dropped hopelessly out of the running. A few duller girls found her interesting, and one or two young men came to the house with the object of meeting other young women; but she was rapidly becoming one of the social supernumeraries who are asked out only because they are on people's lists.

The blow was bitter to Mrs. Lethbury; but she consoled herself with the idea that Jane had failed because she was too clever. Jane probably shared this conviction; at all events she betrayed no consciousness of failure. She had developed a pronounced taste for society, and went out, unweariedly and obstinately, winter after winter, while Mrs. Lethbury toiled in her wake, showering attentions on oblivious hostesses. To Lethbury there was something at once tragic and exasperating in the sight of their two figures, the one conciliatory, the other dogged, both pursuing with unabated zeal the elusive prize of popularity. He even began to feel a personal stake in the pursuit, not as it concerned Jane, but as it affected his wife. He saw that the latter was the victim of Jane's disappointment: that Jane was not above the crude satisfaction of "taking it out" of her mother. Experience checked the impulse to come to his wife's defence; and when his resentment was at its height, Jane disarmed him by giving up the struggle.

Nothing was said to mark her capitulation; but Lethbury noticed that the visiting ceased, and that the dressmaker's bills diminished. At the same time, Mrs. Lethbury made it known that Jane had taken up charities; and before long Jane's conversation confirmed this announcement. At first Lethbury congratulated himself on the change; but Jane's domesticity soon began to weigh on him. During the day she was sometimes absent on errands of mercy; but in the evening she was always there. At first she and Mrs. Lethbury sat in the drawing–room together, and Lethbury smoked in the library; but presently Jane formed the habit of joining him there, and he began to suspect that he was included among the objects of her philanthropy.

Mrs. Lethbury confirmed the suspicion. "Jane has grown very serious−minded lately," she said. "She imagines that she used to neglect you, and she is trying to make up for it. Don't discourage her," she added innocently.

Such a plea delivered Lethbury helpless to his daughter's ministrations: and he found himself measuring the hours he spent with her by the amount of relief they must be affording her mother. There were even moments when he read a furtive gratitude in Mrs. Lethbury's eye.

But Lethbury was no hero, and he had nearly reached the limit of vicarious endurance when something wonderful happened. They never quite knew afterward how it had come about, or who first perceived it; but Mrs. Lethbury one day gave tremulous voice to their inferences.

"Of course," she said, "he comes here because of Elise." The young lady in question, a friend of Jane's, was possessed of attractions which had already been found to explain the presence of masculine visitors.

Lethbury risked a denial. "I don't think he does," he declared.

"But Elise is thought very pretty," Mrs. Lethbury insisted.

"I can't help that," said Lethbury doggedly.

He saw a faint light in his wife's eyes; but she remarked carelessly: "Mr. Budd would be a very good match for Elise."

Lethbury could hardly repress a chuckle: he was so exquisitely aware that she was trying to propitiate the gods.

For a few weeks neither said a word; then Mrs. Lethbury once more reverted to the subject.

"It is a month since Elise went abroad," she said.

"Is it?"

"And Mr. Budd seems to come here just as often — "

"Ah," said Lethbury with heroic indifference; and his wife hastily changed the subject.

Mr. Winstanley Budd was a young man who suffered from an excess of manner. Politeness gushed from him in the driest seasons. He was always performing feats of drawing–room chivalry, and the approach of the most unobtrusive female threw him into attitudes which endangered the furniture. His features, being of the cherubic order, did not lend themselves to this role; but there were moments when he appeared to dominate them, to force them into compliance with an aquiline ideal. The range of Mr. Budd's social benevolence made its object hard to distinguish. He spread his cloak so indiscriminately that one could not always interpret the gesture, and Jane's impassive manner had the effect of increasing his demonstrations: she threw him into paroxysms of politeness.

At first he filled the house with his amenities; but gradually it became apparent that his most dazzling effects were directed exclusively to Jane. Lethbury and his wife held their breath and looked away from each other. They pretended not to notice the frequency of Mr. Budd's visits, they struggled against an imprudent inclination to leave the young people too much alone. Their conclusions were the result of indirect observation, for neither of them dared to be caught watching Mr. Budd: they behaved like naturalists on the trail of a rare butterfly.

In his efforts not to notice Mr. Budd, Lethbury centred his attentions on Jane; and Jane, at this crucial moment, wrung from him a reluctant admiration. While her parents went about dissembling their emotions, she seemed to have none to conceal. She betrayed neither eagerness nor surprise; so complete was her unconcern that there were moments when Lethbury feared it was obtuseness, when he could hardly help whispering to her that now was the moment to lower the net.

Meanwhile the velocity of Mr. Budd's gyrations increased with the ardor of courtship: his politeness became incandescent, and Jane found herself the centre of a pyrotechnical display culminating in the "set piece" of an offer of marriage.

Mrs. Lethbury imparted the news to her husband one evening after their daughter had gone to bed. The announcement was made and received with an air of detachment, as though both feared to be betrayed into unseemly exultation; but Lethbury, as his wife ended, could not repress the inquiry, "Have they decided on a day?"

Mrs. Lethbury's superior command of her features enabled her to look shocked. "What can you be thinking of? He only offered himself at five!"

"Of course — of course — " stammered Lethbury — "but nowadays people marry after such short engagements — "

"Engagement!" said his wife solemnly. "There is no engagement."

Lethbury dropped his cigar. "What on earth do you mean?"

"Jane is thinking it over."

"Thinking it over?"

"She has asked for a month before deciding."

Lethbury sank back with a gasp. Was it genius or was it madness? He felt incompetent to decide; and Mrs. Lethbury's next words showed that she shared his difficulty.

"Of course I don't want to hurry Jane — "

"Of course not," he acquiesced.

"But I pointed out to her that a young man of Mr. Budd's impulsive temperament might — might be easily discouraged — "

"Yes; and what did she say?"

"She said that if she was worth winning she was worth waiting for."

VI

The period of Mr. Budd's probation could scarcely have cost him as much mental anguish as it caused his would–be parents–in–law.

Mrs. Lethbury, by various ruses, tried to shorten the ordeal, but Jane remained inexorable; and each morning Lethbury came down to breakfast with the certainty of finding a letter of withdrawal from her discouraged suitor.

When at length the decisive day came, and Mrs. Lethbury, at its close, stole into the library with an air of chastened joy, they stood for a moment without speaking; then Mrs. Lethbury paid a fitting tribute to the proprieties by faltering out: "It will be dreadful to have to give her up — "

Lethbury could not repress a warning gesture; but even as it escaped him, he realized that his wife's grief was genuine.

"Of course, of course," he said, vainly sounding his own emotional shallows for an answering regret. And yet it was his wife who had suffered most from Jane!

He had fancied that these sufferings would be effaced by the milder atmosphere of their last weeks together; but felicity did not soften Jane. Not for a moment did she relax her dominion: she simply widened it to include a new subject. Mr. Budd found himself under orders with the others; and a new fear assailed Lethbury as he saw Jane assume prenuptial control of her betrothed. Lethbury had never felt any strong personal interest in Mr. Budd; but, as Jane's prospective husband, the young man excited his sympathy. To his surprise, he found that Mrs. Lethbury shared the feeling.

"I'm afraid he may find Jane a little exacting," she said, after an evening dedicated to a stormy discussion of the wedding arrangements. "She really ought to make some concessions. If he wants to be married in a black frock–coat instead of a dark gray one — " She paused and looked doubtfully at Lethbury.

"What can I do about it?" he said.

"You might explain to him — tell him that Jane isn't always — "

Lethbury made an impatient gesture. "What are you afraid of? His finding her out or his not finding her out?"

Mrs. Lethbury flushed. "You put it so dreadfully!"

Her husband mused for a moment; then he said with an air of cheerful hypocrisy: "After all, Budd is old enough to take care of himself."

But the next day Mrs. Lethbury surprised him. Late in the afternoon she entered the library, so breathless and inarticulate that he scented a catastrophe.

"I've done it!" she cried.

"Done what?"

"Told him." She nodded toward the door. "He's just gone. Jane is out, and I had a chance to talk to him alone."

Lethbury pushed a chair forward and she sank into it.

"What did you tell him? That she is not always — "

Mrs. Lethbury lifted a tragic eye. "No; I told him that she always is — "

"Always is — ?"

"Yes."

There was a pause. Lethbury made a call on his hoarded philosophy. He saw Jane suddenly reinstated in her evening seat by the library fire; but an answering chord in him thrilled at his wife's heroism.

"Well — what did he say?"

Mrs. Lethbury's agitation deepened. It was clear that the blow had fallen.

"He . . . he said . . . that we . . . had never understood Jane . . . or appreciated her . . ." The final syllables were lost in her handkerchief, and she left him marvelling at the mechanism of a woman.

After that, Lethbury faced the future with an undaunted eye. They had done their duty — at least his wife had done hers — and they were reaping the usual harvest of ingratitude with a zest seldom accorded to such reaping. There was a marked change in Mr. Budd's manner, and his increasing coldness sent a genial glow through Lethbury's system. It was easy to bear with Jane in the light of Mr. Budd's disapproval.

There was a good deal to be borne in the last days, and the brunt of it fell on Mrs. Lethbury. Jane marked her transition to the married state by an appropriate but incongruous display of nerves. She became sentimental, hysterical and reluctant. She quarrelled with her betrothed and threatened to return the ring. Mrs. Lethbury had to intervene, and Lethbury felt the hovering sword of destiny. But the blow was suspended. Mr. Budd's chivalry was proof against all his bride's caprices, and his devotion throve on her cruelty. Lethbury feared that he was too faithful, too enduring, and longed to urge him to vary his tactics. Jane presently reappeared with the ring on her finger, and consented to try on the wedding–dress; but her uncertainties, her reactions, were prolonged till the final day.

When it dawned, Lethbury was still in an ecstasy of apprehension. Feeling reasonably sure of the principal actors, he had centred his fears on incidental possibilities. The clergyman might have a stroke, or the church might burn down, or there might be something wrong with the license. He did all that was humanly possible to avert such contingencies, but there remained that incalculable factor known as the hand of God. Lethbury seemed to feel it groping for him.

In the church it almost had him by the nape. Mr. Budd was late; and for five immeasurable minutes Lethbury and Jane faced a churchful of conjecture. Then the bridegroom appeared, flushed but chivalrous, and explaining to his father–in–law under cover of the ritual that he had torn his glove and had to go back for another.

"You'll be losing the ring next," muttered Lethbury; but Mr. Budd produced this article punctually, and a moment or two later was bearing its wearer captive down the aisle.

At the wedding–breakfast Lethbury caught his wife's eye fixed on him in mild disapproval, and understood that his hilarity was exceeding the bounds of fitness. He pulled himself together, and tried to subdue his tone; but his jubilation bubbled over like a champagne–glass perpetually refilled. The deeper his draughts, the higher it rose.

It was at the brim when, in the wake of the dispersing guests, Jane came down in her travelling–dress and fell on her mother's neck.

"I can't leave you!" she wailed, and Lethbury felt as suddenly sobered as a man under a douche. But if the bride was reluctant her captor was relentless. Never had Mr. Budd been more dominant, more aquiline. Lethbury's last fears were dissipated as the young man snatched Jane from her mother's bosom and bore her off to the brougham.

The brougham rolled away, the last milliner's girl forsook her post by the awning, the red carpet was folded up, and the house door closed. Lethbury stood alone in the hall with his wife. As he turned toward her, he noticed the look of tired heroism in her eyes, the deepened lines of her face. They reflected his own symptoms too accurately not to appeal to him. The nervous tension had been horrible. He went up to her, and an answering impulse made her lay a hand on his arm. He held it there a moment.

"let us go off and have a jolly little dinner at a restaurant," he proposed.

There had been a time when such a suggestion would have surprised her to the verge of disapproval; but now she agreed to it at once.

"Oh, that would be so nice," she murmured with a great sigh of relief and assuagement.

Jane had fulfilled her mission after all: she had drawn them together at last.

The Reckoning

I

"THE marriage law of the new dispensation will be: Thou shalt not be unfaithful — to thyself."

A discreet murmur of approval filled the studio, and through the haze of cigarette smoke Mrs. Clement Westall, as her husband descended from his improvised platform, saw him merged in a congratulatory group of ladies. Westall's informal talks on "The New Ethics" had drawn about him an eager following of the mentally unemployed — those who, as he had once phrased it, liked to have their brain–food cut up for them. The talks had begun by accident. Westall's ideas were known to be "advanced," but hitherto their advance had not been in the direction of publicity. He had been, in his wife's opinion, almost pusillanimously careful not to let his personal views endanger his professional standing. Of late, however, he had shown a puzzling tendency to dogmatize, to throw down the gauntlet, to flaunt his private code in the face of society; and the relation of the sexes being a topic always sure of an audience, a few admiring friends had persuaded him to give his after–dinner opinions a larger circulation by summing them up in a series of talks at the Van Sideren studio.

The Herbert Van Siderens were a couple who subsisted, socially, on the fact that they had a studio. Van Sideren's pictures were chiefly valuable as accessories to the mise en scene which differentiated his wife's "afternoons" from the blighting functions held in long New York drawing–rooms, and permitted her to offer their friends whiskey–and–soda instead of tea. Mrs. Van Sideren, for her part, was skilled in making the most of the kind of atmosphere which a lay–figure and an easel create; and if at times she found the illusion hard to maintain, and lost courage to the extent of almost wishing that Herbert could paint, she promptly overcame such moments of weakness by calling in some fresh talent, some extraneous re–enforcement of the "artistic" impression. It was in quest of such aid that she had seized on Westall, coaxing him, somewhat to his wife's surprise, into a flattered participation in her fraud. It was vaguely felt, in the Van Sideren circle, that all the audacities were artistic, and that a teacher who pronounced marriage immoral was somehow as distinguished as a painter who depicted purple grass and a green sky. The Van Sideren set were tired of the conventional color–scheme in art and conduct.

Julia Westall had long had her own views on the immorality of marriage; she might indeed have claimed her husband as a disciple. In the early days of their union she had secretly resented his disinclination to proclaim himself a follower of the new creed; had been inclined to tax him with moral cowardice, with a failure to live up to the convictions for which their marriage was supposed to stand. That was in the first burst of propagandism, when, womanlike, she wanted to turn her disobedience into a law. Now she felt differently. She could hardly account for the change, yet being a woman who never allowed her impulses to remain unaccounted for, she tried to do so by saying that she did not care to have the articles of her faith misinterpreted by the vulgar. In this connection, she was beginning to think that almost every one was vulgar; certainly there were few to whom she would have cared to intrust the defence of so esoteric a doctrine. And it was precisely at this point that Westall, discarding his unspoken principles, had chosen to descend from the heights of privacy, and stand hawking his convictions at the street–corner!

It was Una Van Sideren who, on this occasion, unconsciously focussed upon herself Mrs. Westall's wandering resentment. In the first place, the girl had no business to be there. It was "horrid" — Mrs. Westall found herself slipping back into the old feminine vocabulary — simply "horrid" to think of a young girl's being allowed to listen to such talk. The fact that Una smoked cigarettes and sipped an occasional cocktail did not in the least tarnish a certain radiant innocency which made her appear the victim, rather than the accomplice, of her parents' vulgarities. Julia Westall felt in a hot helpless way that something ought to be done — that some one ought to speak to the girl's mother. And just then Una glided up.

"Oh, Mrs. Westall, how beautiful it was!" Una fixed her with large limpid eyes. "You believe it all, I suppose?" she asked with seraphic gravity.

"All — what, my dear child?"

The girl shone on her. "About the higher life — the freer expansion of the individual — the law of fidelity to one's self," she glibly recited.

Mrs. Westall, to her own wonder, blushed a deep and burning blush.

"My dear Una," she said, "you don't in the least understand what it's all about!"

Miss Van Sideren stared, with a slowly answering blush. "Don't you, then?" she murmured.

Mrs. Westall laughed. "Not always — or altogether! But I should like some tea, please."

Una led her to the corner where innocent beverages were dispensed. As Julia received her cup she scrutinized the girl more carefully. It was not such a girlish face, after all — definite lines were forming under the rosy haze of youth. She reflected that Una must be six–and–twenty, and wondered why she had not married. A nice stock of ideas she would have as her dower! If they were to be a part of the modern girl's trousseau —

Mrs. Westall caught herself up with a start. It was as though some one else had been speaking — a stranger who had borrowed her own voice: she felt herself the dupe of some fantastic mental ventriloquism. Concluding suddenly that the room was stifling and Una's tea too sweet, she set down her cup, and looked about for Westall: to meet his eyes had long been her refuge from every uncertainty. She met them now, but only, as she felt, in transit; they included her parenthetically in a larger flight. She followed the flight, and it carried her to a corner to which Una had withdrawn — one of the palmy nooks to which Mrs. Van Sideren attributed the success of her Saturdays. Westall, a moment later, had overtaken his look, and found a place at the girl's side. She bent forward, speaking eagerly; he leaned back, listening, with the depreciatory smile which acted as a filter to flattery, enabling him to swallow the strongest doses without apparent grossness of appetite. Julia winced at her own definition of the smile.

On the way home, in the deserted winter dusk, Westall surprised his wife by a sudden boyish pressure of her arm. "Did I open their eyes a bit? Did I tell them what you wanted me to?" he asked gaily.

Almost unconsciously, she let her arm slip from his. "What I wanted — ?"

"Why, haven't you — all this time?" She caught the honest wonder of his tone. "I somehow fancied you'd rather blamed me for not talking more openly — before — You've made me feel, at times, that I was sacrificing principles to expediency."

She paused a moment over her reply; then she asked quietly: "What made you decide not to — any longer?"

She felt again the vibration of a faint surprise. "Why — the wish to please you!" he answered, almost too simply.

"I wish you would not go on, then," she said abruptly.

He stopped in his quick walk, and she felt his stare through the darkness.

"Not go on — ?"

"Call a hansom, please. I'm tired," broke from her with a sudden rush of physical weariness.

Instantly his solicitude enveloped her. The room had been infernally hot — and then that confounded cigarette smoke — he had noticed once or twice that she looked pale — she mustn't come to another Saturday. She felt herself yielding, as she always did, to the warm influence of his concern for her, the feminine in her leaning on the man in him with a conscious intensity of abandonment. He put her in the hansom, and her hand stole into his in the darkness. A tear or two rose, and she let them fall. It was so delicious to cry over imaginary troubles!

That evening, after dinner, he surprised her by reverting to the subject of his talk. He combined a man's dislike of uncomfortable questions with an almost feminine skill in eluding them; and she knew that if he returned to the subject he must have some special reason for doing so.

"You seem not to have cared for what I said this afternoon. Did I put the case badly?"

"No — you put it very well."

"Then what did you mean by saying that you would rather not have me go on with it?"

She glanced at him nervously, her ignorance of his intention deepening her sense of helplessness.

"I don't think I care to hear such things discussed in public."

"I don't understand you," he exclaimed. Again the feeling that his surprise was genuine gave an air of obliquity to her own attitude. She was not sure that she understood herself.

"Won't you explain?" he said with a tinge of impatience.

Her eyes wandered about the familiar drawing–room which had been the scene of so many of their evening confidences. The shaded lamps, the quiet–colored walls hung with mezzotints, the pale spring flowers scattered here and there in Venice glasses and bowls of old Sevres, recalled, she hardly knew why, the apartment in which the evenings of her first marriage had been passed — a wilderness of rosewood and upholstery, with a picture of a Roman peasant above the mantel–piece, and a Greek slave in "statuary marble" between the folding–doors of the back drawing–room. It was a room with which she had never been able to establish any closer relation than that between a traveller and a railway station; and now, as she looked about at the surroundings which stood for her deepest affinities — the room for which she had left that other room — she was startled by the same sense of strangeness and unfamiliarity. The prints, the flowers, the subdued tones of the old porcelains, seemed to typify a superficial refinement that had no relation to the deeper significances of life.

Suddenly she heard her husband repeating his question.

"I don't know that I can explain," she faltered.

He drew his arm–chair forward so that he faced her across the hearth. The light of a reading–lamp fell on his finely drawn face, which had a kind of surface–sensitiveness akin to the surface–refinement of its setting.

"Is it that you no longer believe in our ideas?" he asked.

"In our ideas — ?"

"The ideas I am trying to teach. The ideas you and I are supposed to stand for." He paused a moment. "The ideas on which our marriage was founded."

The blood rushed to her face. He had his reasons, then — she was sure now that he had his reasons! In the ten years of their marriage, how often had either of them stopped to

111

consider the ideas on which it was founded? How often does a man dig about the basement of his house to examine its foundation? The foundation is there, of course — the house rests on it — but one lives abovestairs and not in the cellar. It was she, indeed, who in the beginning had insisted on reviewing the situation now and then, on recapitulating the reasons which justified her course, on proclaiming, from time to time, her adherence to the religion of personal independence; but she had long ceased to feel the need of any such ideal standards, and had accepted her marriage as frankly and naturally as though it had been based on the primitive needs of the heart, and needed no special sanction to explain or justify it.

"Of course I still believe in our ideas!" she exclaimed.

"Then I repeat that I don't understand. It was a part of your theory that the greatest possible publicity should be given to our view of marriage. Have you changed your mind in that respect?"

She hesitated. "It depends on circumstances — on the public one is addressing. The set of people that the Van Siderens get about them don't care for the truth or falseness of a doctrine. They are attracted simply by its novelty."

"And yet it was in just such a set of people that you and I met, and learned the truth from each other."

"That was different."

"In what way?"

"I was not a young girl, to begin with. It is perfectly unfitting that young girls should be present at — at such times — should hear such things discussed — "

"I thought you considered it one of the deepest social wrongs that such things never are discussed before young girls; but that is beside the point, for I don't remember seeing any young girl in my audience to–day — "

"Except Una Van Sideren!"

He turned slightly and pushed back the lamp at his elbow.

"Oh, Miss Van Sideren — naturally — "

"Why naturally?"

"The daughter of the house — would you have had her sent out with her governess?"

"If I had a daughter I should not allow such things to go on in my house!"

Westall, stroking his mustache, leaned back with a faint smile. "I fancy Miss Van Sideren is quite capable of taking care of herself."

"No girl knows how to take care of herself — till it's too late."

"And yet you would deliberately deny her the surest means of self–defence?"

"What do you call the surest means of self–defence?"

"Some preliminary knowledge of human nature in its relation to the marriage tie."

She made an impatient gesture. "How should you like to marry that kind of a girl?"

"Immensely — if she were my kind of girl in other respects."

She took up the argument at another point.

"You are quite mistaken if you think such talk does not affect young girls. Una was in a state of the most absurd exaltation — " She broke off, wondering why she had spoken.

Westall reopened a magazine which he had laid aside at the beginning of their discussion. "What you tell me is immensely flattering to my oratorical talent — but I fear you overrate its effect. I can assure you that Miss Van Sideren doesn't have to have her thinking done for her. She's quite capable of doing it herself."

"You seem very familiar with her mental processes!" flashed unguardedly from his wife.

He looked up quietly from the pages he was cutting.

"I should like to be," he answered. "She interests me."

II

If there be a distinction in being misunderstood, it was one denied to Julia Westall when she left her first husband. Every one was ready to excuse and even to defend her. The world she adorned agreed that John Arment was "impossible," and hostesses gave a sigh of relief at the thought that it would no longer be necessary to ask him to dine.

There had been no scandal connected with the divorce: neither side had accused the other of the offence euphemistically described as "statutory." The Arments had indeed been obliged to transfer their allegiance to a State which recognized desertion as a cause for divorce, and construed the term so liberally that the seeds of desertion were shown to exist in every union. Even Mrs. Arment's second marriage did not make traditional morality stir in its sleep. It was known that she had not met her second husband till after she had parted from the first, and she had, moreover, replaced a rich man by a poor one. Though Clement Westall was acknowledged to be a rising lawyer, it was generally felt that his fortunes would not rise as rapidly as his reputation. The Westalls would probably always have to live quietly and go out to dinner in cabs. Could there be better evidence of Mrs. Arment's complete disinterestedness?

If the reasoning by which her friends justified her course was somewhat cruder and less complex than her own elucidation of the matter, both explanations led to the same conclusion: John Arment was impossible. The only difference was that, to his wife, his impossibility was something deeper than a social disqualification. She had once said, in ironical defence of her marriage, that it had at least preserved her from the necessity of sitting next to him at dinner; but she had not then realized at what cost the immunity was purchased. John Arment was impossible; but the sting of his impossibility lay in the fact that he made it impossible for those about him to be other than himself. By an unconscious process of elimination he had excluded from the world everything of which he did not feel a personal need: had become, as it were, a climate in which only his own requirements survived. This might seem to imply a deliberate selfishness; but there was nothing deliberate about Arment. He was as instinctive as an animal or a child. It was this childish element in his nature which sometimes for a moment unsettled his wife's estimate of him. Was it possible that he was simply undeveloped, that he had delayed, somewhat longer than is usual, the laborious process of growing up? He had the kind of sporadic shrewdness which causes it to be said of a dull man that he is "no fool"; and it was this quality that his wife found most trying. Even to the naturalist it is annoying to have his deductions disturbed by some unforeseen aberrancy of form or function; and how much more so to the wife whose estimate of herself is inevitably bound up with her judgment of her husband!

Arment's shrewdness did not, indeed, imply any latent intellectual power; it suggested, rather, potentialities of feeling, of suffering, perhaps, in a blind rudimentary way, on which Julia's sensibilities naturally declined to linger. She so fully understood her own reasons for leaving him that she disliked to think they were not as comprehensible to her husband. She was haunted, in her analytic moments, by the look of perplexity, too inarticulate for words, with which he had acquiesced to her explanations.

These moments were rare with her, however. Her marriage had been too concrete a misery to be surveyed philosophically. If she had been unhappy for complex reasons, the unhappiness was as real as though it had been uncomplicated. Soul is more bruisable than flesh, and Julia was wounded in every fibre of her spirit. Her husband's personality seemed to be closing gradually in on her, obscuring the sky and cutting off the air, till she felt herself shut up among the decaying bodies of her starved hopes. A sense of having been decoyed by some world−old conspiracy into this bondage of body and soul filled her with despair. If marriage was the slow life−long acquittal of a debt contracted in ignorance, then marriage was a crime against human nature. She, for one, would have no share in maintaining the pretence of which she had been a victim: the pretence that a man and a woman, forced into the narrowest of personal relations, must remain there till the end, though they may have outgrown the span of each other's natures as the mature tree outgrows the iron brace about the sapling.

It was in the first heat of her moral indignation that she had met Clement Westall. She had seen at once that he was "interested," and had fought off the discovery, dreading any influence that should draw her back into the bondage of conventional relations. To ward off the peril she had, with an almost crude precipitancy, revealed her opinions to him. To her surprise, she found that he shared them. She was attracted by the frankness of a suitor who, while pressing his suit, admitted that he did not believe in marriage. Her worst audacities did not seem to surprise him: he had thought out all that she had felt, and they had reached the same conclusion. People grew at varying rates, and the yoke that was an easy fit for the one might soon become galling to the other. That was what divorce was for: the readjustment of personal relations. As soon as their necessarily transitive nature was recognized they would gain in dignity as well as in harmony. There would be no farther need of the ignoble concessions and connivances, the perpetual sacrifice of personal delicacy and moral pride, by means of which imperfect marriages were now held together. Each partner to the contract would be on his mettle, forced to live up to the highest standard of self-development, on pain of losing the other's respect and affection. The low nature could no longer drag the higher down, but must struggle to rise, or remain alone on its inferior level. The only necessary condition to a harmonious marriage was a frank recognition of this truth, and a solemn agreement between the contracting parties to keep faith with themselves, and not to live together for a moment after complete accord had ceased to exist between them. The new adultery was unfaithfulness to self.

It was, as Westall had just reminded her, on this understanding that they had married. The ceremony was an unimportant concession to social prejudice: now that the door of divorce stood open, no marriage need be an imprisonment, and the contract therefore no longer involved any diminution of self-respect. The nature of their attachment placed them so far beyond the reach of such contingencies that it was easy to discuss them with an open mind; and Julia's sense of security made her dwell with a tender insistence on Westall's promise to claim his release when he should cease to love her. The exchange of these vows seemed to make them, in a sense, champions of the new law, pioneers in the forbidden realm of individual freedom: they felt that they had somehow achieved beatitude without martyrdom.

This, as Julia now reviewed the past, she perceived to have been her theoretical attitude toward marriage. It was unconsciously, insidiously, that her ten years of happiness with Westall had developed another conception of the tie; a reversion, rather, to the old instinct of passionate dependency and possessorship that now made her blood revolt at the mere hint of change. Change? Renewal? Was that what they had called it, in their foolish jargon? Destruction, extermination rather — this rending of a myriad fibres interwoven with another's being! Another? But he was not other! He and she were one, one in the mystic sense which alone gave marriage its significance. The new law was not for them, but for the disunited creatures forced into a mockery of union. The gospel she had felt called on to proclaim had no bearing on her own case. . . . She sent for the doctor and told him she was sure she needed a nerve tonic.

She took the nerve tonic diligently, but it failed to act as a sedative to her fears. She did not know what she feared; but that made her anxiety the more pervasive. Her husband had not reverted to the subject of his Saturday talks. He was unusually kind and considerate, with a softening of his quick manner, a touch of shyness in his consideration, that sickened her with new fears. She told herself that it was because she looked badly — because he knew about the doctor and the nerve tonic — that he showed this deference to her wishes, this eagerness to screen her from moral draughts; but the explanation simply cleared the way for fresh inferences.

The week passed slowly, vacantly, like a prolonged Sunday. On Saturday the morning post brought a note from Mrs. Van Sideren. Would dear Julia ask Mr. Westall to come half an hour earlier than usual, as there was to be some music after his "talk"? Westall was just leaving for his office when his wife read the note. She opened the drawing–room door and called him back to deliver the message.

He glanced at the note and tossed it aside. "What a bore! I shall have to cut my game of racquets. Well, I suppose it can't be helped. Will you write and say it's all right?"

Julia hesitated a moment, her hand stiffening on the chair–back against which she leaned.

"You mean to go on with these talks?" she asked.

"I — why not?" he returned; and this time it struck her that his surprise was not quite unfeigned. The discovery helped her to find words.

"You said you had started them with the idea of pleasing me — "

"Well?"

"I told you last week that they didn't please me."

"Last week? Oh — " He seemed to make an effort of memory. "I thought you were nervous then; you sent for the doctor the next day."

"It was not the doctor I needed; it was your assurance — "

"My assurance?"

Suddenly she felt the floor fail under her. She sank into the chair with a choking throat, her words, her reasons slipping away from her like straws down a whirling flood.

"Clement," she cried, "isn't it enough for you to know that I hate it?"

He turned to close the door behind them; then he walked toward her and sat down. "What is it that you hate?" he asked gently.

She had made a desperate effort to rally her routed argument.

"I can't bear to have you speak as if — as if — our marriage — were like the other kind — the wrong kind. When I heard you there, the other afternoon, be−fore all those inquisitive gossiping people, proclaiming that husbands and wives had a right to leave each other whenever they were tired — or had seen some one else — "

Westall sat motionless, his eyes fixed on a pattern of the carpet.

"You have ceased to take this view, then?" he said as she broke off. "You no longer believe that husbands and wives are justified in separating — under such conditions?"

"Under such conditions?" she stammered. "Yes — I still believe that — but how can we judge for others? What can we know of the circumstances — ?"

He interrupted her. "I thought it was a fundamental article of our creed that the special circumstances produced by marriage were not to interfere with the full assertion of individual liberty." He paused a moment. "I thought that was your reason for leaving Arment."

She flushed to the forehead. It was not like him to give a personal turn to the argument.

"It was my reason," she said simply.

"Well, then — why do you refuse to recognize its validity now?"

"I don't — I don't — I only say that one can't judge for others."

He made an impatient movement. "This is mere hair–splitting. What you mean is that, the doctrine having served your purpose when you needed it, you now repudiate it."

"Well," she exclaimed, flushing again, "what if I do? What does it matter to us?"

Westall rose from his chair. He was excessively pale, and stood before his wife with something of the formality of a stranger.

"It matters to me," he said in a low voice, "because I do not repudiate it."

"Well — ?"

"And because I had intended to invoke it as" —

He paused and drew his breath deeply. She sat silent, almost deafened by her heart–beats.

— "as a complete justification of the course I am about to take."

Julia remained motionless. "What course is that?" she asked.

He cleared his throat. "I mean to claim the fulfilment of your promise."

For an instant the room wavered and darkened; then she recovered a torturing acuteness of vision. Every detail of her surroundings pressed upon her: the tick of the clock, the slant of sunlight on the wall, the hardness of the chair–arms that she grasped, were a separate wound to each sense.

"My promise — " she faltered.

"Your part of our mutual agreement to set each other free if one or the other should wish to be released."

119

She was silent again. He waited a moment, shifting his position nervously; then he said, with a touch of irritability: "You acknowledge the agreement?"

The question went through her like a shock. She lifted her head to it proudly. "I acknowledge the agreement," she said.

"And — you don't mean to repudiate it?"

A log on the hearth fell forward, and mechanically he advanced and pushed it back.

"No," she answered slowly, "I don't mean to repudiate it."

There was a pause. He remained near the hearth, his elbow resting on the mantel−shelf. Close to his hand stood a little cup of jade that he had given her on one of their wedding anniversaries. She wondered vaguely if he noticed it.

"You intend to leave me, then?" she said at length.

His gesture seemed to deprecate the crudeness of the allusion.

"To marry some one else?"

Again his eye and hand protested. She rose and stood before him.

"Why should you be afraid to tell me? Is it Una Van Sideren?"

He was silent.

"I wish you good luck," she said.

III

She looked up, finding herself alone. She did not remember when or how he had left the room, or how long afterward she had sat there. The fire still smouldered on the hearth, but the slant of sunlight had left the wall.

Her first conscious thought was that she had not broken her word, that she had fulfilled the very letter of their bargain. There had been no crying out, no vain appeal to the past, no attempt at temporizing or evasion. She had marched straight up to the guns.

Now that it was over, she sickened to find herself alive. She looked about her, trying to recover her hold on reality. Her identity seemed to be slipping from her, as it disappears in a physical swoon. "This is my room — this is my house," she heard herself saying. Her room? Her house? She could almost hear the walls laugh back at her.

She stood up, a dull ache in every bone. The silence of the room frightened her. She remembered, now, having heard the front door close a long time ago: the sound suddenly re-echoed through her brain. Her husband must have left the house, then — her husband? She no longer knew in what terms to think: the simplest phrases had a poisoned edge. She sank back into her chair, overcome by a strange weakness. The clock struck ten — it was only ten o'clock! Suddenly she remembered that she had not ordered dinner . . . or were they dining out that evening? Dinner — dining out — the old meaningless phraseology pursued her! She must try to think of herself as she would think of some one else, a some one dissociated from all the familiar routine of the past, whose wants and habits must gradually be learned, as one might spy out the ways of a strange animal. . .

The clock struck another hour — eleven. She stood up again and walked to the door: she thought she would go up stairs to her room. Her room? Again the word derided her. She opened the door, crossed the narrow hall, and walked up the stairs. As she passed, she noticed Westall's sticks and umbrellas: a pair of his gloves lay on the hall table. The same stair-carpet mounted between the same walls; the same old French print, in its narrow black frame, faced her on the landing. This visual continuity was intolerable. Within, a gaping chasm; without, the same untroubled and familiar surface. She must get away from it before she could attempt to think. But, once in her room, she sat down on the lounge, a stupor creeping over her. . .

Gradually her vision cleared. A great deal had happened in the interval — a wild marching and countermarching of emotions, arguments, ideas — a fury of insurgent impulses that fell back spent upon themselves. She had tried, at first, to rally, to organize these chaotic forces. There must be help somewhere, if only she could master the inner tumult. Life could not be broken off short like this, for a whim, a fancy; the law itself would side with her, would defend her. The law? What claim had she upon it? She was the prisoner of her own choice: she had been her own legislator, and she was the predestined victim of the code she had devised. But this was grotesque, intolerable — a mad mistake, for which she could not be held accountable! The law she had despised was still there, might still be invoked . . . invoked, but to what end? Could she ask it to chain Westall to her side? She had been allowed to go free when she claimed her freedom — should she show less magnanimity than she had exacted? Magnanimity? The word lashed her with its irony — one does not strike an attitude when one is fighting for life! She would threaten, grovel, cajole . . . she would yield anything to keep her hold on happiness. Ah, but the difficulty lay deeper! The law could not help her — her own apostasy could not help her. She was the victim of the theories she renounced. It was as though some giant machine of her own making had caught her up in its wheels and was grinding her to atoms. . .

It was afternoon when she found herself out–of–doors. She walked with an aimless haste, fearing to meet familiar faces. The day was radiant, metallic: one of those searching American days so calculated to reveal the shortcomings of our street–cleaning and the excesses of our architecture. The streets looked bare and hideous; everything stared and glittered. She called a passing hansom, and gave Mrs. Van Sideren's address. She did not know what had led up to the act; but she found herself suddenly resolved to speak, to cry out a warning. it was too late to save herself — but the girl might still be told. The hansom rattled up Fifth Avenue; she sat with her eyes fixed, avoiding recognition. At the Van Siderens' door she sprang out and rang the bell. Action had cleared her brain, and she felt calm and self–possessed. She knew now exactly what she meant to say.

The ladies were both out . . . the parlor–maid stood waiting for a card. Julia, with a vague murmur, turned away from the door and lingered a moment on the sidewalk. Then she remembered that she had not paid the cab–driver. She drew a dollar from her purse and handed it to him. He touched his hat and drove off, leaving her alone in the long empty street. She wandered away westward, toward strange thoroughfares, where she was not likely to meet acquaintances. The feeling of aimlessness had returned. Once she found herself in the afternoon torrent of Broadway, swept past tawdry shops and flaming theatrical posters, with a succession of meaningless faces gliding by in the opposite direction. . .

A feeling of faintness reminded her that she had not eaten since morning. She turned into a side street of shabby houses, with rows of ash–barrels behind bent area railings. In a basement window she saw the sign Ladies' Restaurant: a pie and a dish of doughnuts lay against the dusty pane like petrified food in an ethnological museum. She entered, and a young woman with a weak mouth and a brazen eye cleared a table for her near the window. The table was covered with a red and white cotton cloth and adorned with a bunch of celery in a thick tumbler and a salt–cellar full of grayish lumpy salt. Julia ordered tea, and sat a long time waiting for it. She was glad to be away from the noise and confusion of the streets. The low–ceilinged room was empty, and two or three waitresses with thin pert faces lounged in the background staring at her and whispering together. At last the tea was brought in a discolored metal teapot. Julia poured a cup and drank it hastily. It was black and bitter, but it flowed through her veins like an elixir. She was almost dizzy with exhilaration. Oh, how tired, how unutterably tired she had been!

She drank a second cup, blacker and bitterer, and now her mind was once more working clearly. She felt as vigorous, as decisive, as when she had stood on the Van Siderens' door–step — but the wish to return there had subsided. She saw now the futility of such an attempt — the humiliation to which it might have exposed her. . . The pity of it was that she did not know what to do next. The short winter day was fading, and she realized that she could not remain much longer in the restaurant without attracting notice. She paid for her tea and went out into the street. The lamps were alight, and here and there a basement shop cast an oblong of gas–light across the fissured pavement. In the dusk there was something sinister about the aspect of the street, and she hastened back toward Fifth Avenue. She was not used to being out alone at that hour.

At the corner of Fifth Avenue she paused and stood watching the stream of carriages. At last a policeman caught sight of her and signed to her that he would take her across. She had not meant to cross the street, but she obeyed automatically, and presently found herself on the farther corner. There she paused again for a moment; but she fancied the policeman was watching her, and this sent her hastening down the nearest side street. . . After that she walked a long time, vaguely. . . Night had fallen, and now and then, through the windows of a passing carriage, she caught the expanse of an evening waistcoat or the shimmer of an opera cloak. . .

Suddenly she found herself in a familiar street. She stood still a moment, breathing quickly. She had turned the corner without noticing whither it led; but now, a few yards ahead of her, she saw the house in which she had once lived — her first husband's house. The blinds were drawn, and only a faint translucence marked the windows and the transom above the door. As she stood there she heard a step behind her, and a man walked by in the direction of the house. He walked slowly, with a heavy middle–aged gait, his head sunk a little between the shoulders, the red crease of his neck visible above the fur collar of his overcoat. He crossed the street, went up the steps of the house, drew forth a latch–key, and let himself in. . .

There was no one else in sight. Julia leaned for a long time against the area–rail at the corner, her eyes fixed on the front of the house. The feeling of physical weariness had returned, but the strong tea still throbbed in her veins and lit her brain with an unnatural clearness. Presently she heard another step draw near, and moving quickly away, she too crossed the street and mounted the steps of the house. The impulse which had carried her there prolonged itself in a quick pressure of the electric bell — then she felt suddenly weak and tremulous, and grasped the balustrade for support. The door opened and a young footman with a fresh inexperienced face stood on the threshold. Julia knew in an instant that he would admit her.

"I saw Mr. Arment going in just now," she said. "Will you ask him to see me for a moment?"

The footman hesitated. "I think Mr. Arment has gone up to dress for dinner, madam."

Julia advanced into the hall. "I am sure he will see me — I will not detain him long," she said. She spoke quietly, authoritatively, in the tone which a good servant does not mistake. The footman had his hand on the drawing–room door.

"I will tell him, madam. What name, please?"

Julia trembled: she had not thought of that. "Merely say a lady," she returned carelessly.

The footman wavered and she fancied herself lost; but at that instant the door opened from within and John Arment stepped into the hall. He drew back sharply as he saw her, his florid face turning sallow with the shock; then the blood poured back to it, swelling the veins on his temples and reddening the lobes of his thick ears.

It was long since Julia had seen him, and she was startled at the change in his appearance. He had thickened, coarsened, settled down into the enclosing flesh. But she noted this insensibly: her one conscious thought was that, now she was face to face with him, she must not let him escape till he had heard her. Every pulse in her body throbbed with the urgency of her message.

She went up to him as he drew back. "I must speak to you," she said.

Arment hesitated, red and stammering. Julia glanced at the footman, and her look acted as a warning. The instinctive shrinking from a "scene" predominated over every other impulse, and Arment said slowly: "Will you come this way?"

He followed her into the drawing–room and closed the door. Julia, as she advanced, was vaguely aware that the room at least was unchanged: time had not mitigated its horrors. The contadina still lurched from the chimney–breast, and the Greek slave obstructed the threshold of the inner room. The place was alive with memories: they started out from every fold of the yellow satin curtains and glided between the angles of the rosewood furniture. But while some subordinate agency was carrying these impressions to her brain, her whole conscious effort was centred in the act of dominating Arment's will. The fear that he would refuse to hear her mounted like fever to her brain. She felt her purpose melt before it, words and arguments running into each other in the heat of her longing. For a moment her voice failed her, and she imagined herself thrust out before she could speak; but as she was struggling for a word, Arment pushed a chair forward, and said quietly: "You are not well."

The sound of his voice steadied her. It was neither kind nor unkind — a voice that suspended judgment, rather, awaiting unforeseen developments. She supported herself against the back of the chair and drew a deep breath. "Shall I send for something?" he continued, with a cold embarrassed politeness.

Julia raised an entreating hand. "No — no — thank you. I am quite well."

He paused midway toward the bell and turned on her. "Then may I ask — ?"

"Yes," she interrupted him. "I came here because I wanted to see you. There is something I must tell you."

Arment continued to scrutinize her. "I am surprised at that," he said. "I should have supposed that any communication you may wish to make could have been made through our lawyers."

"Our lawyers!" She burst into a little laugh. "I don't think they could help me — this time."

Arment's face took on a barricaded look. "If there is any question of help — of course — "

It struck her, whimsically, that she had seen that look when some shabby devil called with a subscription–book. Perhaps he thought she wanted him to put his name down for so much in sympathy — or even in money. . . The thought made her laugh again. She saw his look change slowly to perplexity. All his facial changes were slow, and she remembered, suddenly, how it had once diverted her to shift that lumbering scenery with a word. For the first time it struck her that she had been cruel. "There is a question of help," she said in a softer key: "you can help me; but only by listening. . . I want to tell you something. . ."

Arment's resistance was not yielding. "Would it not be easier to — write?" he suggested.

She shook her head. "There is no time to write . . . and it won't take long." She raised her head and their eyes met. "My husband has left me," she said.

"Westall — ?" he stammered, reddening again.

"Yes. This morning. Just as I left you. Because he was tired of me."

The words, uttered scarcely above a whisper, seemed to dilate to the limit of the room. Arment looked toward the door; then his embarrassed glance returned to Julia.

"I am very sorry," he said awkwardly.

"Thank you," she murmured.

"But I don't see — "

"No — but you will — in a moment. Won't you listen to me? Please!" Instinctively she had shifted her position putting herself between him and the door. "It happened this morning," she went on in short breathless phrases. "I never suspected anything — I thought we were — perfectly happy... Suddenly he told me he was tired of me ... there is a girl he likes better... He has gone to her..." As she spoke, the lurking anguish rose upon her, possessing her once more to the exclusion of every other emotion. Her eyes ached, her throat swelled with it, and two painful tears burnt a way down her face.

Arment's constraint was increasing visibly. "This — this is very unfortunate," he began. "But I should say the law — "

"The law?" she echoed ironically. "When he asks for his freedom?"

"You are not obliged to give it."

"You were not obliged to give me mine — but you did."

He made a protesting gesture.

"You saw that the law couldn't help you — didn't you?" she went on. "That is what I see now. The law represents material rights — it can't go beyond. If we don't recognize an inner law ... the obligation that love creates ... being loved as well as loving ... there is nothing to prevent our spreading ruin unhindered ... is there?" She raised her head plaintively, with the look of a bewildered child. "That is what I see now ... what I wanted to tell you. He leaves me because he's tired ... but I was not tired; and I don't understand why he is. That's the dreadful part of it — the not understanding: I hadn't realized what it meant. But I've been thinking of it all day, and things have come back to me — things I hadn't noticed ... when you and I..." She moved closer to him, and fixed her eyes on his with the gaze that tries to reach beyond words. "I see now that you didn't understand — did you?"

Their eyes met in a sudden shock of comprehension: a veil seemed to be lifted between them. Arment's lip trembled.

"No," he said, "I didn't understand."

She gave a little cry, almost of triumph. "I knew it! I knew it! You wondered — you tried to tell me — but no words came. . . You saw your life falling in ruins . . . the world slipping from you . . . and you couldn't speak or move!"

She sank down on the chair against which she had been leaning. "Now I know — now I know," she repeated.

"I am very sorry for you," she heard Arment stammer.

She looked up quickly. "That's not what I came for. I don't want you to be sorry. I came to ask you to forgive me . . . for not understanding that you didn't understand. . . That's all I wanted to say." She rose with a vague sense that the end had come, and put out a groping hand toward the door.

Arment stood motionless. She turned to him with a faint smile.

"You forgive me?"

"There is nothing to forgive — "

"Then will you shake hands for good–by?" She felt his hand in hers: it was nerveless, reluctant.

"Good–by," she repeated. "I understand now."

She opened the door and passed out into the hall. As she did so, Arment took an impulsive step forward; but just then the footman, who was evidently alive to his obligations, advanced from the background to let her out. She heard Arment fall back. The footman threw open the door, and she found herself outside in the darkness.

The Letter

I

COLONEL ALINGDON died in Florence in 1890.

For many years he had lived withdrawn from the world in which he had once played so active and even turbulent a part. The study of Tuscan art was his only pursuit, and it was to help him in the classification of his notes and documents that I was first called to his villa. Colonel Alingdon had then the look of a very old man, though his age can hardly have exceeded seventy. He was small and bent, with a finely wrinkled face which still wore the tan of youthful exposure. But for this dusky redness it would have been hard to reconstruct from the shrunken recluse, with his low fastidious voice and carefully tended hands, an image of that young knight of adventure whose sword had been at the service of every uprising which stirred the uneasy soil of Italy in the first half of the nineteenth century.

Though I was more of a proficient in Colonel Alingdon's later than his earlier pursuits, the thought of his soldiering days was always coming between me and the pacific work of his old age. As we sat collating papers and comparing photographs, I had the feeling that this dry and quiet old man had seen even stranger things than people said: that he knew more of the inner history of Europe than half the diplomatists of his day.

I was not alone in this conviction; and the friend who had engaged me for Colonel Alingdon had appended to his instructions the injunction to "get him to talk." But this was what no one could do. Colonel Alingdon was ready to discuss by the hour the date of a Giottesque triptych, or the attribution of a disputed master; but on the history of his early life he was habitually silent.

It was perhaps because I recognized this silence and respected it that it afterward came to be broken for me. Or it was perhaps merely because, as the failure of Colonel Alingdon's sight cut him off from his work, he felt the natural inclination of age to revert from the empty present to the crowded past. For one cause or another he did talk to me in the last year of his life; and I felt myself mingled, to an extent inconceivable to the mere reader of history, with the passionate scenes of the Italian struggle for liberty. Colonel Alingdon had been mixed with it in all its phases: he had known the last Carbonari and the Young Italy of Mazzini; he had been in Perugia when the mercenaries of a liberal Pope slaughtered women and children in the streets; he had been in Sicily with the Thousand, and in Milan during the Cinque Giornate.

"They say the Italians didn't know how to fight," he said one day, musingly — "that the French had to come down and do their work for them. People forget how long it was since they had had any fighting to do. But they hadn't forgotten how to suffer and hold their tongues; how to die and take their secrets with them. The Italian war of independence was really carried on underground: it was one of those awful silent struggles which are so much more terrible than the roar of a battle. It's a deuced sight easier to charge with your regiment than to lie rotting in an Austrian prison and know that if you give up the name of a friend or two you can go back scot-free to your wife and children. And thousands and thousands of Italians had the choice given them — and hardly one went back."

He sat silent, his meditative fingertips laid together, his eyes fixed on the past which was the now only thing clearly visible to them.

"And the women?" I said. "Were they as brave as the men?"

I had not spoken quite at random. I had always heard that there had been as much of love as of war in Colonel Alingdon's early career, and I hoped that my question might give a personal turn to his reminiscences.

"The women?" he repeated. "They were braver — for they had more to bear and less to do. Italy could never have been saved without them."

His eye had kindled and I detected in it the reflection of some vivid memory. It was then that I asked him what was the bravest thing he had ever known of a woman's doing.

The question was such a vague one that I hardly knew why I had put it, but to my surprise he answered almost at once, as though I had touched on a subject of frequent meditation.

"The bravest thing I ever saw done by a woman," he said, "was brought about by an act of my own — and one of which I am not particularly proud. For that reason I have never spoken of it before — there was a time when I didn't even care to think of it — but all that is past now. She died years ago, and so did the Jack Alingdon she knew, and in telling you the story I am no more than the mouthpiece of an old tradition which some ancestor might have handed down to me."

He leaned back, his clear blind gaze fixed smilingly on me, and I had the feeling that, in groping through the labyrinth of his young adventures, I had come unawares upon their central point.

II

(COLONEL ALINGDON'S STORY)

When I was in Milan in 'forty–seven an unlucky thing happened to me.

I had been sent there to look over the ground by some of my Italian friends in England. As an English officer I had no difficulty in getting into Milanese society, for England had for years been the refuge of the Italian fugitives, and I was known to be working in their interests. It was just the kind of job I liked, and I never enjoyed life more than I did in those days. There was a great deal going on — good music, balls and theatres. Milan kept up her gayety to the last. The English were shocked by the insouciance of a race who could dance under the very nose of the usurper; but those who understood the situation knew that Milan was playing Brutus, and playing it uncommonly well.

I was in the thick of it all — it was just the atmosphere to suit a young fellow of nine–and–twenty, with a healthy passion for waltzing and fighting. But, as I said, an unlucky thing happened to me. I was fool enough to fall in love with Donna Candida Falco. You have heard of her, of course: you know the share she had in the great work. In a different way she was what the terrible Princess Belgioioso had been to an earlier generation. But Donna Candida was not terrible. She was quiet, discreet and charming. When I knew her she was a widow of thirty, her husband, Andrea Falco, having died ten years previously, soon after their marriage. The marriage had been notoriously unhappy, and his death was a release to Donna Candida. Her family were of Modena, but they had come to live in Milan soon after the execution of Ciro Menotti and his companions. You remember the details of that business? The Duke of Modena, one of the most adroit villains in Europe, had been bitten with the hope of uniting the Italian states under his rule. It was a vision of Italian liberation — of a sort. A few madmen were dazzled by it, and Ciro Menotti was one of them. You know the end. The Duke of Modena, who had counted on Louis Philippe's backing, found that that astute sovereign had betrayed him to Austria. Instantly, he saw that his first business was to get rid of the conspirators he had created. There was nothing easier than for a Hapsburg Este to turn on a friend. Ciro Menotti had staked his life for the Duke — and the Duke took it. You may remember that, on the night when seven hundred men and a cannon attacked Menotti's house, the Duke was seen looking on at the slaughter from an arcade across the square.

Well, among the lesser fry taken that night was a lad of eighteen, Emilio Verna, who was the only brother of Donna Candida. The Verna family was one of the most respected in Modena. It consisted, at that time, of the mother, Countess Verna, of young Emilio and his sister. Count Verna had been in Spielberg in the twenties. He had never recovered from his sufferings there, and died in exile, without seeing his wife and children again. Countess Verna had been an ardent patriot in her youth, but the failure of the first attempts against Austria had discouraged her. She thought that in losing her husband she had sacrificed enough for her country, and her one idea was to keep Emilio on good terms with the government. But the Verna blood was not tractable, and his father's death was not likely to make Emilio a good subject of the Estes. Not that he had as yet taken any active share in the work of the conspirators: he simply hadn't had time. At his trial there was nothing to show that he had been in Menotti's confidence; but he had been seen once or twice coming out of what the ducal police called "suspicious" houses, and in his desk were found some verses to Italy. That was enough to hang a man in Modena, and Emilio Verna was hanged.

The Countess never recovered from the blow. The circumstances of her son's death were too abominable, to unendurable. If he had risked his life in the conspiracy, she might have been reconciled to his losing it. But he was a mere child, who had sat at home, chafing but powerless, while his seniors plotted and fought. He had been sacrificed to the Duke's insane fear, to his savage greed for victims, and the Countess Verna was not to be consoled.

As soon as possible, the mother and daughter left Modena for Milan. There they lived in seclusion till Candida's marriage. During her girlhood she had had to accept her mother's view of life: to shut herself up in the tomb in which the poor woman brooded over her martyrs. But that was not the girl's way of honoring the dead. At the moment when the first shot was fired on Menotti's house she had been reading Petrarch's Ode to the Lords of Italy, and the lines

l'antico valor Ne Vitalici cor non e ancor morto had lodged like a bullet in her brain. From the day of her marriage she began to take a share in the silent work which was going on throughout Italy. Milan was at that time the centre of the movement, and Candida Falco threw herself into it with all the passion which her unhappy marriage left unsatisfied. At first she had to act with great reserve, for her husband was a prudent man, who did not care to have his habits disturbed by political complications; but after his death there was nothing to restrain her, except the exquisite tact which enabled her to work night and day in the Italian cause without giving the Austrian authorities a pretext for interference.

When I first knew Donna Candida, her mother was still living: a tragic woman, prematurely bowed, like an image of death in the background of the daughter's brilliant life. The Countess, since her son's death, had become a patriot again, though in a narrower sense than Candida. The mother's first thought was that her dead must be avenged, the daughter's that Italy must be saved; but from different motives they worked for the same end. Candida felt for the Countess that protecting tenderness with which Italian children so often regard their parents, a feeling heightened by the reverence which the mother's sufferings inspired. Countess Verna, as the wife and mother of martyrs, had done what Candida longed to do: she had given her utmost to Italy. There must have been moments when the self–absorption of her grief chilled her daughter's ardent spirit; but Candida revered in her mother the image of their afflicted country.

"It was too terrible," she said, speaking of what the Countess had suffered after Emilio's death. "All the circumstances were too unmerciful. It seemed as if God had turned His face from my mother; as if she had been singled out to suffer more than any of the others. All the other families received some message or token of farewell from the prisoners. One of them bribed the gaoler to carry a letter — another sent a lock of hair by the chaplain. But Emilio made no sign, sent no word. My mother felt as though he had turned his back on us. She used to sit for hours, saying again and again, 'Why was he the only one to forget his mother?' I tried to comfort her, but it was useless: she had suffered too much. Now I never reason with her; I listen, and let her ease her poor heart. Do you know, she still asks me sometimes if I think he may have left a letter — if there is no way of finding out if he left one? She forgets that I have tried again and again: that I have sent bribes and messages to the gaoler, the chaplain, to every one who came near him. The answer is always the same — no one has ever heard of a letter. I suppose the poor boy was stunned, and did not think of writing. Who knows what was passing through his poor bewildered brain? But it would have been a great help to my mother to have a word from him. If I had known how to imitate his writing I should have forged a letter."

I knew enough of the Italians to understand how her boy's silence must have aggravated the Countess's grief. Precious as a message from a dying son would be to any mother, such signs of tenderness have to the Italians a peculiar significance. The Latin race is rhetorical: it possesses the gift of death–bed eloquence, the knack of saying the effective thing on momentous occasions. The letters which the Italian patriots sent home from their prisons or from the scaffold are not the halting farewells that anguish would have wrung from a less expressive race: they are veritable "compositions," saved from affectation only by the fact that fluency and sonority are a part of the Latin inheritance. Such letters, passed from hand to hand among the bereaved families, were not only a comfort to the survivors but an incentive to fresh sacrifices. They were the "seed of the martyrs" with which Italy was being sown; and I knew what it meant to the Countess Verna to have no such treasure in her bosom, to sit silent while other mothers quoted their sons' last words.

I said just now that it was an unlucky day for me when I fell in love with Donna Candida; and no doubt you have guessed the reason. She was in love with some one else. It was the old situation of Heine's song. That other loved another — loved Italy, and with an undivided passion. His name was Fernando Briga, and at that time he was one of the foremost liberals in Italy. He came of a middle–class Modenese family. His father was a doctor, a prudent man, engrossed in his profession and unwilling to compromise it by meddling in politics. His irreproachable attitude won the confidence of the government, and the Duke conferred on him the sinister office of physician to the prisons of Modena. It was this Briga who attended Emilio Falco, and several of the other prisoners who were executed at the same time.

Under shelter of his father's loyalty young Fernando conspired in safety. He was studying medicine, and every one supposed him to be absorbed in his work; but as a matter of fact he was fast ripening into one of Mazzini's ablest lieutenants. His career belongs to history, so I need not enlarge on it here. In 1847 he was in Milan, and had become one of the leading figures in the liberal group which was working for a coalition with Piedmont. Like all the ablest men of his day, he had cast off Mazziniism and pinned his faith to the house of Savoy. The Austrian government had an eye on him, but he had inherited his father's prudence, though he used it for nobler ends, and his discretion enabled him to do far more for the cause than a dozen enthusiasts could have accomplished. No one understood this better than Donna Candida. She had a share of his caution, and he trusted her with secrets which he would not have confided to many men. Her drawing–room was the centre of the Piedmontese party, yet so clever was she in averting suspicion that more than one hunted conspirator hid in her house, and was helped across the Alps by her agents.

Briga relied on her as he did on no one else; but he did not love her, and she knew it. Still, she was young, she was handsome, and he loved no one else: how could she give up hoping? From her intimate friends she made no secret of her feelings: Italian women are not reticent in such matters, and Donna Candida was proud of loving a hero. You will see at once that I had no chance; but if she could not give up hope, neither could I. Perhaps in her desire to secure my services for the cause she may have shown herself overkind; or perhaps I was still young enough to set down to my own charms a success due to quite different causes. At any rate, I persuaded myself that if I could manage to do something conspicuous for Italy I might yet make her care for me. With such an incentive you will not wonder that I worked hard; but though Donna Candida was full of gratitude she continued to adore my rival.

One day we had a hot scene. I began, I believe, by reproaching her with having led me on; and when she defended herself, I retaliated by taunting her with Briga's indifference. She grew pale at that, and said it was enough to love a hero, even without hope of return; and as she said it she herself looked so heroic, so radiant, so unattainably the woman I wanted, that a sneer may have escaped me: — was she so sure then that Briga was a hero? I remember her proud silence and our wretched parting. I went away feeling that at last I had really lost her; and the thought made me savage and vindictive.

Soon after, as it happened, came the Five Days, and Milan was free. I caught a distant glimpse of Donna Candida in the hospital to which I was carried after the fight; but my wound was a slight one and in twenty–four hours I was about again on crutches. I hoped she might send for me, but she did not, and I was too sulky to make the first advance. A day or two later I heard there had been a commotion in Modena, and not being in fighting trim I got leave to go over there with one or two men whom the Modenese liberals had called in to help them. When we arrived the precious Duke had been swept out and a provisional government set up. One of my companions, who was a Modenese, was made a member, and knowing that I wanted something to do, he commissioned me to look up some papers in the ducal archives. It was fascinating work, for in the pursuit of my documents I uncovered the hidden springs of his late Highness's paternal administration. The principal papers relative to the civil and criminal administration of Modena have since been published, and the world knows how that estimable sovereign cared for the material and spiritual welfare of his subjects.

Well — in the course of my search, I came across a file of old papers marked: "Taken from political prisoners. A.D. 1831." It was the year of Menotti's conspiracy, and everything connected with that date was thrilling. I loosened the band and ran over the letters. Suddenly I came across one which was docketed: "Given by Doctor Briga's son to the warder of His Highness's prisons." Doctor Briga's son? That could be no other than Fernando: I knew he was an only child. But how came such a paper into his hands, and how had it passed from them into those of the Duke's warder? My own hands shook as I opened the letter — I felt the man suddenly in my power.

Then I began to read. "My adored mother, even in this lowest circle of hell all hearts are not closed to pity, and I have been given the hope that these last words of farewell may reach you. . . ." My eyes ran on over pages of plaintive rhetoric. "Embrace for me my adored Candida . . . let her never forget the cause for which her father and brother perished . . . let her keep alive in her breast the thought of Spielberg and Reggio. Do not grieve that I die so young . . . though not with those heroes in deed I was with them in spirit, and am worthy to be enrolled in the sacred phalanx . . ." and so on. Before I reached the signature I knew the letter was from Emilio Verna.

I put it in my pocket, finished my work and started immediately for Milan. I didn't quite know what I meant to do — my head was in a whirl. I saw at once what must have happened. Fernando Briga, then a lad of fifteen or sixteen, had attended his father in prison during Emilio Verna's last hours, and the latter, perhaps aware of the lad's liberal sympathies, had found an opportunity of giving him the letter. But why had Briga given it up to the warder? That was the puzzling question. The docket said: " Given by Doctor Briga's son" — but it might mean "taken from." Fernando might have been seen to receive the letter and might have been searched on leaving the prison. But that would not account for his silence afterward. How was it that, if he knew of the letter, he had never told Emilio's family of it? There was only one explanation. If the letter had been taken from him by force he would have had no reason for concealing its existence; and his

136

silence was clear proof that he had given it up voluntarily, no doubt in the hope of standing well with the authorities. But then he was a traitor and a coward; the patriot of 'forty–eight had begun life as an informer! But does innate character ever change so radically that the lad who has committed a base act at fifteen may grow up into an honorable man? A good man may be corrupted by life, but can the years turn a born sneak into a hero?

You may fancy how I answered my own questions. . . . If Briga had been false and cowardly then, was he not sure to be false and cowardly still? In those days there were traitors under every coat, and more than one brave fellow had been sold to the police by his best friend. . . . You will say that Briga's record was unblemished, that he had exposed himself to danger too frequently, had stood by his friends too steadfastly, to permit of a rational doubt of his good faith. So reason might have told me in a calmer moment, but she was not allowed to make herself heard just then. I was young, I was angry, I chose to think I had been unfairly treated, and perhaps at my rival's instigation. It was not unlikely that Briga knew of my love for Donna Candida, and had encouraged her to use it in the good cause. Was she not always at his bidding? My blood boiled at the thought, and reaching Milan in a rage I went straight to Donna Candida.

I had measured the exact force of the blow I was going to deal. The triumph of the liberals in Modena had revived public interest in the unsuccessful struggle of their predecessors, the men who, sixteen years earlier, had paid for the same attempt with their lives. The victors of 'forty–eight wished to honor the vanquished of 'thirty–two. All the families exiled by the ducal government were hastening back to recover possession of their confiscated property and of the graves of their dead. Already it had been decided to raise a monument to Menotti and his companions. There were to be speeches, garlands, a public holiday: the thrill of the commemoration would run through Europe. You see what it would have meant to the poor Countess to appear on the scene with her boy's letter in her hand; and you see also what the memorandum on the back of the letter would have meant to Donna Candida. Poor Emilio's farewell would be published in all the journals of Europe: the finding of the letter would be on every one's lips. And how conceal those fatal words on the back? At the moment, it seemed to me that fortune could not have given me a handsomer chance of destroying my rival than in letting me find the letter which he stood convicted of having suppressed.

My sentiment was perhaps not a strictly honorable one; yet what could I do but give the letter to Donna Candida? To keep it back was out of the question; and with the best will in the world I could not have erased Briga's name from the back. The mistake I made was in thinking it lucky that the paper had fallen into my hands.

Donna Candida was alone when I entered. We had parted in anger, but she held out her hand with a smile of pardon, and asked what news I brought from Modena. The smile exasperated me: I felt as though she were trying to get me into her power again.

"I bring you a letter from your brother," I said, and handed it to her. I had purposely turned the superscription downward, so that she should not see it.

She uttered an incredulous cry and tore the letter open. A light struck up from it into her face as she read — a radiance that smote me to the soul. For a moment I longed to snatch the paper from her and efface the name on the back. It hurt me to think how short–lived her happiness must be.

Then she did a fatal thing. She came up to me, caught my two hands and kissed them. "Oh, thank you — bless you a thousand times! He died thinking of us — he died loving Italy!"

I put her from me gently: it was not the kiss I wanted, and the touch of her lips hardened me.

She shone on me through her happy tears. "What happiness — what consolation you have brought my poor mother! This will take the bitterness from her grief. And that it should come to her now! Do you know, she had a presentiment of it? When we heard of the Duke's flight her first word was: 'Now we may find Emilio's letter.' At heart she was always sure that he had written — I suppose some blessed instinct told her so." She dropped her face on her hands, and I saw her tears fall on the wretched letter.

In a moment she looked up again, with eyes that blessed and trusted me. "Tell me where you found it," she said.

I told her.

"Oh, the savages! They took it from him — "

My opportunity had come. "No," I said, "it appears they did not take it from him."

"Then how — "

I waited a moment. "The letter," I said, looking full at her, "was given up to the warder of the prison by the son of Doctor Briga."

She stared, repeating the words slowly. "The son of Doctor Briga? But that is — Fernando," she said.

"I have always understood," I replied, "that your friend was an only son."

I had expected an outcry of horror; if she had uttered it I could have forgiven her anything. But I heard, instead, an incredulous exclamation: my statement was really too preposterous! I saw that her mind had flashed back to our last talk, and that she charged me with something too nearly true to be endurable.

"My brother's letter? Given to the prison warder by Fernando Briga? My dear Captain Alingdon — on what authority do you expect me to believe such a tale?"

Her incredulity had in it an evident implication of bad faith, and I was stung to a quick reply.

"If you will turn over the letter you will see."

She continued to gaze at me a moment: then she obeyed. I don't think I ever admired her more than I did then. As she read the name a tremor crossed her face; and that was all. Her mind must have reached out instantly to the farthest consequences of the discovery, but the long habit of self-command enabled her to steady her muscles at once. If I had not been on the alert I should have seen no hint of emotion.

For a while she looked fixedly at the back of the letter; then she raised her eyes to mine.

"Can you tell me who wrote this?" she asked.

Her composure irritated me. She had rallied all her forces to Briga's defence, and I felt as though my triumph were slipping from me.

"Probably one of the clerks of the archives," I answered. "It is written in the same hand as all the other memoranda relating to the political prisoners of that year."

"But it is a lie!" she exclaimed. "He was never admitted to the prisons."

"Are you sure?"

"How should he have been?"

"He might have gone as his father's assistant."

"But if he had seen my poor brother he would have told me long ago."

"Not if he had really given up this letter," I retorted.

I supposed her quick intelligence had seized this from the first; but I saw now that it came to her as a shock. She stood motionless, clenching the letter in her hands, and I could guess the rapid travel of her thoughts.

Suddenly she came up to me. "Colonel Alingdon," she said, "you have been a good friend of mine, though I think you have not liked me lately. But whether you like me or not, I know you will not deceive me. On your honor, do you think this memorandum may have been written later than the letter?"

I hesitated. If she had cried out once against Briga I should have wished myself out of the business; but she was too sure of him.

"On my honor," I said, "I think it hardly possible. The ink has faded to the same degree."

She made a rapid comparison and folded the letter with a gesture of assent.

"It may have been written by an enemy," I went on, wishing to clear myself of any appearance of malice.

She shook her head. "He was barely fifteen — and his father was on the side of the government. Besides, this would have served him with the government, and the liberals would never have known of it."

This was unanswerable — and still not a word of revolt against the man whose condemnation she was pronouncing!

"Then — " I said with a vague gesture.

She caught me up. "Then — ?"

"You have answered my objections," I returned.

"Your objections?"

"To thinking that Signor Briga could have begun his career as a patriot by betraying a friend."

I had brought her to the test at last, but my eyes shrank from her face as I spoke. There was a dead silence, which I broke by adding lamely: "But no doubt Signor Briga could explain."

She lifted her head, and I saw that my triumph was to be short. She stood erect, a few paces from me, resting her hand on a table, but not for support.

"Of course he can explain," she said; "do you suppose I ever doubted it? But — " she paused a moment, fronting me nobly — "he need not, for I understand it all now."

"Ah," I murmured with a last flicker of irony.

"I understand," she repeated. It was she, now, who sought my eyes and held them. "It is quite simple — he could not have done otherwise."

This was a little too oracular to be received with equanimity. I suppose I smiled.

"He could not have done otherwise," she repeated with tranquil emphasis. "He merely did what is every Italian's duty — he put Italy before himself and his friends." She waited a moment, and then went on with growing passion: "Surely you must see what I mean? He was evidently in the prison with his father at the time of my poor brother's death. Emilio perhaps guessed that he was a friend — or perhaps appealed to him because he was young and looked kind. But don't you see how dangerous it would have been for Briga to bring this letter to us, or even to hide it in his father's house? It is true that he was not yet suspected of liberalism, but he was already connected with Young Italy, and it is just because he managed to keep himself so free of suspicion that he was able to do such good work for the cause." She paused, and then went on with a firmer voice. "You don't know the danger we all lived in. The government spies were everywhere. The laws were set aside as the Duke pleased — was not Emilio hanged for having an ode to Italy in his desk? After Menotti's conspiracy the Duke grew mad with fear — he was haunted by the dread of assassination. The police, to prove their zeal, had to trump up false charges and arrest innocent persons — you remember the case of poor Ricci? Incriminating papers were smuggled into people's houses — they were condemned to death on the paid evidence of brigands and galley–slaves. The families of the revolutionists were under the closest observation and were shunned by all who wished to stand well with the government. If Briga had been seen going into our house he would at once have been suspected. If he had hidden Emilio's letter at home, its discovery might have ruined his family as well as himself. It was his duty to consider all these things. In those days no man could serve two masters, and he had to choose between endangering the cause and failing to serve a friend. He chose the latter — and he was right."

I stood listening, fascinated by the rapidity and skill with which she had built up the hypothesis of Briga's defence. But before she ended a strange thing happened — her argument had convinced me. It seemed to me quite likely that Briga had in fact been actuated by the motives she suggested.

I suppose she read the admission in my face, for hers lit up victoriously.

"You see?" she exclaimed. "Ah, it takes one brave man to understand another."

Perhaps I winced a little at being thus coupled with her hero; at any rate, some last impulse of resistance made me say: "I should be quite convinced, if Briga had only spoken of the letter afterward. If brave people understand each other, I cannot see why he

142

should have been afraid of telling you the truth."

She colored deeply, and perhaps not quite resentfully.

"You are right," she said; "he need not have been afraid. But he does not know me as I know him. I was useful to Italy, and he may have feared to risk my friendship."

"You are the most generous woman I ever knew!" I exclaimed.

She looked at me intently. "You also are generous," she said.

I stiffened instantly, suspecting a pur—pose behind her praise. "I have given you small proof of it!" I said.

She seemed surprised. "In bringing me this letter? What else could you do?" She sighed deeply. "You can give me proof enough now."

She had dropped into a chair, and I saw that we had reached the most difficult point in our interview.

"Captain Alingdon," she said, "does any one else know of this letter?"

"No. I was alone in the archives when I found it."

"And you spoke of it to no one?"

"To no one."

"Then no one must know."

I bowed. "It is for you to decide."

She paused. "Not even my mother," she continued, with a painful blush.

I looked at her in amazement. "Not even — ?"

She shook her head sadly. "You think me a cruel daughter? Well — he was a cruel friend. What he did was done for Italy: shall I allow myself to be surpassed?"

I felt a pang of commiseration for the mother. "But you will at least tell the Countess — "

Her eyes filled with tears. "My poor mother — don't make it more difficult for me!"

"But I don't understand — "

"Don't you see that she might find it impossible to forgive him? She has suffered so much! And I can't risk that — for in her anger she might speak. And even if she forgave him, she might be tempted to show the letter. Don't you see that, even now, a word of this might ruin him? I will trust his fate to no one. If Italy needed him then she needs him far more to–day."

She stood before me magnificently, in the splendor of her great refusal; then she turned to the writing–table at which she had been seated when I came in. Her sealing–taper was still alight, and she held her brother's letter to the flame.

I watched her in silence while it burned; but one more question rose to my lips.

"You will tell him, then, what you have done for him?" I cried.

And at that the heroine turned woman, melted and pressed unhappy hands in mine.

"Don't you see that I can never tell him what I do for him? That is my gift to Italy," she said.

The Dilettante.

IT was on an impulse hardly needing the arguments he found himself advancing in its favor, that Thursdale, on his way to the club, turned as usual into Mrs. Vervain's street.

The "as usual" was his own qualification of the act; a convenient way of bridging the interval — in days and other sequences — that lay between this visit and the last. It was characteristic of him that he instinctively excluded his call two days earlier, with Ruth Gaynor, from the list of his visits to Mrs. Vervain: the special conditions attending it had made it no more like a visit to Mrs. Vervain than an engraved dinner invitation is like a personal letter. Yet it was to talk over his call with Miss Gaynor that he was now returning to the scene of that episode; and it was because Mrs. Vervain could be trusted to handle the talking over as skilfully as the interview itself that, at her corner, he had felt the dilettante's irresistible craving to take a last look at a work of art that was passing out of his possession.

On the whole, he knew no one better fitted to deal with the unexpected than Mrs. Vervain. She excelled in the rare art of taking things for granted, and Thursdale felt a pardonable pride in the thought that she owed her excellence to his training. Early in his career Thursdale had made the mistake, at the outset of his acquaintance with a lady, of telling her that he loved her and exacting the same avowal in return. The latter part of that episode had been like the long walk back from a picnic, when one has to carry all the crockery one has finished using: it was the last time Thursdale ever allowed himself to be encumbered with the debris of a feast. He thus incidentally learned that the privilege of loving her is one of the least favors that a charming woman can accord; and in seeking to avoid the pitfalls of sentiment he had developed a science of evasion in which the woman of the moment became a mere implement of the game. He owed a great deal of delicate enjoyment to the cultivation of this art. The perils from which it had been his refuge became naively harmless: was it possible that he who now took his easy way along the levels had once preferred to gasp on the raw heights of emotion? Youth is a high–colored season; but he had the satisfaction of feeling that he had entered earlier than most into that chiar'oscuro of sensation where every half–tone has its value.

As a promoter of this pleasure no one he had known was comparable to Mrs. Vervain. He had taught a good many women not to betray their feelings, but he had never before had such fine material to work in. She had been surprisingly crude when he first knew her; capable of making the most awkward inferences, of plunging through thin ice, of recklessly undressing her emotions; but she had acquired, under the discipline of his reticences and evasions, a skill almost equal to his own, and perhaps more remarkable in that it involved keeping time with any tune he played and reading at sight some uncommonly difficult passages.

It had taken Thursdale seven years to form this fine talent; but the result justified the effort. At the crucial moment she had been perfect: her way of greeting Miss Gaynor had made him regret that he had announced his engagement by letter. it was an evasion that confessed a difficulty; a deviation implying an obstacle, where, by common consent, it was agreed to see none; it betrayed, in short, a lack of confidence in the completeness of his method. It had been his pride never to put himself in a position which had to be quitted, as it were, by the back door; but here, as he perceived, the main portals would have opened for him of their own accord. All this, and much more, he read in the finished naturalness with which Mrs. Vervain had met Miss Gaynor. He had never seen a better piece of work: there was no over–eagerness, no suspicious warmth, above all (and this gave her art the grace of a natural quality) there were none of those damnable implications whereby a woman, in welcoming her friend's betrothed, may keep him on pins and needles while she laps the lady in complacency. So masterly a performance, indeed, hardly needed the offset of Miss Gaynor's door–step words — "To be so kind to me, how she must have liked you!" — though he caught himself wishing it lay within the bounds of fitness to transmit them, as a final tribute, to the one woman he knew who was unfailingly certain to enjoy a good thing. It was perhaps the one drawback to his new situation that it might develop good things which it would be impossible to hand on to Margaret Vervain.

The fact that he had made the mistake of underrating his friend's powers, the consciousness that his writing must have betrayed his distrust of her efficiency, seemed an added reason for turning down her street instead of going on to the club. He would show her that he knew how to value her; he would ask her to achieve with him a feat infinitely rarer and more delicate than the one he had appeared to avoid. Incidentally, he would also dispose of the interval of time before dinner: ever since he had seen Miss Gaynor off, an hour earlier, on her return journey to Buffalo, he had been wondering how he should put in the rest of the afternoon. It was absurd, how he missed the girl. . . . Yes, that was it; the desire to talk about her was, after all, at the bottom of his impulse to call on Mrs. Vervain! It was absurd, if you like — but it was delightfully rejuvenating. He could recall the time when he had been afraid of being obvious: now he felt that this return to the primitive emotions might be as restorative as a holiday in the Canadian woods. And it was precisely by the girl's candor, her directness, her lack of complications, that he was taken. The sense that she might say something rash at any moment was positively exhilarating: if she had thrown her arms about him at the station he would not have given a thought to his crumpled dignity. It surprised Thursdale to find

146

what freshness of heart he brought to the adventure; and though his sense of irony prevented his ascribing his intactness to any conscious purpose, he could but rejoice in the fact that his sentimental economies had left him such a large surplus to draw upon.

Mrs. Vervain was at home — as usual. When one visits the cemetery one expects to find the angel on the tombstone, and it struck Thursdale as another proof of his friend's good taste that she had been in no undue haste to change her habits. The whole house appeared to count on his coming; the footman took his hat and overcoat as naturally as though there had been no lapse in his visits; and the drawing–room at once enveloped him in that atmosphere of tacit intelligence which Mrs. Vervain imparted to her very furniture.

It was a surprise that, in this general harmony of circumstances, Mrs. Vervain should herself sound the first false note.

"You?" she exclaimed; and the book she held slipped from her hand.

It was crude, certainly; unless it were a touch of the finest art. The difficulty of classifying it disturbed Thursdale's balance.

"Why not?" he said, restoring the book. "Isn't it my hour?" And as she made no answer, he added gently, "Unless it's some one else's?"

She laid the book aside and sank back into her chair. "Mine, merely," she said.

"I hope that doesn't mean that you're unwilling to share it?"

"With you? By no means. You're welcome to my last crust."

He looked at her reproachfully. "Do you call this the last?"

She smiled as he dropped into the seat across the hearth. "It's a way of giving it more flavor!"

He returned the smile. "A visit to you doesn't need such condiments."

She took this with just the right measure of retrospective amusement.

147

"Ah, but I want to put into this one a very special taste," she confessed.

Her smile was so confident, so reassuring, that it lulled him into the imprudence of saying, "Why should you want it to be different from what was always so perfectly right?"

She hesitated. "Doesn't the fact that it's the last constitute a difference?"

"The last — my last visit to you?"

"Oh, metaphorically, I mean — there's a break in the continuity."

Decidedly, she was pressing too hard: unlearning his arts already!

"I don't recognize it," he said. "Unless you make me — " he added, with a note that slightly stirred her attitude of languid attention.

She turned to him with grave eyes. "You recognize no difference whatever?"

"None — except an added link in the chain."

"An added link?"

"In having one more thing to like you for — your letting Miss Gaynor see why I had already so many." He flattered himself that this turn had taken the least hint of fatuity from the phrase.

Mrs. Vervain sank into her former easy pose. "Was it that you came for?" she asked, almost gaily.

"If it is necessary to have a reason — that was one."

"To talk to me about Miss Gaynor?"

"To tell you how she talks about you."

"That will be very interesting — especially if you have seen her since her second visit to me."

"Her second visit?" Thursdale pushed his chair back with a start and moved to another. "She came to see you again?"

"This morning, yes — by appointment."

He continued to look at her blankly. "You sent for her?"

"I didn't have to — she wrote and asked me last night. But no doubt you have seen her since."

Thursdale sat silent. He was trying to separate his words from his thoughts, but they still clung together inextricably. "I saw her off just now at the station."

"And she didn't tell you that she had been here again?"

"There was hardly time, I suppose — there were people about — " he floundered.

"Ah, she'll write, then."

He regained his composure. "Of course she'll write: very often, I hope. You know I'm absurdly in love," he cried audaciously.

She tilted her head back, looking up at him as he leaned against the chimney–piece. He had leaned there so often that the attitude touched a pulse which set up a throbbing in her throat. "Oh, my poor Thursdale!" she murmured.

"I suppose it's rather ridiculous," he owned; and as she remained silent, he added, with a sudden break — "Or have you another reason for pitying me?"

Her answer was another question. "Have you been back to your rooms since you left her?"

"Since I left her at the station? I came straight here."

"Ah, yes — you could: there was no reason — " Her words passed into a silent musing.

Thursdale moved nervously nearer. "You said you had something to tell me?"

"Perhaps I had better let her do so. There may be a letter at your rooms."

"A letter? What do you mean? A letter from her? What has happened?"

His paleness shook her, and she raised a hand of reassurance. "Nothing has happened — perhaps that is just the worst of it. You always hated, you know," she added incoherently, "to have things happen: you never would let them."

"And now — ?"

"Well, that was what she came here for: I supposed you had guessed. To know if anything had happened."

"Had happened?" He gazed at her slowly. "Between you and me?" he said with a rush of light.

The words were so much cruder than any that had ever passed between them that the color rose to her face; but she held his startled gaze.

"You know girls are not quite as unsophisticated as they used to be. Are you surprised that such an idea should occur to her?"

His own color answered hers: it was the only reply that came to him.

Mrs. Vervain went on, smoothly: "I supposed it might have struck you that there were times when we presented that appearance."

He made an impatient gesture. "A man's past is his own!"

"Perhaps — it certainly never belongs to the woman who has shared it. But one learns such truths only by experience; and Miss Gaynor is naturally inexperienced."

"Of course — but — supposing her act a natural one — " he floundered lamentably among his innuendoes — "I still don't see — how there was anything — "

"Anything to take hold of? There wasn't — "

"Well, then — ?" escaped him, in crude satisfaction; but as she did not complete the sentence he went on with a faltering laugh: "She can hardly object to the existence of a mere friendship between us!"

"But she does," said Mrs. Vervain.

Thursdale stood perplexed. He had seen, on the previous day, no trace of jealousy or resentment in his betrothed: he could still hear the candid ring of the girl's praise of Mrs. Vervain. If she were such an abyss of insincerity as to dissemble distrust under such frankness, she must at least be more subtle than to bring her doubts to her rival for solution. The situation seemed one through which one could no longer move in a penumbra, and he let in a burst of light with the direct query: "Won't you explain what you mean?"

Mrs. Vervain sat silent, not provokingly, as though to prolong his distress, but as if, in the attenuated phraseology he had taught her, it was difficult to find words robust enough to meet his challenge. It was the first time he had ever asked her to explain anything; and she had lived so long in dread of offering elucidations which were not wanted, that she seemed unable to produce one on the spot.

At last she said slowly: "She came to find out if you were really free."

Thursdale colored again. "Free?" he stammered, with a sense of physical disgust at contact with such crassness.

"Yes — if I had quite done with you." She smiled in recovered security. "It seems she likes clear outlines; she has a passion for definitions."

"Yes — well?" he said, wincing at the echo of his own subtlety.

"Well — and when I told her that you had never belonged to me, she wanted me to define my status — to know exactly where I had stood all along."

Thursdale sat gazing at her intently; his hand was not yet on the clue. "And even when you had told her that — "

"Even when I had told her that I had had no status — that I had never stood anywhere, in any sense she meant," said Mrs. Vervain, slowly — "even then she wasn't satisfied, it seems."

He uttered an uneasy exclamation. "She didn't believe you, you mean?"

"I mean that she did believe me: too thoroughly."

"Well, then — in God's name, what did she want?"

"Something more — those were the words she used."

"Something more? Between — between you and me? Is it a conundrum?" He laughed awkwardly.

"Girls are not what they were in my day; they are no longer forbidden to contemplate the relation of the sexes."

"So it seems!" he commented. "But since, in this case, there wasn't any — " he broke off, catching the dawn of a revelation in her gaze.

"That's just it. The unpardonable offence has been — in our not offending."

He flung himself down despairingly. "I give it up! — What did you tell her?" he burst out with sudden crudeness.

"The exact truth. If I had only known," she broke off with a beseeching tenderness, "won't you believe that I would still have lied for you?"

"Lied for me? Why on earth should you have lied for either of us?"

152

"To save you — to hide you from her to the last! As I've hidden you from myself all these years!" She stood up with a sudden tragic import in her movement. "You believe me capable of that, don't you? If I had only guessed — but I have never known a girl like her; she had the truth out of me with a spring."

"The truth that you and I had never — "

"Had never — never in all these years! Oh, she knew why — she measured us both in a flash. She didn't suspect me of having haggled with you — her words pelted me like hail. 'He just took what he wanted — sifted and sorted you to suit his taste. Burnt out the gold and left a heap of cinders. And you let him — you let yourself be cut in bits' — she mixed her metaphors a little — 'be cut in bits, and used or discarded, while all the while every drop of blood in you belonged to him! But he's Shylock — and you have bled to death of the pound of flesh he has cut out of you.' But she despises me the most, you know — far the most — " Mrs. Vervain ended.

The words fell strangely on the scented stillness of the room: they seemed out of harmony with its setting of afternoon intimacy, the kind of intimacy on which at any moment, a visitor might intrude without perceptibly lowering the atmosphere. It was as though a grand opera–singer had strained the acoustics of a private music–room.

Thursdale stood up, facing his hostess. Half the room was between them, but they seemed to stare close at each other now that the veils of reticence and ambiguity had fallen.

His first words were characteristic. "She does despise me, then?" he exclaimed.

"She thinks the pound of flesh you took was a little too near the heart."

He was excessively pale. "Please tell me exactly what she said of me."

"She did not speak much of you: she is proud. But I gather that while she understands love or indifference, her eyes have never been opened to the many intermediate shades of feeling. At any rate, she expressed an unwillingness to be taken with reservations — she thinks you would have loved her better if you had loved some one else first. The point of view is original — she insists on a man with a past!"

"Oh, a past — if she's serious — I could rake up a past!" he said with a laugh.

"So I suggested: but she has her eyes on his particular portion of it. She insists on making it a test case. She wanted to know what you had done to me; and before I could guess her drift I blundered into telling her."

Thursdale drew a difficult breath. "I never supposed — your revenge is complete," he said slowly.

He heard a little gasp in her throat. "My revenge? When I sent for you to warn you — to save you from being surprised as I was surprised?"

"You're very good — but it's rather late to talk of saving me." He held out his hand in the mechanical gesture of leave–taking.

"How you must care! — for I never saw you so dull," was her answer. "Don't you see that it's not too late for me to help you?" And as he continued to stare, she brought out sublimely: "Take the rest — in imagination! Let it at least be of that much use to you. Tell her I lied to her — she's too ready to believe it! And so, after all, in a sense, I sha'n't have been wasted."

His stare hung on her, widening to a kind of wonder. She gave the look back brightly, unblushingly, as though the expedient were too simple to need oblique approaches. It was extraordinary how a few words had swept them from an atmosphere of the most complex dissimulations to this contact of naked souls.

It was not in Thursdale to expand with the pressure of fate; but something in him cracked with it, and the rift let in new light. He went up to his friend and took her hand.

"You would do it — you would do it!"

She looked at him, smiling, but her hand shook.

"Good–by," he said, kissing it.

"Good–by? You are going — ?"

"To get my letter."

"Your letter? The letter won't matter, if you will only do what I ask."

He returned her gaze. "I might, I suppose, without being out of character. Only, don't you see that if your plan helped me it could only harm her?"

"Harm her?"

"To sacrifice you wouldn't make me different. I shall go on being what I have always been — sifting and sorting, as she calls it. Do you want my punishment to fall on her?"

She looked at him long and deeply. "Ah, if I had to choose between you — !"

"You would let her take her chance? But I can't, you see. I must take my punishment alone."

She drew her hand away, sighing. "Oh, there will be no punishment for either of you."

"For either of us? There will be the reading of her letter for me."

She shook her head with a slight laugh. "There will be no letter."

Thursdale faced about from the threshold with fresh life in his look. "No letter? You don't mean — "

"I mean that she's been with you since I saw her — she's seen you and heard your voice. If there is a letter, she has recalled it — from the first station, by telegraph."

He turned back to the door, forcing an answer to her smile. "But in the mean while I shall have read it," he said.

The door closed on him, and she hid her eyes from the dreadful emptiness of the room.

The Quicksand

I

AS Mrs. Quentin's victoria, driving homeward, turned from the Park into Fifth Avenue, she divined her son's tall figure walking ahead of her in the twilight. His long stride covered the ground more rapidly than usual, and she had a premonition that, if he were going home at that hour, it was because he wanted to see her.

Mrs. Quentin, though not a fanciful woman, was sometimes aware of a sixth sense enabling her to detect the faintest vibrations of her son's impulses. She was too shrewd to fancy herself the one mother in possession of this faculty, but she permitted herself to think that few could exercise it more discreetly. If she could not help overhearing Alan's thoughts, she had the courage to keep her discoveries to herself, the tact to take for granted nothing that lay below the surface of their spoken intercourse: she knew that most people would rather have their letters read than their thoughts. For this superfeminine discretion Alan repaid her by — being Alan. There could have been no completer reward. He was the key to the meaning of life, the justification of what must have seemed as incomprehensible as it was odious, had it not all–sufficingly ended in himself. He was a perfect son, and Mrs. Quentin had always hungered for perfection.

Her house, in a minor way, bore witness to the craving. One felt it to be the result of a series of eliminations: there was nothing fortuitous in its blending of line and color. The almost morbid finish of every material detail of her life suggested the possibility that a diversity of energies had, by some pressure of circumstance, been forced into the channel of a narrow dilettanteism. Mrs. Quentin's fastidiousness had, indeed, the flaw of being too one–sided. Her friends were not always worthy of the chairs they sat in, and she overlooked in her associates defects she would not have tolerated in her bric–a–brac. Her house was, in fact, never so distinguished as when it was empty; and it was at its best in the warm fire–lit silence that now received her.

Her son, who had overtaken her on the door–step, followed her into the drawing–room, and threw himself into an armchair near the fire, while she laid off her furs and busied herself about the tea table. For a while neither spoke; but glancing at him across the kettle, his mother noticed that he sat staring at the embers with a look she had never seen on his face, though its arrogant young outline was as familiar to her as her own thoughts. The look extended itself to his negligent attitude, to the droop of his long fine hands, the dejected tilt of his head against the cushions. It was like the moral equivalent of physical fatigue: he looked, as he himself would have phrased it, dead—beat, played out. Such an air was so foreign to his usual bright indomitableness that Mrs. Quentin had the sense of an unfamiliar presence, in which she must observe herself, must raise hurried barriers against an alien approach. It was one of the drawbacks of their excessive intimacy that any break in it seemed a chasm.

She was accustomed to let his thoughts circle about her before they settled into speech, and she now sat in motionless expectancy, as though a sound might frighten them away.

At length, without turning his eyes from the fire, he said: "I'm so glad you're a nice old—fashioned intuitive woman. It's painful to see them think."

Her apprehension had already preceded him. "Hope Fenno — ?" she faltered.

He nodded. "She's been thinking — hard. It was very painful — to me, at least; and I don't believe she enjoyed it: she said she didn't." He stretched his feet to the fire. "The result of her cogitations is that she won't have me. She arrived at this by pure ratiocination — it's not a question of feeling, you understand. I'm the only man she's ever loved — but she won't have me. What novels did you read when you were young, dear? I'm convinced it all turns on that. If she'd been brought up on Trollope and Whyte—Melville, instead of Tolstoi and Mrs. Ward, we should have now been vulgarly sitting on a sofa, trying on the engagement—ring."

Mrs. Quentin at first was kept silent by the mother's instinctive anger that the girl she has not wanted for her son should have dared to refuse him. Then she said, "Tell me, dear."

"My good woman, she has scruples."

"Scruples?"

"Against the paper. She objects to me in my official capacity as owner of the Radiator."

His mother did not echo his laugh.

157

"She had found a solution, of course — she overflows with expedients. I was to chuck the paper, and we were to live happily ever afterward on canned food and virtue. She even had an alternative ready — women are so full of resources! I was to turn the Radiator into an independent organ, and run it at a loss to show the public what a model newspaper ought to be. On the whole, I think she fancied this plan more than the other — it commended itself to her as being more uncomfortable and aggressive. It's not the fashion nowadays to be good by stealth."

Mrs. Quentin said to herself, "I didn't know how much he cared!" Aloud she murmured, "You must give her time."

"Time?"

"To move out the old prejudices and make room for new ones."

"My dear mother, those she has are brand−new; that's the trouble with them. She's tremendously up−to−date. She takes in all the moral fashion−papers, and wears the newest thing in ethics."

Her resentment lost its way in the intricacies of his metaphor. "Is she so very religious?"

"You dear archaic woman! She's hopelessly irreligious; that's the difficulty. You can make a religious woman believe almost anything: there's the habit of credulity to work on. But when a girl's faith in the Deluge has been shaken, it's very hard to inspire her with confidence. She makes you feel that, before believing in you, it's her duty as a conscientious agnostic to find out whether you're not obsolete, or whether the text isn't corrupt, or somebody hasn't proved conclusively that you never existed, anyhow.

Mrs. Quentin was again silent. The two moved in that atmosphere of implications and assumptions where the lightest word may shake down the dust of countless stored impressions; and speech was sometimes more difficult between them than had their union been less close.

Presently she ventured, "It's impossible?"

"Impossible?"

She seemed to use her words cautiously, like weapons that might slip and inflict a cut. "What she suggests."

Her son, raising himself, turned to look at her for the first time. Their glance met in a shock of comprehension. He was with her against the girl, then! Her satisfaction overflowed in a murmur of tenderness.

"Of course not, dear. One can't change — change one's life. . . ."

"One's self," he emended. "That's what I tell her. What's the use of my giving up the paper if I keep my point of view?"

The psychological distinction attracted her. "Which is it she minds most?"

"Oh, the paper — for the present. She undertakes to modify the point of view afterward. All she asks is that I shall renounce my heresy: the gift of grace will come later."

Mrs. Quentin sat gazing into her untouched cup. Her son's first words had produced in her the hallucinated sense of struggling in the thick of a crowd that he could not see. It was horrible to feel herself hemmed in by influences imperceptible to him; yet if anything could have increased her misery it would have been the discovery that her ghosts had become visible.

As though to divert his attention, she precipitately asked, "And you — ?"

His answer carried the shock of an evocation. "I merely asked her what she thought of you."

"Of me?"

"She admires you immensely, you know."

For a moment Mrs. Quentin's cheek showed the lingering light of girlhood: praise transmitted by her son acquired something of the transmitter's merit. "Well — ?" she smiled.

"Well — you didn't make my father give up the Radiator, did you?"

His mother, stiffening, made a circuitous return: "She never comes here. How can she know me?"

"She's so poor! She goes out so little." He rose and leaned against the mantel–piece, dislodging with impatient fingers a slender bronze wrestler poised on a porphyry base, between two warm–toned Spanish ivories. "And then her mother — " he added, as if involuntarily.

"Her mother has never visited me," Mrs. Quentin finished for him.

He shrugged his shoulders. "Mrs. Fenno has the scope of a wax doll. Her rule of conduct is taken from her grandmother's sampler."

"But the daughter is so modern — and yet — "

"The result is the same? Not exactly. She admires you — oh, immensely!" He replaced the bronze and turned to his mother with a smile. "Aren't you on some hospital committee together? What especially strikes her is your way of doing good. She says philanthropy is not a line of conduct, but a state of mind — and it appears that you are one of the elect."

As, in the vague diffusion of physical pain, relief seems to come with the acuter pang of a single nerve, Mrs. Quentin felt herself suddenly eased by a rush of anger against the girl. "If she loved you — " she began.

His gesture checked her. "I'm not asking you to get her to do that."

The two were again silent, facing each other in the disarray of a common catastrophe — as though their thoughts, at the summons of danger, had rushed naked into action. Mrs. Quentin, at this revealing moment, saw for the first time how many elements of her son's character had seemed comprehensible simply because they were familiar: as, in reading a foreign language, we take the meaning of certain words for granted till the context corrects us. Often as in a given case, her maternal musings had figured his conduct, she now found herself at a loss to forecast it; and with this failure of intuition came a sense of the subserviency which had hitherto made her counsels but the anticipation of his wish.

Her despair escaped in the moan, "What is it you ask me?"

"To talk to her."

"Talk to her?"

"Show her — tell her — make her understand that the paper has always been a thing outside your life — that hasn't touched you — that needn't touch her. Only, let her hear you — watch you — be with you — she'll see . . . she can't help seeing. . ."

His mother faltered. "But if she's given you her reasons — ?"

"Let her give them to you! If she can — when she sees you. . . ." His impatient hand again displaced the wrestler. "I care abominably," he confessed.

II

On the Fenno threshold a sudden sense of the futility of the attempt had almost driven Mrs. Quentin back to her carriage; but the door was already opening, and a parlor–maid who believed that Miss Fenno was in led the way to the depressing drawing–room. It was the kind of room in which no member of the family is likely to be found except after dinner or after death. The chairs and tables looked like poor relations who had repaid their keep by a long career of grudging usefulness: they seemed banded together against intruders in a sullen conspiracy of discomfort. Mrs. Quentin, keenly susceptible to such influences, read failure in every angle of the upholstery. She was incapable of the vulgar error of thinking that Hope Fenno might be induced to marry Alan for his money; but between this assumption and the inference that the girl's imagination might be touched by the finer possibilities of wealth, good taste admitted a distinction. The Fenno furniture, however, presented to such reasoning the obtuseness of its black–walnut chamferings; and something in its attitude suggested that its owners would be as uncompromising. The room showed none of the modern attempts at palliation, no apologetic draping of facts; and Mrs. Quentin, provisionally perched on a green–reps Gothic sofa with which it was clearly impossible to establish any closer relations, concluded that, had Mrs. Fenno needed another seat of the same size, she would have set out placidly to match the one on which her visitor now languished.

To Mrs. Quentin's fancy, Hope Fenno's opinions, presently imparted in a clear young voice from the opposite angle of the Gothic sofa, partook of the character of their surroundings. The girl's mind was like a large light empty place, scantily furnished with a few massive prejudices, not designed to add to any one's comfort but too ponderous to be easily moved. Mrs. Quentin's own intelligence, in which its owner, in an artistically shaded half–light, had so long moved amid a delicate complexity of sensations, seemed in comparison suddenly close and crowded; and in taking refuge there from the glare of the young girl's candor, the older woman found herself stumbling in an unwonted obscurity. Her uneasiness resolved itself into a sense of irritation against her listener. Mrs. Quentin knew that the momentary value of any argument lies in the capacity of the mind to which it is addressed, and as her shafts of persuasion spent themselves against Miss Fenno's obduracy, she said to herself that, since conduct is governed by emotions rather than ideas, the really strong people are those who mistake their sensations for opinions. Viewed in this light, Miss Fenno was certainly very strong: there was an unmistakable ring of finality in the tone with which she declared,

"It's impossible."

Mrs. Quentin's answer veiled the least shade of feminine resentment. "I told Alan that, where he had failed, there was no chance of my making an impression."

Hope Fenno laid on her visitor's an almost reverential hand. "Dear Mrs. Quentin, it's the impression you make that confirms the impossibility."

Mrs. Quentin waited a moment: she was perfectly aware that, where her feelings were concerned, her sense of humor was not to be relied on. "Do I make such an odious impression?" she asked at length, with a smile that seemed to give the girl her choice of two meanings.

"You make such a beautiful one! It's too beautiful — it obscures my judgment."

Mrs. Quentin looked at her thoughtfully. "Would it be permissible, I wonder, for an older woman to suggest that, at your age, it isn't always a misfortune to have what one calls one's judgment temporarily obscured?"

Miss Fenno flushed. "I try not to judge others — "

"You judge Alan."

"Ah, he is not others," she murmured, with an accent that touched the older woman.

"You judge his mother."

"I don't; I don't!"

Mrs. Quentin pressed her point. "You judge yourself, then, as you would be in my position — and your verdict condemns me."

"How can you think it? It's because I appreciate the difference in our point of view that I find it so difficult to defend myself — "

"Against what?"

"The temptation to imagine that I might be as you are — feeling as I do."

Mrs. Quentin rose with a sigh. "My child, in my day love was less subtle." She added, after a moment, "Alan is a perfect son."

"Ah, that again — that makes it worse!"

"Worse?"

"Just as your goodness does, your sweetness, your immense indulgence in letting me discuss things with you in a way that must seem almost an impertinence."

Mrs. Quentin's smile was not without irony. "You must remember that I do it for Alan."

"That's what I love you for!" the girl instantly returned; and again her tone touched her listener.

"And yet you're sacrificing him — and to an idea!"

"Isn't it to ideas that all the sacrifices that were worth while have been made?"

"One may sacrifice one's self."

Miss Fenno's color rose. "That's what I'm doing," she said gently.

Mrs. Quentin took her hand. "I believe you are," she answered. "And it isn't true that I speak only for Alan. Perhaps I did when I began; but now I want to plead for you too — against yourself." She paused, and then went on with a deeper note: "I have let you, as you say, speak your mind to me in terms that some women might have resented, because I wanted to show you how little, as the years go on, theories, ideas, abstract conceptions of life, weigh against the actual, against the particular way in which life presents itself to us — to women especially. To decide beforehand exactly how one ought to behave in given circumstances is like deciding that one will follow a certain direction in crossing an unexplored country. Afterward we find that we must turn out for the obstacles — cross the rivers where they're shallowest — take the tracks that others have beaten — make all sorts of unexpected concessions. Life is made up of compromises: that is what youth refuses to understand. I've lived long enough to doubt whether any real good ever came of sacrificing beautiful facts to even more beautiful theories. Do I seem casuistical? I don't know — there may be losses either way . . . but the love of the man one loves . . . of the child one loves . . . that makes up for everything. . . ."

She had spoken with a thrill which seemed to communicate itself to the hand her listener had left in hers. Her eyes filled suddenly, but through their dimness she saw the girl's lips shape a last desperate denial:

"Don't you see it's because I feel all this that I mustn't — that I can't?"

III

Mrs. Quentin, in the late spring afternoon, had turned in at the doors of the Metropolitan Museum. She had been walking in the Park, in a solitude oppressed by the ever-present sense of her son's trouble, and had suddenly remembered that some one had added a Beltraffio to the collection. It was an old habit of Mrs. Quentin's to seek in the enjoyment of the beautiful the distraction that most of her acquaintances appeared to find in each other's company. She had few friends, and their society was welcome to her only in her more superficial moods; but she could drug anxiety with a picture as some women can soothe it with a bonnet.

During the six months that had elapsed since her visit to Miss Fenno she had been conscious of a pain of which she had supposed herself no longer capable: as a man will continue to feel the ache of an amputated arm. She had fancied that all her centres of feeling had been transferred to Alan; but she now found herself subject to a kind of dual suffering, in which her individual pang was the keener in that it divided her from her son's. Alan had surprised her: she had not foreseen that he would take a sentimental rebuff so hard. His disappointment took the uncommunicative form of a sterner application to work. He threw himself into the concerns of the Radiator with an aggressiveness that almost betrayed itself in the paper. Mrs. Quentin never read the Radiator, but from the glimpses of it reflected in the other journals she gathered that it was at least not being subjected to the moral reconstruction which had been one of Miss Fenno's alternatives.

Mrs. Quentin never spoke to her son of what had happened. She was superior to the cheap satisfaction of avenging his injury by depreciating its cause. She knew that in sentimental sorrows such consolations are as salt in the wound. The avoidance of a subject so vividly present to both could not but affect the closeness of their relation. An invisible presence hampered their liberty of speech and thought. The girl was always between them; and to hide the sense of her intrusion they began to be less frequently together. It was then that Mrs. Quentin measured the extent of her isolation. Had she ever dared to forecast such a situation, she would have proceeded on the conventional theory that her son's suffering must draw her nearer to him; and this was precisely the relief that was denied her. Alan's uncommunicativeness extended below the level of speech, and his mother, reduced to the helplessness of dead–reckoning, had not even the solace of adapting her sympathy to his needs. She did not know what he felt: his course was incalculable to her. She sometimes wondered if she had become as incomprehensible to him; and it was to find a moment's refuge from the dogging misery of such conjectures that she had now turned in at the Museum.

The long line of mellow canvases seemed to receive her into the rich calm of an autumn twilight. She might have been walking in an enchanted wood where the footfall of care never sounded. So deep was the sense of seclusion that, as she turned from her prolonged communion with the new Beltraffio, it was a surprise to find she was not alone.

A young lady who had risen from the central ottoman stood in suspended flight as Mrs. Quentin faced her. The older woman was the first to regain her self-possession.

"Miss Fenno!" she said.

The girl advanced with a blush. As it faded, Mrs. Quentin noticed a change in her. There had always been something bright and bannerlike in her aspect, but now her look drooped, and she hung at half-mast, as it were. Mrs. Quentin, in the embarrassment of surprising a secret that its possessor was doubtless unconscious of betraying, reverted hurriedly to the Beltraffio.

"I came to see this," she said. "It's very beautiful."

Miss Fenno's eye travelled incuriously over the mystic blue reaches of the landscape. "I suppose so," she assented; adding, after another tentative pause, "You come here often, don't you?"

"Very often," Mrs. Quentin answered. "I find pictures a great help."

"A help?"

"A rest, I mean . . . if one is tired or out of sorts."

"Ah," Miss Fenno murmured, looking down.

"This Beltraffio is new, you know," Mrs. Quentin continued. "What a wonderful background, isn't it? Is he a painter who interests you?"

The girl glanced again at the dusky canvas, as though in a final endeavor to extract from it a clue to the consolations of art. "I don't know," she said at length; "I'm afraid I don't understand pictures." She moved nearer to Mrs. Quentin and held out her hand.

"You're going?"

"Yes."

Mrs. Quentin looked at her. "Let me drive you home," she said, impulsively. She was feeling, with a shock of surprise, that it gave her, after all, no pleasure to see how much the girl had suffered.

Miss Fenno stiffened perceptibly. "Thank you; I shall like the walk."

Mrs. Quentin dropped her hand with a corresponding movement of withdrawal, and a momentary wave of antagonism seemed to sweep the two women apart. Then, as Mrs. Quentin, bowing slightly, again addressed herself to the picture, she felt a sudden touch on her arm.

"Mrs. Quentin," the girl faltered, "I really came here because I saw your carriage." Her eyes sank, and then fluttered back to her hearer's face. "I've been horribly unhappy!" she exclaimed.

Mrs. Quentin was silent. If Hope Fenno had expected an immediate response to her appeal, she was disappointed. The older woman's face was like a veil dropped before her thoughts.

"I've thought so often," the girl went on precipitately, "of what you said that day you came to see me last autumn. I think I understand now what you meant — what you tried to make me see. . . . Oh, Mrs. Quentin," she broke out, "I didn't mean to tell you this — I never dreamed of it till this moment — but you do remember what you said, don't you? You must remember it! And now that I've met you in this way, I can't help telling you that I believe — I begin to believe — that you were right, after all."

Mrs. Quentin had listened without moving; but now she raised her eyes with a slight smile. "Do you wish me to say this to Alan?" she asked.

The girl flushed, but her glance braved the smile. "Would he still care to hear it?" she said fearlessly.

Mrs. Quentin took momentary refuge in a renewed inspection of the Beltraffio; then, turning, she said, with a kind of reluctance: "He would still care."

"Ah!" broke from the girl.

During this exchange of words the two speakers had drifted unconsciously toward one of the benches. Mrs. Quentin glanced about her: a custodian who had been hovering in the doorway sauntered into the adjoining gallery, and they remained alone among the silvery Vandykes and flushed bituminous Halses. Mrs. Quentin sank down on the bench and reached a hand to the girl.

"Sit by me," she said.

Miss Fenno dropped beside her. In both women the stress of emotion was too strong for speech. The girl was still trembling, and Mrs. Quentin was the first to regain her composure.

"You say you've suffered," she began at last. "Do you suppose I haven't?"

"I knew you had. That made it so much worse for me — that I should have been the cause of your suffering for Alan!"

Mrs. Quentin drew a deep breath. "Not for Alan only," she said. Miss Fenno turned on her a wondering glance. "Not for Alan only. That pain every woman expects — and knows how to bear. We all know our children must have such disappointments, and to suffer with them is not the deepest pain. It's the suffering apart — in ways they don't understand." She breathed deeply. "I want you to know what I mean. You were right — that day — and I was wrong."

"Oh," the girl faltered.

Mrs. Quentin went on in a voice of passionate lucidity. "I knew it then — I knew it even while I was trying to argue with you — I've always known it! I didn't want my son to marry you till I heard your reasons for refusing him; and then — then I longed to see you his wife!"

"Oh, Mrs. Quentin!"

"I longed for it; but I knew it mustn't be."

"Mustn't be?"

Mrs. Quentin shook her head sadly, and the girl, gaining courage from this mute negation, cried with an uncontrollable escape of feeling:

"It's because you thought me hard, obstinate narrow-minded? Oh, I understand that so well! My self-righteousness must have seemed so petty! A girl who could sacrifice a man's future to her own moral vanity — for it was a form of vanity; you showed me that plainly enough — how you must have despised me! But I am not that girl now — indeed I'm not. I'm not impulsive — I think things out. I've thought this out. I know Alan loves me — I know how he loves me — and I believe I can help him — oh, not in the ways I had fancied before — but just merely by loving him." She paused, but Mrs. Quentin made no sign. "I see it all so differently now. I see what an influence love itself may be — how my believing in him, loving him, accepting him just as he is, might help him more than any theories, any arguments. I might have seen this long ago in looking at you — as he often told me — in seeing how you'd kept yourself apart from — from — Mr. Quentin's work and his — been always the beautiful side of life to them — kept their faith alive in spite of themselves — not by interfering, preaching, reforming, but by — just loving them and being there — " She looked at Mrs. Quentin with a simple nobleness. "It isn't as if I cared for the money, you know; if I cared for that, I should be afraid — "

"You will care for it in time," Mrs. Quentin said suddenly.

Miss Fenno drew back, releasing her hand. "In time?"

"Yes; when there's nothing else left." She stared a moment at the pictures. "My poor child," she broke out, "I've heard all you say so often before!"

"You've heard it?"

"Yes — from myself. I felt as you do, I argued as you do, I acted as I mean to prevent your doing, when I married Alan's father."

The long empty gallery seemed to reverberate with the girl's startled exclamation — "Oh, Mrs. Quentin — "

"Hush; let me speak. Do you suppose I'd do this if you were the kind of pink–and–white idiot he ought to have married? It's because I see you're alive, as I was, tingling with beliefs, ambitions, energies, as I was — that I can't see you walled up alive, as I was, without stretching out a hand to save you!" She sat gazing rigidly forward, her eyes on the pictures, speaking in the low precipitate tone of one who tries to press the meaning of a lifetime into a few breathless sentences.

"When I met Alan's father," she went on, "I knew nothing of his — his work. We met abroad, where I had been living with my mother. That was twenty–six years ago, when the Radiator was less — less notorious than it is now. I knew my husband owned a newspaper — a great newspaper — and nothing more. I had never seen a copy of the Radiator; I had no notion what it stood for, in politics — or in other ways. We were married in Europe, and a few months afterward we came to live here. People were already beginning to talk about the Radiator. My husband, on leaving college, had bought it with some money an old uncle had left him, and the public at first was merely curious to see what an ambitious, stirring young man without any experience of journalism was going to make out of his experiment. They found first of all that he was going to make a great deal of money out of it. I found that out too. I was so happy in other ways that it didn't make much difference at first; though it was pleasant to be able to help my mother, to be generous and charitable, to live in a nice house, and wear the handsome gowns he liked to see me in. But still it didn't really count — it counted so little that when, one day, I learned what the Radiator was, I would have gone out into the streets barefooted rather than live another hour on the money it brought in. . . ." Her voice sank, and she paused to steady it. The girl at her side did not speak or move. "I shall never forget that day," she began again. "The paper had stripped bare some family scandal — some miserable bleeding secret that a dozen unhappy people had been struggling to keep out of print — that would have been kept out if my husband had not — Oh, you must guess the rest! I can't go on!"

She felt a hand on hers. "You mustn't go on, Mrs. Quentin," the girl whispered.

"Yes, I must — I must! You must be made to understand." She drew a deep breath. "My husband was not like Alan. When he found out how I felt about it he was surprised at first — but gradually he began to see — or at least I fancied he saw — the hatefulness of it. At any rate he saw how I suffered, and he offered to give up the whole thing — to sell the paper. It couldn't be done all of a sudden, of course — he made me see that — for he had put all his money in it, and he had no special aptitude for any other kind of work. He was a born journalist — like Alan. It was a great sacrifice for him to give up the paper, but he promised to do it — in time — when a good opportunity offered. Meanwhile, of course, he wanted to build it up, to increase the circulation — and to do that he had to keep on in the same way — he made that clear to me. I saw that we were in a vicious circle. The paper, to sell well, had to be made more and more detestable and disgraceful. At first I rebelled — but somehow — I can't tell you how it was — after that first concession the ground seemed to give under me: with every struggle I sank deeper. And then — then Alan was born. He was such a delicate baby that there was very little hope of saving him. But money did it — the money from the paper. I took him abroad to see the best physicians — I took him to a warm climate every winter. In hot weather the doctors recommended sea air, and we had a yacht and cruised every summer. I owed his life to the Radiator. And when he began to grow stronger the habit was formed — the habit of luxury. He could not get on without the things he had always been used to. He pined in bad air; he drooped under monotony and discomfort; he throve on variety, amusement, travel, every kind of novelty and excitement. And all I wanted for him his inexhaustible foster–mother was there to give!

"My husband said nothing, but he must have seen how things were going. There was no more talk of giving up the Radiator. He never reproached me with my inconsistency, but I thought he must despise me, and the thought made me reckless. I determined to ignore the paper altogether — to take what it gave as though I didn't know where it came from. And to excuse this I invented the theory that one may, so to speak, purify money by putting it to good uses. I gave away a great deal in charity — I indulged myself very little at first. All the money that was not spent on Alan I tried to do good with. But gradually, as my boy grew up, the problem became more complicated. How was I to protect Alan from the contamination I had let him live in? I couldn't preach by example — couldn't hold up his father as a warning, or denounce the money we were living on. All I could do was to disguise the inner ugliness of life by making it beautiful outside — to build a wall of beauty between him and the facts of life, turn his tastes and interests another way, hide the Radiator from him as a smiling woman at a ball may hide a cancer in her breast! Just as Alan was entering college his father died. Then I saw my way clear. I had loved my husband — and yet I drew my first free breath in years. For the Radiator had been left to Alan outright — there was nothing on earth to prevent his selling it when he came of age. And there was no excuse for his not selling it. I had brought him up to depend on money, but the paper had given us enough money to gratify all his tastes. At last we could turn on the monster that had nourished us. I felt a savage joy in the thought — I could hardly bear to wait till Alan came of age. But I had never spoken to him of the paper, and I didn't dare speak of it now. Some false shame kept me back, some vague belief in his ignorance. I would wait till he was twenty–one, and then we should be free.

"I waited — the day came, and I spoke. You can guess his answer, I suppose. He had no idea of selling the Radiator. It wasn't the money he cared for — it was the career that tempted him. He was a born journalist, and his ambition, ever since he could remember, had been to carry on his father's work, to develop, to surpass it. There was nothing in the world as interesting as modern journalism. He couldn't imagine any other kind of life that wouldn't bore him to death. A newspaper like the Radiator might be made one of the biggest powers on earth, and he loved power, and meant to have all he could get. I listened to him in a kind of trance. I couldn't find a word to say. His father had had scruples — he had none. I seemed to realize at once that argument would be useless. I don't know that I even tried to plead with him — he was so bright and hard and inaccessible! Then I saw that he was, after all, what I had made him — the creature of my concessions, my connivances, my evasions. That was the price I had paid for him — I had kept him at that cost!

"Well — I had kept him, at any rate. That was the feeling that survived. He was my boy, my son, my very own — till some other woman took him. Meanwhile the old life must go on as it could. I gave up the struggle. If at that point he was inaccessible, at others he was close to me. He has always been a perfect son. Our tastes grew together — we enjoyed the same books, the same pictures, the same people. All I had to do was to look at him in profile to see the side of him that was really mine. At first I kept thinking of the dreadful other side — but gradually the impression faded, and I kept my mind turned from it, as one does from a deformity in a face one loves. I thought I had made my last compromise with life — had hit on a modus vivendi that would last my time.

"And then he met you. I had always been prepared for his marrying, but not a girl like you. I thought he would choose a sweet thing who would never pry into his closets — he hated women with ideas! But as soon as I saw you I knew the struggle would have to begin again. He is so much stronger than his father — he is full of the most monstrous convictions. And he has the courage of them, too — you saw last year that his love for you never made him waver. He believes in his work; he adores it — it is a kind of hideous idol to which he would make human sacrifices! He loves you still — I've been

172

honest with you — but his love wouldn't change him. It is you who would have to change — to die gradually, as I have died, till there is only one live point left in me. Ah, if one died completely — that's simple enough! But something persists — remember that — a single point, an aching nerve of truth. Now and then you may drug it — but a touch wakes it again, as your face has waked it in me. There's always enough of one's old self left to suffer with. . . ."

She stood up and faced the girl abruptly. "What shall I tell Alan?" she said.

Miss Fenno sat motionless, her eyes on the ground. Twilight was falling on the gallery — a twilight which seemed to emanate not so much from the glass dome overhead as from the crepuscular depths into which the faces of the pictures were receding. The custodian's step sounded warningly down the corridor. When the girl looked up she was alone.

A Venetian Night's Entertainment

THIS is the story that, in the dining–room of the old Beacon Street house (now the Aldebaran Club), Judge Anthony Bracknell, of the famous East India firm of Bracknell &Saulsbee, when the ladies had withdrawn to the oval parlour (and Maria's harp was throwing its gauzy web of sound across the Common), used to relate to his grandsons, about the year that Buonaparte marched upon Moscow.

I

"Him Venice!" said the Lascar with the big earrings; and Tony Bracknell, leaning on the high gunwale of his father's East Indiaman, the Hepzibah B., saw far off, across the morning sea, a faint vision of towers and domes dissolved in golden air.

It was a rare February day of the year 1760, and a young Tony, newly of age, and bound on the grand tour aboard the crack merchantman of old Bracknell's fleet, felt his heart leap up as the distant city trembled into shape. Venice! The name, since childhood, had been a magician's wand to him. In the hall of the old Bracknell house at Salem there hung a series of yellowing prints which Uncle Richard Saulsbee had brought home from one of his long voyages: views of heathen mosques and palaces, of the Grand Turk's Seraglio, of St. Peter's Church in Rome; and, in a corner — the corner nearest the rack where the old flintlocks hung — a busy merry populous scene, entitled: St. Mark's Square in Venice. This picture, from the first, had singularly taken little Tony's fancy. His unformulated criticism on the others was that they lacked action. True, in the view of St. Peter's an experienced–looking gentleman in a full–bottomed wig was pointing out the fairly obvious monument to a bashful companion, who had presumably not ventured to raise his eyes to it; while, at the doors of the Seraglio, a group of turbaned infidels observed with less hesitancy the approach of a veiled lady on a camel. But in Venice so many things were happening at once — more, Tony was sure, than had ever happened in Boston in a twelve–month or in Salem in a long lifetime. For here, by their garb, were people of every nation on earth, Chinamen, Turks, Spaniards, and many more, mixed with a parti–coloured throng of gentry, lacqueys, chapmen, hucksters, and tall personages in parsons' gowns who stalked through the crowd with an air of mastery, a string of parasites at their heels. And all these people seemed to be diverting themselves hugely, chaffering with the hucksters, watching the antics of trained dogs and monkeys, distributing doles to maimed beggars or having their pockets picked by slippery–looking fellows in black — the whole with such an air of ease and good–humour that one felt the cut–purses to be as much a part of the show as the tumbling acrobats and animals.

As Tony advanced in years and experience this childish mumming lost its magic; but not so the early imaginings it had excited. For the old picture had been but the spring–board of fancy, the first step of a cloud–ladder leading to a land of dreams. With these dreams the name of Venice remained associated; and all that observation or report subsequently brought him concerning the place seemed, on a sober warranty of fact, to confirm its claim to stand midway between reality and illusion. There was, for instance, a slender Venice glass, gold–powdered as with lily–pollen or the dust of sunbeams, that, standing in the corner cabinet betwixt two Lowestoft caddies, seemed, among its lifeless neighbours, to palpitate like an impaled butterfly. There was, farther, a gold chain of his mother's, spun of that same sun–pollen, so thread–like, impalpable, that it slipped through the fingers like light, yet so strong that it carried a heavy pendant which seemed held in air as if by magic. Magic! That was the word which the thought of Venice evoked. It was the kind of place, Tony felt, in which things elsewhere impossible might naturally happen, in which two and two might make five, a paradox elope with a syllogism, and a conclusion give the lie to its own premiss. Was there ever a young heart that did not, once and again, long to get away into such a world as that? Tony, at least, had felt the longing from the first hour when the axioms in his horn–book had brought home to him his heavy responsibilities as a Christian and a sinner. And now here was his wish taking shape before him, as the distant haze of gold shaped itself into towers and domes across the morning sea!

The Reverend Ozias Mounce, Tony's governor and bear–leader, was just putting a hand to the third clause of the fourth part of a sermon on Free–Will and Predestination as the Hepzibah B.'s anchor rattled overboard. Tony, in his haste to be ashore, would have made one plunge with the anchor; but the Reverend Ozias, on being roused from his lucubrations, earnestly protested against leaving his argument in suspense. What was the trifle of an arrival at some Papistical foreign city, where the very churches wore turbans like so many Moslem idolators, to the important fact of Mr. Mounce's summing up his conclusions before the Muse of Theology took flight? He should be happy, he said, if the tide served, to visit Venice with Mr. Bracknell the next morning.

The next morning, ha! — Tony murmured a submissive "Yes, sir," winked at the subjugated captain, buckled on his sword, pressed his hat down with a flourish, and before the Reverend Ozias had arrived at his next deduction, was skimming merrily shoreward in the Hepzibah's gig.

A moment more and he was in the thick of it! Here was the very world of the old print, only suffused with sunlight and colour, and bubbling with merry noises. What a scene it was! A square enclosed in fantastic painted buildings, and peopled with a throng as fantastic: a bawling, laughing, jostling, sweating mob, parti–coloured, parti–speeched, crackling and sputtering under the hot sun like a dish of fritters over a kitchen fire. Tony, agape, shouldered his way through the press, aware at once that, spite of the tumult, the shrillness, the gesticulation, there was no undercurrent of clownishness, no tendency to horse–play, as in such crowds on market–day at home, but a kind of facetious suavity which seemed to include everybody in the circumference of one huge joke. In such an air the sense of strangeness soon wore off, and Tony was beginning to feel himself vastly at home, when a lift of the tide bore him against a droll–looking bell–ringing fellow who carried above his head a tall metal tree hung with sherbet–glasses.

The encounter set the glasses spinning and three or four spun off and clattered to the stones. The sherbet–seller called on all the saints, and Tony, clapping a lordly hand to his pocket, tossed him a ducat by mistake for a sequin. The fellow's eyes shot out of their orbits, and just then a personable–looking young man who had observed the transaction stepped up to Tony and said pleasantly, in English:

175

"I perceive, sir, that you are not familiar with our currency."

"Does he want more?" says Tony, very lordly; whereat the other laughed and replied: "You have given him enough to retire from his business and open a gaming—house over the arcade."

Tony joined in the laugh, and this incident bridging the preliminaries, the two young men were presently hobnobbing over a glass of Canary in front of one of the coffee—houses about the square. Tony counted himself lucky to have run across an English—speaking companion who was good—natured enough to give him a clue to the labyrinth; and when he had paid for the Canary (in the coin his friend selected) they set out again to view the town. The Italian gentleman, who called himself Count Rialto, appeared to have a very numerous acquaintance, and was able to point out to Tony all the chief dignitaries of the state, the men of ton and ladies of fashion, as well as a number of other characters of a kind not openly mentioned in taking a census of Salem.

Tony, who was not averse from reading when nothing better offered, had perused the "Merchant of Venice" and Mr. Otway's fine tragedy; but though these pieces had given him a notion that the social usages of Venice differed from those at home, he was unprepared for the surprising appearance and manners of the great people his friend named to him. The gravest Senators of the Republic went in prodigious striped trousers, short cloaks and feathered hats. One nobleman wore a ruff and doctor's gown, another a black velvet tunic slashed with rose—colour; while the President of the dreaded Council of Ten was a terrible strutting fellow with a rapier—like nose, a buff leather jerkin and a trailing scarlet cloak that the crowd was careful not to step on.

It was all vastly diverting, and Tony would gladly have gone on forever; but he had given his word to the captain to be at the landing—place at sunset, and here was dusk already creeping over the skies! Tony was a man of honour; and having pressed on the Count a handsome damascened dagger selected from one of the goldsmiths' shops in a narrow street lined with such wares, he insisted on turning his face toward the Hepzibah's gig. The Count yielded reluctantly; but as they came out again on the square they were caught in a great throng pouring toward the doors of the cathedral.

"They go to Benediction," said the Count. "A beautiful sight, with many lights and flowers. It is a pity you cannot take a peep at it."

Tony thought so too, and in another minute a legless beggar had pulled back the leathern flap of the cathedral door, and they stood in a haze of gold and perfume that seemed to rise and fall on the mighty undulations of the organ. Here the press was as thick as without; and as Tony flattened himself against a pillar, he heard a pretty voice at his elbow: — "Oh, sir, oh, sir, your sword!"

He turned at sound of the broken English, and saw a girl who matched the voice trying to disengage her dress from the tip of his scabbard. She wore one of the voluminous black hoods which the Venetian ladies affected, and under its projecting eaves her face spied out at him as sweet as a nesting bird.

In the dusk their hands met over the scabbard, and as she freed herself a shred of her lace flounce clung to Tony's enchanted fingers. Looking after her, he saw she was on the arm of a pompous-looking graybeard in a long black gown and scarlet stockings, who, on perceiving the exchange of glances between the young people, drew the lady away with a threatening look.

The Count met Tony's eye with a smile. "One of our Venetian beauties," said he; "the lovely Polixena Cador. She is thought to have the finest eyes in Venice."

"She spoke English," stammered Tony.

"Oh — ah — precisely: she learned the language at the Court of Saint James's, where her father, the Senator, was formerly accredited as Ambassador. She played as an infant with the royal princes of England."

"And that was her father?"

"Assuredly: young ladies of Donna Polixena's rank do not go abroad save with their parents or a duenna."

Just then a soft hand slid into Tony's. His heart gave a foolish bound, and he turned about half-expecting to meet again the merry eyes under the hood; but saw instead a slender brown boy, in some kind of fanciful page's dress, who thrust a folded paper between his fingers and vanished in the throng. Tony, in a tingle, glanced surreptitiously at the Count, who appeared absorbed in his prayers. The crowd, at the ringing of a bell, had in fact

177

been overswept by a sudden wave of devotion; and Tony seized the moment to step beneath a lighted shrine with his letter.

"I am in dreadful trouble and implore your help. Polixena" — he read; but hardly had he seized the sense of the words when a hand fell on his shoulder, and a stern–looking man in a cocked hat, and bearing a kind of rod or mace, pronounced a few words in Venetian.

Tony, with a start, thrust the letter in his breast, and tried to jerk himself free; but the harder he jerked the tighter grew the other's grip, and the Count, presently perceiving what had happened, pushed his way through the crowd, and whispered hastily to his companion: "For God's sake, make no struggle. This is serious. Keep quiet and do as I tell you."

Tony was no chicken–heart. He had something of a name for pugnacity among the lads of his own age at home, and was not the man to stand in Venice what he would have resented in Salem; but the devil of it was that this black fellow seemed to be pointing to the letter in his breast; and this suspicion was confirmed by the Count's agitated whisper.

"This is one of the agents of the Ten. — For God's sake, no outcry." He exchanged a word or two with the mace–bearer and again turned to Tony. "You have been seen concealing a letter about your person — "

"And what of that?" says Tony furiously.

"Gently, gently, my master. A letter handed to you by the page of Donna Polixena Cador. — A black business! Oh, a very black business! This Cador is one of the most powerful nobles in Venice — I beseech you, not a word, sir! Let me think — deliberate — "

His hand on Tony's shoulder, he carried on a rapid dialogue with the potentate in the cocked hat.

"I am sorry, sir — but our young ladies of rank are as jealously guarded as the Grand Turk's wives, and you must be answerable for this scandal. The best I can do is to have you taken privately to the Palazzo Cador, instead of being brought before the Council. I have pleaded your youth and inexperience" — Tony winced at this — "and I think the business may still be arranged."

178

Meanwhile the agent of the Ten had yielded his place to a sharp−featured shabby−looking fellow in black, dressed somewhat like a lawyer's clerk, who laid a grimy hand on Tony's arm, and with many apologetic gestures steered him through the crowd to the doors of the church. The Count held him by the other arm, and in this fashion they emerged on the square, which now lay in darkness save for the many lights twinkling under the arcade and in the windows of the gaming−rooms above it.

Tony by this time had regained voice enough to declare that he would go where they pleased, but that he must first say a word to the mate of the Hepzibah, who had now been awaiting him some two hours or more at the landing−place.

The Count repeated this to Tony's custodian, but the latter shook his head and rattled off a sharp denial.

"Impossible, sir," said the Count. "I entreat you not to insist. Any resistance will tell against you in the end."

Tony fell silent. With a rapid eye he was measuring his chances of escape. In wind and limb he was more than a mate for his captors, and boyhood's ruses were not so far behind him but he felt himself equal to outwitting a dozen grown men; but he had the sense to see that at a cry the crowd would close in on him. Space was what he wanted: a clear ten yards, and he would have laughed at Doge and Council. But the throng was thick as glue, and he walked on submissively, keeping his eye alert for an opening. Suddenly the mob swerved aside after some new show. Tony's fist shot out at the black fellow's chest, and before the latter could right himself the young New Englander was showing a clean pair of heels to his escort. On he sped, cleaving the crowd like a flood−tide in Gloucester bay, diving under the first arch that caught his eye, dashing down a lane to an unlit water−way, and plunging across a narrow hump−back bridge which landed him in a black pocket between walls. But now his pursuers were at his back, reinforced by the yelping mob. The walls were too high to scale, and for all his courage Tony's breath came short as he paced the masonry cage in which ill−luck had landed him. Suddenly a gate opened in one of the walls, and a slip of a servant wench looked out and beckoned him. There was no time to weigh chances. Tony dashed through the gate, his rescuer slammed and bolted it, and the two stood in a narrow paved well between high houses.

II

THE servant picked up a lantern and signed to Tony to follow her. They climbed a squalid stairway of stone, felt their way along a corridor, and entered a tall vaulted room feebly lit by an oil–lamp hung from the painted ceiling. Tony discerned traces of former splendour in his surroundings, but he had no time to examine them, for a figure started up at his approach and in the dim light he recognized the girl who was the cause of all his troubles.

She sprang toward him with outstretched hands, but as he advanced her face changed and she shrank back abashed.

"This is a misunderstanding — a dreadful misunderstanding," she cried out in her pretty broken English. "Oh, how does it happen that you are here?"

"Through no choice of my own, madam, I assure you!" retorted Tony, not over–pleased by his reception.

"But why — how — how did you make this unfortunate mistake?"

"Why, madam, if you'll excuse my candour, I think the mistake was yours — "

"Mine?"

— "in sending me a letter — "

" You — a letter?"

— "by a simpleton of a lad, who must needs hand it to me under your father's very nose — "

The girl broke in on him with a cry. "What! It was you who received my letter?" She swept round on the little maid–servant and submerged her under a flood of Venetian. The latter volleyed back in the same jargon, and as she did so, Tony's astonished eye detected in her the doubleted page who had handed him the letter in Saint Mark's.

"What!" he cried, "the lad was this girl in disguise?"

Polixena broke off with an irrepressible smile; but her face clouded instantly and she returned to the charge.

"This wicked, careless girl — she has ruined me, she will be my undoing! Oh, sir, how can I make you understand? The letter was not intended for you — it was meant for the English Ambassador, an old friend of my mother's, from whom I hoped to obtain assistance — oh, how can I ever excuse myself to you?"

"No excuses are needed, madam," said Tony, bowing; "though I am surprised, I own, that any one should mistake me for an ambassador."

Here a wave of mirth again overran Polixena's face. "Oh, sir, you must pardon my poor girl's mistake. She heard you speaking English, and — and — I had told her to hand the letter to the handsomest foreigner in the church." Tony bowed again, more profoundly. "The English Ambassador," Polixena added simply, "is a very handsome man."

"I wish, madam, I were a better proxy!"

She echoed his laugh, and then clapped her hands together with a look of anguish. "Fool that I am! How can I jest at such a moment? I am in dreadful trouble, and now perhaps I have brought trouble on you also — Oh, my father! I hear my father coming!" She turned pale and leaned tremblingly upon the little servant.

Footsteps and loud voices were in fact heard outside, and a moment later the red–stockinged Senator stalked into the room attended by half–a–dozen of the magnificoes whom Tony had seen abroad in the square. At sight of him, all clapped hands to their swords and burst into furious outcries; and though their jargon was unintelligible to the young man, their tones and gestures made their meaning unpleasantly plain. The Senator, with a start of anger, first flung himself on the intruder; then, snatched back by his companions, turned wrathfully on his daughter, who, at his feet, with outstretched arms and streaming face, pleaded her cause with all the eloquence of young distress. Meanwhile the other nobles gesticulated vehemently among themselves, and one, a truculent–looking personage in ruff and Spanish cape, stalked apart, keeping a jealous eye on Tony. The latter was at his wit's end how to comport himself, for the

181

lovely Polixena's tears had quite drowned her few words of English, and beyond guessing that the magnificoes meant him a mischief he had no notion what they would be at.

At this point, luckily, his friend Count Rialto suddenly broke in on the scene, and was at once assailed by all the tongues in the room. He pulled a long face at sight of Tony, but signed to the young man to be silent, and addressed himself earnestly to the Senator. The latter, at first, would not draw breath to hear him; but presently, sobering, he walked apart with the Count, and the two conversed together out of earshot.

"My dear sir," said the Count, at length turning to Tony with a perturbed countenance, "it is as I feared, and you are fallen into a great misfortune."

"A great misfortune! A great trap, I call it!" shouted Tony, whose blood, by this time, was boiling; but as he uttered the word the beautiful Polixena cast such a stricken look on him that he blushed up to the forehead.

"Be careful," said the Count, in a low tone. "Though his Illustriousness does not speak your language, he understands a few words of it, and — "

"So much the better!" broke in Tony; "I hope he will understand me if I ask him in plain English what is his grievance against me."

The Senator, at this, would have burst forth again; but the Count, stepping between, answered quickly: "His grievance against you is that you have been detected in secret correspondence with his daughter, the most noble Polixena Cador, the betrothed bride of this gentleman, the most illustrious Marquess Zanipolo — " and he waved a deferential hand at the frowning hidalgo of the cape and ruff.

"Sir," said Tony, "if that is the extent of my offence, it lies with the young lady to set me free, since by her own avowal — " but here he stopped short, for, to his surprise, Polixena shot a terrified glance at him.

"Sir," interposed the Count, "we are not accustomed in Venice to take shelter behind a lady's reputation."

"No more are we in Salem," retorted Tony in a white heat. "I was merely about to remark that, by the young lady's avowal, she has never seen me before."

Polixena's eyes signalled her gratitude, and he felt he would have died to defend her.

The Count translated his statement, and presently pursued: "His Illustriousness observes that, in that case, his daughter's misconduct has been all the more reprehensible."

"Her misconduct? Of what does he accuse her?"

"Of sending you, just now, in the church of Saint Mark's, a letter which you were seen to read openly and thrust in your bosom. The incident was witnessed by his Illustriousness the Marquess Zanipolo, who, in consequence, has already repudiated his unhappy bride."

Tony stared contemptuously at the black Marquess. "If his Illustriousness is so lacking in gallantry as to repudiate a lady on so trivial a pretext, it is he and not I who should be the object of her father's resentment."

"That, my dear young gentleman, is hardly for you to decide. Your only excuse being your ignorance of our customs, it is scarcely for you to advise us how to behave in matters of punctilio."

It seemed to Tony as though the Count were going over to his enemies, and the thought sharpened his retort.

"I had supposed," said he, "that men of sense had much the same behaviour in all countries, and that, here as elsewhere, a gentleman would be taken at his word. I solemnly affirm that the letter I was seen to read reflects in no way on the honour of this young lady, and has in fact nothing to do with what you suppose."

As he had himself no notion what the letter was about, this was as far as he dared commit himself.

There was another brief consultation in the opposing camp, and the Count then said: — "We all know, sir, that a gentleman is obliged to meet certain enquiries by a denial; but you have at your command the means of immediately clearing the lady. Will you show the letter to her father?"

There was a perceptible pause, during which Tony, while appearing to look straight before him, managed to deflect an interrogatory glance toward Polixena. Her reply was a faint negative motion, accompanied by unmistakable signs of apprehension.

"Poor girl!" he thought, "she is in a worse case than I imagined, and whatever happens I must keep her secret."

He turned to the Senator with a deep bow. "I am not," said he, "in the habit of showing my private correspondence to strangers."

The Count interpreted these words, and Donna Polixena's father, dashing his hand on his hilt, broke into furious invective, while the Marquess continued to nurse his outraged feelings aloof.

The Count shook his head funereally. "Alas, sir, it is as I feared. This is not the first time that youth and propinquity have led to fatal imprudence. But I need hardly, I suppose, point out the obligation incumbent upon you as a man of honour."

Tony stared at him haughtily, with a look which was meant for the Marquess. "And what obligation is that?"

"To repair the wrong you have done — in other words, to marry the lady."

Polixena at this burst into tears, and Tony said to himself: "Why in heaven does she not bid me show the letter?" Then he remembered that it had no superscription, and that the words it contained, supposing them to have been addressed to himself, were hardly of a nature to disarm suspicion. The sense of the girl's grave plight effaced all thought of his own risk, but the Count's last words struck him as so preposterous that he could not repress a smile.

"I cannot flatter myself," said he, "that the lady would welcome this solution."

The Count's manner became increasingly ceremonious. "Such modesty," he said, "becomes your youth and inexperience; but even if it were justified it would scarcely

184

alter the case, as it is always assumed in this country that a young lady wishes to marry the man whom her father has selected."

"But I understood just now," Tony interposed, "that the gentleman yonder was in that enviable position."

"So he was, till circumstances obliged him to waive the privilege in your favour."

"He does me too much honour; but if a deep sense of my unworthiness obliges me to decline — "

"You are still," interrupted the Count, "labouring under a misapprehension. Your choice in the matter is no more to be consulted than the lady's. Not to put too fine a point on it, it is necessary that you should marry her within the hour."

Tony, at this, for all his spirit, felt the blood run thin in his veins. He looked in silence at the threatening visages between himself and the door, stole a side–glance at the high barred windows of the apartment, and then turned to Polixena, who had fallen sobbing at her father's feet.

"And if I refuse?" said he.

The Count made a significant gesture. "I am not so foolish as to threaten a man of your mettle. But perhaps you are unaware what the consequences would be to the lady."

Polixena, at this, struggling to her feet, addressed a few impassioned words to the Count and her father; but the latter put her aside with an obdurate gesture.

The Count turned to Tony. "The lady herself pleads for you — at what cost you do not guess — but as you see it is vain. In an hour his Illustriousness's chaplain will be here. Meanwhile his Illustriousness consents to leave you in the custody of your betrothed."

He stepped back, and the other gentlemen, bowing with deep ceremony to Tony, stalked out one by one from the room. Tony heard the key turn in the lock, and found himself alone with Polixena.

III

THE girl had sunk into a chair, her face hidden, a picture of shame and agony. So moving was the sight that Tony once again forgot his own extremity in the view of her distress. He went and kneeled beside her, drawing her hands from her face.

"Oh, don't make me look at you!" she sobbed; but it was on his bosom that she hid from his gaze. He held her there a breathing–space, as he might have clasped a weeping child; then she drew back and put him gently from her.

"What humiliation!" she lamented.

"Do you think I blame you for what has happened?"

"Alas, was it not my foolish letter that brought you to this plight? And how nobly you defended me! How generous it was of you not to show the letter! If my father knew I had written to the Ambassador to save me from this dreadful marriage his anger against me would be even greater."

"Ah — it was that you wrote for?" cried Tony with unaccountable relief.

"Of course — what else did you think?"

"But is it too late for the Ambassador to save you?"

"From you?" A smile flashed through her tears. "Alas, yes." She drew back and hid her face again, as though overcome by a fresh wave of shame.

Tony glanced about him. "If I could wrench a bar out of that window — " he muttered.

"Impossible! The court is guarded. You are a prisoner, alas. — Oh, I must speak!" She sprang up and paced the room. "But indeed you can scarce think worse of me than you do already — "

"I think ill of you?"

"Alas, you must! To be unwilling to marry the man my father has chosen for me — "

"Such a beetle–browed lout! It would be a burning shame if you married him."

"Ah, you come from a free country. Here a girl is allowed no choice."

"It is infamous, I say — infamous!"

"No, no — I ought to have resigned myself, like so many others."

"Resigned yourself to that brute! Impossible!"

"He has a dreadful name for violence — his gondolier has told my little maid such tales of him! But why do I talk of myself, when it is of you I should be thinking?"

"Of me, poor child?" cried Tony, losing his head.

"Yes, and how to save you — for I can save you! But every moment counts — and yet what I have to say is so dreadful."

"Nothing from your lips could seem dreadful."

"Ah, if he had had your way of speaking!"

"Well, now at least you are free of him," said Tony, a little wildly; but at this she stood up and bent a grave look on him.

"No, I am not free," she said; "but you are, if you will do as I tell you."

Tony, at this, felt a sudden dizziness; as though, from a mad flight through clouds and darkness, he had dropped to safety again, and the fall had stunned him.

"What am I to do?" he said.

"Look away from me, or I can never tell you."

He thought at first that this was a jest, but her eyes commanded him, and reluctantly he walked away and leaned in the embrasure of the window. She stood in the middle of the room, and as soon as his back was turned she began to speak in a quick monotonous voice, as though she were reciting a lesson.

"You must know that the Marquess Zanipolo, though a great noble, is not a rich man. True, he has large estates, but he is a desperate spendthrift and gambler, and would sell his soul for a round sum of ready money. — If you turn round I shall not go on! — He wrangled horribly with my father over my dowry — he wanted me to have more than either of my sisters, though one married a Procurator and the other a grandee of Spain. But my father is a gambler too — oh, such fortunes as are squandered over the arcade yonder! And so — and so — don't turn, I implore you — oh, do you begin to see my meaning?"

She broke off sobbing, and it took all his strength to keep his eyes from her.

"Go on," he said.

"Will you not understand? Oh, I would say anything to save you! You don't know us Venetians — we're all to be bought for a price. It is not only the brides who are marketable — sometimes the husbands sell themselves too. And they think you rich — my father does, and the others — I don't know why, unless you have shown your money too freely — and the English are all rich, are they not? And — oh, oh — do you understand? Oh, I can't bear your eyes!"

She dropped into a chair, her head on her arms, and Tony in a flash was at her side.

"My poor child, my poor Polixena!" he cried, and wept and clasped her.

"You are rich, are you not? You would promise them a ransom?" she persisted.

"To enable you to marry the Marquess?"

"To enable you to escape from this place. Oh, I hope I may never see your face again." She fell to weeping once more, and he drew away and paced the floor in a fever.

188

Presently she sprang up with a fresh air of resolution, and pointed to a clock against the wall. "The hour is nearly over. It is quite true that my father is gone to fetch his chaplain. Oh, I implore you, be warned by me! There is no other way of escape."

"And if I do as you say — ?"

"You are safe! You are free! I stake my life on it."

"And you — you are married to that villain?"

"But I shall have saved you. Tell me your name, that I may say it to myself when I am alone."

"My name is Anthony. But you must not marry that fellow."

"You forgive me, Anthony? You don't think too badly of me?"

"I say you must not marry that fellow."

She laid a trembling hand on his arm. "Time presses," she adjured him, "and I warn you there is no other way."

For a moment he had a vision of his mother, sitting very upright, on a Sunday evening, reading Dr. Tillotson's sermons in the best parlour at Salem; then he swung round on the girl and caught both her hands in his. "Yes, there is," he cried, "if you are willing. Polixena, let the priest come!"

She shrank back from him, white and radiant. "Oh, hush, be silent!" she said. `"I am no noble Marquess, and have no great estates," he cried. "My father is a plain India merchant in the colony of Massachusetts — but if you — "

"Oh, hush, I say! I don't know what your long words mean. But I bless you, bless you, bless you on my knees!" And she knelt before him, and fell to kissing his hands.

He drew her up to his breast and held her there.

"You are willing, Polixena?" he said.

"No, no!" She broke from him with outstretched hands. "I am not willing. You mistake me. I must marry the Marquess, I tell you!"

"On my money?" he taunted her; and her burning blush rebuked him.

"Yes, on your money," she said sadly.

"Why? Because, much as you hate him, you hate me still more?"

She was silent.

"If you hate me, why do you sacrifice yourself for me?" he persisted.

"You torture me! And I tell you the hour is past."

"Let it pass. I'll not accept your sacrifice. I will not lift a finger to help another man to marry you."

"Oh, madman, madman!" she murmured.

Tony, with crossed arms, faced her squarely, and she leaned against the wall a few feet off from him. Her breast throbbed under its lace and falbalas, and her eyes swam with terror and entreaty.

"Polixena, I love you!" he cried.

A blush swept over her throat and bosom, bathing her in light to the verge of her troubled brows.

"I love you! I love you!" he repeated.

And now she was on his breast again, and all their youth was in their lips. But her embrace was as fleeting as a bird's poise and before he knew it he clasped empty air, and half the room was between them.

She was holding up a little coral charm and laughing. "I took it from your fob," she said. "It is of no value, is it? And I shall not get any of the money, you know."

She continued to laugh strangely, and the rouge burned like fire in her ashen face.

"What are you talking of?" he said.

"They never give me anything but the clothes I wear. And I shall never see you again, Anthony!" She gave him a dreadful look. "Oh, my poor boy, my poor love — ' I love you, I love you, Polixena!'"

He thought she had turned light-headed, and advanced to her with soothing words; but she held him quietly at arm's length, and as he gazed he read the truth in her face.

He fell back from her, and a sob broke from him as he bowed his head on his hands.

"Only, for God's sake, have the money ready, or there may be foul play here," she said.

As she spoke there was a great tramping of steps outside and a burst of voices on the threshold.

"It is all a lie," she gasped out, "about my marriage, and the Marquess, and the Ambassador, and the Senator — but not, oh, not about your danger in this place — or about my love," she breathed to him. And as the key rattled in the door she laid her lips on his brow.

The key rattled, and the door swung open — but the black-cassocked gentleman who stepped in, though a priest indeed, was no votary of idolatrous rites, but that sound orthodox divine, the Reverend Ozias Mounce, looking very much perturbed at his surroundings, and very much on the alert for the Scarlet Woman. He was supported, to his evident relief, by the captain of the Hepzibah B., and the procession was closed by an escort of stern-looking fellows in cocked hats and small-swords, who led between them Tony's late friends the magnificoes, now as sorry a looking company as the law ever landed in her net.

The captain strode briskly into the room, uttering a grunt of satisfaction as he clapped eyes on Tony.

"So, Mr. Bracknell," said he, "you have been seeing the Carnival with this pack of mummers, have you? And this is where your pleasuring has landed you? H'm — a pretty establishment, and a pretty lady at the head of it." He glanced about the apartment and doffed his hat with mock ceremony to Polixena, who faced him like a princess.

"Why, my girl," said he, amicably, "I think I saw you this morning in the square, on the arm of the Pantaloon yonder; and as for that Captain Spavent — " and he pointed a derisive finger at the Marquess — "I've watched him drive his bully's trade under the arcade ever since I first dropped anchor in these waters. Well, well," he continued, his indignation subsiding, "all's fair in Carnival, I suppose, but this gentleman here is under sailing orders, and I fear we must break up your little party."

At this Tony saw Count Rialto step forward, looking very small and explanatory, and uncovering obsequiously to the captain.

"I can assure you, sir," said the Count in his best English, "that this incident is the result of an unfortunate misunderstanding, and if you will oblige us by dismissing these myrmidons, any of my friends here will be happy to offer satisfaction to Mr. Bracknell and his companions."

Mr. Mounce shrank visibly at this, and the captain burst into a loud guffaw.

"Satisfaction?" says he. "Why, my cock, that's very handsome of you, considering the rope's at your throats. But we'll not take advantage of your generosity, for I fear Mr. Bracknell has already trespassed on it too long. You pack of galley-slaves, you!" he spluttered suddenly, "decoying young innocents with that devil's bait of yours — " His eye fell on Polixena, and his voice softened unaccountably. "Ah, well, we must all see the Carnival once, I suppose," he said. "All's well that ends well, as the fellow says in the play; and now, if you please, Mr. Bracknell, if you'll take the reverend gentleman's arm there, we'll bid adieu to our hospitable entertainers, and right about face for the Hepzibah."

Printed in the United States
74675LV00004B/51

9 781419 158964